APPEAL

Also by Lynda La Plante

Jane Tennison series
Tennison
Hidden Killers
Good Friday
Murder Mile
The Dirty Dozen
Blunt Force
Unholy Murder
Dark Rooms
Taste of Blood
Whole Life Sentence

DC Jack Warr series
Buried
Judas Horse
Vanished
Pure Evil
Crucified

CSI Jessica Russell series
The Scene of the Crime

Widows series
Widows
Widows' Revenge
She's Out

Trial & Retribution series
Trial & Retribution
Alibi
Accused
Appeal

Getting Away with Murder: My Unexpected Life on Page, Stage and Screen

For a complete list of Lynda's works, please visit:
www.lyndalaplante.com/books

Lynda La Plante was born in Liverpool. She trained for the stage at RADA and worked with the National Theatre and RSC before becoming a television actress. She then turned to writing and made her breakthrough with the phenomenally successful TV series *Widows*. She has written over thirty international novels, all of which have been bestsellers, and is the creator of the Anna Travis, Lorraine Page and *Trial and Retribution* series. Her original script for the much-acclaimed *Prime Suspect* won awards from BAFTA, Emmy, British Broadcasting and the Royal Television Society, as well as the 1993 Edgar Allan Poe Award.

Lynda is one of the only three screenwriters to have been made an honorary fellow of the British Film Institute and was awarded the BAFTA Dennis Potter Best Writer Award in 2000. In 2008, she was awarded a CBE in the Queen's Birthday Honours List for services to Literature, Drama and Charity.

✉ Join the Lynda La Plante Readers' Club at
www.bit.ly/LyndaLaPlanteClub
www.lyndalaplante.com
Facebook @LyndaLaPlanteCBE
@LaPlanteLynda

APPEAL

LYNDA LA PLANTE

ZAFFRE

First published in 2000 by Macmillan

This edition published in 2025 by
ZAFFRE
An imprint of Bonnier Books UK
5th Floor, HYLO, 105 Bunhill Row,
London, EC1Y 8LZ

A CIP catalogue record for this book is
available from the British Library.

ISBN: 978-1-80418-949-8

Also available as an ebook and an audiobook

1 3 5 7 9 10 8 6 4 2

Typeset by IDSUK (Data Connection) Ltd
Printed and bound by CPI (UK) Ltd, Croydon CR0 4YY

The authorised representative in the EEA is Bonnier Books
UK (Ireland) Limited.
Registered office address: Floor 3, Block 3, Miesian Plaza,
Dublin 2, D02 Y754, Ireland
compliance@bonnierbooks.ie
www.bonnierbooks.co.uk

CHAPTER 1

FRIDAY, 28 JANUARY

It could not be said that Friday afternoon in HM Prison Garton is much like it is in the outside world. As a matter of fact, Garton's population of murderers, rapists, muggers, drug dealers and armed robbers could probably do without the seven-day *week* altogether. A single day, of course, weighs heavily enough – no one ignores the rising and the setting of the sun. And then on the longer scale the years, dragging by until the judge's tariff has been served out, are never forgotten. Between these extremes, a month, a week – except when parole is close – mean little enough to the long-term prisoner.

But a week's *end* is a different matter. For one thing the remembered weekends of freedom resonate. Here there may be none of the good prospects he once enjoyed – a pub night, a club-crawl, a football match – but just because it's Saturday or Sunday doesn't change the basic fact of imprisonment. The prison officers' shifts go round eternally. Mealtimes, exercise, association, lock-up continue as before. But, even for lifers, the anticipation that comes with Friday afternoon remains strong, like a vestigial body part that passes down the generations without evolving.

But there is also, in fact, a pattern of life on Saturdays and Sundays which is subtly different from the week. The busy army of civilians who work professionally in the prison, the doctors, teachers, instructors, librarians, psychologists, counsellors and therapists, don't show up. Prisoners are left more to their own devices, which in itself allows for an element of surprise and scandal to enter the life of the place. And, above all, there are visits, from family, friends and lawyers. The family and friends, if you are lucky, offer comfort and love. The lawyer, if you are even luckier, brings something yet more valuable – hope.

Jimmy McCready had served eight years of his life sentence and innocence was his full-time job. For inspiration he read the stories of the Guildford Four, the Birmingham Six, the M25 Three. He worked to make everyone understand his innocence – the padre, the Governor, the doctor, even the art therapist and the bookbinding instructor. Even Wayne, the gorilla who oversaw the weights room in Garton's gym. He studied law. He laid contingency plans for a rooftop protest, should the chance ever arise. He clutched at every straw of hope that blew his way. At times the straws had been few and fragile. But McCready never abandoned hope entirely and now, at last, his determination was paying off. Finally, with a bombardment of letters, he had attracted the attention of Robert Rylands MP and QC Rylands had agreed to be his new counsel and today he was coming to call.

McCready sat in the legal visits room picturing Rylands' arrival. A gleaming black BMW saloon draws up to the prison gate. What is playing on its in-car sound system? Opera, probably. Let's say Puccini. The driver, a clean-shaven, sleekly dressed man in his early fifties, gets out of the car, crosses to the gatehouse and shows a pass. The screw on the gate looks at the pass, checks a list of names and then waves him through. Rylands drives at a stately pace through the gates, which bang shut behind him. He finds the parking space that has been reserved for him. He kills the ignition and *Madame Butterfly* is abruptly cut off.

McCready was aware of his beating heart and pumping adrenalin as he thought of Rylands, now accompanied by a prison officer, swiftly making his way past the cages in the exercise area. Here a few inmates kick a ball around the marked football pitch, supervised by another screw. Play stops momentarily as they watch the immaculate lawyer glide past. They are thinking, *Poncy brief with his shiny shoes and flutey voice.* But that's just envy. This man is Establishment and having people from the Establishment rooting for you is half the battle. Those prats on the football pitch see the Establishment only as the enemy, an attitude which McCready thinks is stupid.

Jimmy had only once met the charismatic barrister who had taken up his case. Rylands had not been a full-time lawyer for several years. Before the last general election he had accepted a safe New Labour seat in London, the story being that he had turned down the bench in order to make it as a politician. Now he was MP first and lawyer second, though always keeping the ability to cherry-pick any high-profile cases that suited his political aspirations. Typically these revolved around gay rights, for during the election Rylands had been outed in the media as gay and with characteristic energy had set about refashioning himself for life outside the closet – with considerable success. The lowering of the homosexual age of consent, the pursuit of homophobic employers, the prosecution of those who beat up gay men on Wimbledon Common and Hampstead Heath, the repeal of Section 28: these were now the sort of cases to which Rylands applied his oratory, charm and incomparable command of legal detail. Jimmy McCready's fitted the bill perfectly.

Jimmy waited. The bare, nondescript room, containing just a table and three chairs, was partly walled in thick glass to assist observation but prevent overhearing. Beside him was a faintly seedy individual in an ill-fitting suit and wearing scuffed brown suede shoes. A bulging briefcase stood on the floor by his side. This was Ben Duffield, Jimmy's long-time solicitor. Every now and then Duffield broke the silence by clearing his throat, an irritating habit. There was a flask of water and Jimmy suddenly snatched it up, poured and pushed the glass at Duffield. Duffield looked surprised but drank.

The footsteps approached at marching speed and through the glass Rylands came into sight. Duffield just had time to say, 'Now, Jimmy, remember what I told you. Don't—'

And, as the door swung open, Rylands strode in with his hand extended. 'Jimmy!' he said. 'Good to see you again. And Mr Duffield.' After shaking hands, Rylands placed his briefcase on the desk and noisily snapped open the catches. And in that confident sound Jimmy imagined he could hear prison doors unlocking themselves.

Looking at the three men through the glass, the screws could see that McCready was keyed up, trying to make a good impression. When Rylands produced a sheaf of handwritten letters on prison notepaper, and spoke at some length about them, McCready was nodding his head all the time. Then suddenly he turned to Duffield and asked him something. Duffield delved into his briefcase and produced a newspaper cutting, which McCready took and pushed across the table towards Rylands. He was talking fast, tapping the cutting for emphasis, the voice muffled and unintelligible until suddenly he raised his voice and they heard it crack with emotion.

'It was an accident! And this proves it. I *didn't* kill him!'

Detective Inspector Pat North was working on her computer, typing up reports. She leant back, yawned, checked the time, swore under her breath and closed down the application. She grabbed her briefcase and jacket and was just about to head out of the office when the phone rang. An internal call. She hesitated, as if she didn't want to answer, but then reached for the receiver.

'Pat North.'

'Hello, Pat, it's Frank.'

'Oh hello,' she said. *Oh shit*, she thought. *What does Bradley want, just when I'm late for Mike's birthday dinner*?

'Pat, are you free to pop in for a minute or two?'

'Yes, sir, I was just off home, actually.'

'You in a rush? I mean it *could* wait—'

'No. No problem. I'll be right with you.' She replaced the receiver. A minute or two with Bradley could extend to sixty if he was in a talkative mood. Mike had done the shopping and she was supposed to do the cooking. Oh well, he'd just have to get started on his own, birthday or no birthday. She reached for her bag and hurried upstairs.

Chief Superintendent Frank Bradley was on the phone. He waved her in. She scanned the maps and photos on his wall as

Bradley politely detached himself from the call. He was North's superior in Vice, a vigorous, kindly boss, always receptive to the latest ideas – some said he was *too* receptive, but at least it kept his team on their toes.

'Pat, thanks for coming up. I need to have a brief word . . .' He opened a file and pulled out a memo with a snazzy printed leaflet paperclipped to it. He pushed it towards Pat and she noticed the Home Office logo prominently displayed. 'It's a matter of staff career development, really. In service training.'

'Oh yes?' said North neutrally.

'They've brought in a new scheme.'

'Who has?'

'The Home Office. They're sponsoring specially selected officers to be the future leaders of the police service.'

Pat had heard rumours of this recently and like many of her colleagues had been on the sceptical side. 'What? With about ten years' experience between them!'

'Not in your case, Pat – the Home Office has picked you! They've looked at your profile and decided to develop that lateral thinking of yours further.'

Instantly North was calculating. What could this mean for her career? Couldn't be bad – or could it? 'This is all a bit sudden, sir,' she said. 'I don't know what to say.'

Bradley looked up at her genially. 'You'll be guaranteed ACPO rank. The job I have in mind for you is a reinvestigation – like a Criminal Case Review, but internal.'

North raised her eyebrows. ACPO rank meant top brass. Anything above Commander – the strategists and policy-makers for the Metropolitan Police. He couldn't mean soon?

This was serious stuff. 'Sounds interesting,' she said, and the curiosity was genuine.

Bradley got up and crossed to a side table, on which a tray and wine glasses were laid out. 'It is.' Smiling broadly he spun around, brandishing a bottle of wine and a stem glass. 'You start on Monday. Fancy a glass of something to celebrate – ma'am?'

Detective Superintendent Mike Walker wasn't much of a cook. In the days of his marriage to Lynn he'd never done anything except make porridge for the kids and even that normally came out lumpy. Since he'd been living with Pat she'd bought him cookbooks and walked him around the kitchen, telling him what everything was.

'This is a colander, Mike. It's for draining cooked vegetables.'

'Pat, I *do* know what a colander is, for Christ's sake!'

She picked up a circular plastic basket and showed it to him. 'What's this, then?'

He screwed up his eyes. 'Another colander?'

'Wrong – part of the salad spinner. See?' And she slotted it back into the thing that he'd thought was a cake storage box. 'You use it for washing salad.'

An aproned Walker was using it now. He was desperate. They'd be here any minute and he wasn't at all sure he wanted Dave Satchell to see him in *chef de cuisine* mode. Or his girlfriend, another one of his blonde conquests – where did he find them? Anyway, the kitchen was shambolic – thick with steam and every surface covered with pans and dishes and food – cooked, uncooked, half-cooked and overcooked. Where *was* Pat?

He tumbled the salad leaves into a bowl and looked around, wiping his wet hands on the apron. The roast was in the oven. He'd done the melon slices, laid the table and got a pot boiling for the peas. What next? The gravy! He glugged some wine into a glass and took a deep draught, then leafed frantically through *Step-by-Step Scottish Cooking*, which North had bought him the previous day.

'Everyone should learn their own ethnic cooking,' she told him.

'Great! You mean cook like my ma?' Give Pat her due, she'd laughed at that.

He found the recipe for gravy, began to skim-read it and gave up halfway through. He ransacked the cupboard. Somewhere he was sure they had some gravy granules. Half the bottle of wine had gone and he had a full glass in his hand as he stirred the suspiciously thin, brown liquid. Would it thicken? And if so, when and how much? He squinted again at the book but it seemed ambiguous. Experimentally, he tipped half the glass of red wine into the saucepan and downed the remainder.

He left the gravy simmering nicely and took the melons through to the table, where four places were set. He lit the candles and was just heading back to the kitchen again when the doorbell rang. 'Shit! Coming . . . Hang on!' As Walker turned towards the front door, the phone rang. He snatched it up and continued to the door.

'Hello! Pat! Where are you? It's after eight . . . What? Hang on . . .' He opened the front door to find Detective Sergeant Dave Satchell trying to hand him a bottle of wine. Beside him was a girl half Walker's age and very blonde, half hidden behind a big bouquet of flowers.

'Hi! Come on in.'

'Happy birthday, Mike!' Satchell thrust the bottle into Walker's free hand and presented his date. 'This is Catrina Roberts. Catrina, Mike Walker.'

Walker stepped back to gesture them in.

'Happy birthday,' said Catrina in a clear, confident voice. She lowered the flowers and held out her hand. Walker, feeling awkward and flustered, took it briefly.

'Thanks. Excuse me, I've got Pat on the line.' Leaving Satchell and Catrina to follow him, he eased back into the living room and resumed his conversation. 'How long are you going to be? I've got everything timed.'

'I've been with Bradley, couldn't get away until now. Sorry, Mike!'

Walker was watching the shapely Catrina as she strolled with her flowers into the kitchen. He whispered urgently into the phone, 'Well, just get here as soon as you can, yeah? OK, bye.'

He slammed the phone down and looked at Satchell, proffering Catrina's coat. 'Where shall I put this, Mike?'

Walker was waving him towards the hall when, from the kitchen, the girl called out cheerfully, 'There's something boiling over in here!'

'Oh shit! Is it the little pan?' He doubled into the kitchen. 'There's wine open, love, help yourself. Use the glasses on the table.' He stood in front of the cooker. Lumpy brown liquid had oozed all over the hob. What was left in the pan was burnt. That was the gravy down the tubes.

North got back at a quarter to nine and ran straight up to the bedroom. She pulled off her work sweater and tugged a blouse from its hanger. Threading her arms in, she grabbed a hairbrush and did a quick once-over before hurrying down. At the foot of the stairs she found her bag and rooted in it for the present she'd got Walker. She cocked an ear. He was talking shop, of course – the new murder inquiry. Boring for Satchell's date, but Walker was oblivious to anything like that.

'He said she went out into the garden to get some mint. I said to him, "How long has your wife been missing?" "Five years," he says . . .'

Through the door she could see they had finished their melon and Walker was upending the almost-empty bottle of red wine into Satchell's glass, while Satchell opened a second bottle. Catrina, drinking orange juice, was staring rather abstractedly at Walker, trying to look interested. Not, North thought, very successfully.

'"Five years?" I said,' Walker was telling them. '"How come you only reported her disappearance last week?" "Because," he says, "I thought she'd done a runner and I was glad to see the back of her." We found her body in his garden shed! Still clutching a sprig of mint!'

'Be dried by that time!' observed Satchell drily. Both were laughing as North appeared, carrying the wrapped gift.

'I'm sorry, I'm so sorry.' She hurried to the table. 'Can I do anything?'

Walker suddenly remembered the kitchen. He shook his head. 'No, no, it's all organised,' he lied. 'Sit down. Pat, this is Catherine.' He doubled back to the kitchen to check on the main course.

'Nice to meet you, Catherine,' said North, sitting down.

'Catrina.'

North smiled and shook hands, casting her eyes upwards at Walker's hopelessness over names. 'Sorry . . . Catrina.'

'Glass of wine, Pat?' said Satchell.

'Yeah, thanks.' She peered across to the kitchen door from where bangs and scrapes were emanating. 'Are you sure I can't do anything, Mike?'

Walker, heaving a roast leg of lamb from the oven, called, 'It's fine, everything's under control . . .' The potatoes were like bullets, but what the hell. 'Eat your melon!' he called out.

North spooned a dripping segment of cantaloupe into her mouth. 'So, Satch,' she went on, when she'd swallowed. 'How's life?'

'Not bad . . .' She could have sworn she'd seen him wink at Catrina. 'Not bad at all . . . apart from this bloody computer course I've been sent on. It's doing my nut! Not only do I have to deal with getting my head around this techno jargon, but I've also been fighting off advances from our batty teacher, Melanie Crass!'

'Melanie Crass? That's not her real name!'

'It is, I'm not joking. Mad Mel we've nicknamed her and she's a total nightmare. And believe me, I should know . . . she sits close, real close!'

A cloud of smoke wafted in from the kitchen with a cry of laughter mixed with despair from Walker. 'Aw, bloody hell, this is burnt!'

Catrina stuck a pert chin in the air and laughed. 'She keeps putting her hand on his leg – doesn't she, Dave?'

'What?' said North. 'And she's supposed to be taking the course?'

Satchell pulled a face. 'Uh-huh! Mind you, she does know her stuff, I'll give her that. Don't know how she does it – fingers like lightning on a keyboard. I tell you, if you ever want to hack into MI5 then Mad Mel's your gal! Oh, here it comes. Food!' Walker was backing through the door and as if on cue turned to the room with the slightly blackened roast as Satchell applauded.

With the main course finished and another bottle of wine opened, Satchell offered his compliments to the chef. The food had been hard chewing but he was gallant.

'Well, I thought it was very nice. I like my meat well done. Roast potatoes got to be crisp!'

'To the chef!' said North, raising her glass.

Walker looked at them a little sullenly as they toasted him. The roast had been a disaster, for God's sake! North bent forward and kissed him, placed his gift in front of him and got up to clear the dishes into the wrecked kitchen. There she opened a cupboard and took out a chocolate cake with one candle stuck in it. Lighting it, she could hear Walker as he opened his present.

'Ah, will you look at this. Pat . . . Pat, this is, it's just . . .' He was holding up a very elegant and pricey Armani watch in admiration as North turned out the lights. The room was lit only by the candles on the table as she made her entrance with the cake, the single candle flickering on top.

She began to sing. '*Happy birthday to you . . .*'

Satchell and Catrina joined in, singing a discordant chorus.

The guests had departed and Walker, by now well inebriated, sprawled contentedly on the bed, still fully clothed. He held the watch high at arm's length, admiring its glistening steel face and polished leather strap. 'I've never had a decent watch before.' North walked in from the bathroom, towelling her face. He turned to her. 'So, why were you so late, then?' He rolled off the bed and wandered into the bathroom. North took off her robe and switched off the main light to leave only a bedside lamp on.

'The Chief called me in to see him. Told me the Home Office have headhunted me.'

Walker reappeared, pasting his toothbrush. 'To do what?'

'For some new scheme. Apparently they've identified some officers "who have the potential to reach the top ranks".' Walker turned back and ran the tap over the toothpaste. She wondered what he was thinking. How would he take the idea that she might be promoted above him one day? She heard him brushing furiously and then his voice, sounding gruff.

'Do you get a new car to go with it?'

'Oh, I doubt it. It *is* the Home Office.'

He was back in the bathroom now, undressing. He was shaking his head. 'Top detectives sponsored by the Home Office! What's the job coming to? In my day you got on by hard work and results!'

North bridled. 'And you're saying I don't work hard?'

'No, I'm not saying that, but Christ! It's just typical. You've got guys like me who've worked their bollocks off from uniform upwards. And now it's elbow time!' He was climbing cautiously into his pyjama bottoms. 'What is it, a feminist thing? "Gender equity", isn't it? Well, I suppose we've got to get you women up the ranks somehow!'

But North was determined not to let him upset her. 'Because it's your birthday, I'll let that one pass.'

'Fine,' he said pugnaciously. 'If you want to give me all the details about your high-rising career, go ahead. I'm all ears.'

She pretended to consider. Obviously, he really wanted to know, she could tell. But she was damned if she would tell him now. 'You know what? I think I'll wait until you're in a better mood.'

CHAPTER 2

MONDAY, 31 JANUARY

Pat North put on her best suit and left early for her first day on the Home Office Sponsorship Scheme. It was a classic 'fast-track', aiming to create a central pool of individuals capable of filling the posts of chief police officers. It allowed senior-ranking officers to be attached to a series of particular inquiries, right across the spectrum of police work. Pat had done some digging over the weekend. She wanted to know what sort of placements were on offer. One, she heard, was to the football hooliganism intelligence unit, another to the National Criminal Intelligence Service. Others were being sent to distant forces where they would learn about rural policing, to the Customs and Excise to uncover VAT fraud, to the channel ports to catch illegal migrants. There were even some being posted to British embassies abroad on liaison with the local power over drug smuggling and asylum seekers.

Her initial assignment was less glamorous. She had been placed on a reinvestigation, a case which the Met had once thought was well wrapped up but which now required review. Today they were to be briefed by the team leader, Detective Chief Inspector George Allard. It had been a hell of a struggle to clear her desk at Vice over the weekend and she couldn't understand why Bradley had fired her into the scheme at such short notice. Had there been a last-minute dropout? Well, it didn't matter. She was in and furthering her career – that was the main thing.

She entered the conference room. Two men in suits were sitting over steaming cups at a long central table. Coffee and biscuits were available by the wall. North greeted her new colleagues, Detective Inspectors Les Pilling and Doug Collins. 'Can I get either of you a top-up?' she said, glancing at their cups. They refused and she was helping herself to coffee and a jammie dodger when the door opened and a fit-looking grey-haired man in his mid-fifties entered after ushering in a companion very well known to North, the black and stunningly beautiful Detective Constable Vivien Watkins.

'I mean, I just can't understand it,' he was saying to Watkins. 'I'm eating low-fat everything and exercising every morning, and I'm still the same weight!'

'Have you tried cutting out carbohydrates? Because I do remember when I—'

North turned with her coffee and caught the newcomer's eye.

'Hello, stranger!' Vivien called out.

'Vivien! What are you doing here?'

'I could ask you the same thing.'

Watkins drew North forward by the arm. 'Sir, this is Pat North. Pat, DCI George Allard.'

They shook hands and Allard smiled. His face had a slightly battered look and North had the impression of a straightforward copper of the old school – the same school Walker had banged on about on the night of his birthday. But this example was milder than Walker and, though probably not as intelligent, better organised and much better mannered. That, however, would not be difficult.

'I gather you're on the Home Office Sponsorship Scheme,' commented Allard.

Watkins raised an eyebrow as she crossed to get a coffee. North shrugged. 'For my sins!'

'Well, congratulations. I hope you're up for the challenge.'

'Oh yes, absolutely.'

As Allard, too, turned to the coffee machine, Watkins passed North on her way back towards the table. 'Home Office, hey?' she said.

'Yep. This is my first assignment.'

'Well, well. Congratulations! How did Mike take it?' In the background, they heard Allard introducing himself to Pilling and Collins. The two women took seats beside each other at the table.

'Don't ask!' Watkins smiled and shook her head. She knew Mike Walker. He was a great detective but in her opinion his social skills definitely needed an upgrade and his competitiveness was exhausting.

By now Allard had sat briskly down at the head of the conference table and cleared his throat to quieten down the rustle of papers and the slap of notebooks. 'Right, let's get started, shall we? I take it introductions have been done?'

They settled themselves as Allard passed out files. 'You may well have heard of this case; James McCready, sentenced to life eight years ago for the murder of his partner, Gary Meadows.'

The four detectives opened their files and began turning the pages as Allard continued.

'The Commissioner has agreed to reinvestigate because several new pieces of evidence have recently come to light. Fiona Meadows, daughter of the deceased, was the only eye-witness to the crime, but she was just seven at the time and too traumatised to give evidence at McCready's trial. She has now come forward with a statement about events leading up to the murder which supports McCready's claim that the stabbing was an accident.'

Allard spooned sugar into his coffee, stirred and took a hurried, noisy slurp.

'As well as this, it's been brought to our attention that the prosecution pathologist, Dr John Foster, whose evidence played a large part in convincing the jury of McCready's guilt, has recently, in a very similar case, argued a directly opposing view to the one he gave at McCready's trial.'

The files had a photocopy of a cutting from a broadsheet newspaper, and a picture of the celebrated pathologist. The photo caption read: *Foster: controversial evidence in murder trial.*

'McCready's also managed to get MP and barrister Robert Rylands on his side, who is pushing the case as a gay rights issue.'

Pilling snorted. 'Huh! No doubt concerned about losing his seat in the next election!'

They all smiled. Rylands represented one of those trendy North London constituencies where to be an active gay rights campaigner was a positive electoral advantage.

'I didn't know you could be an MP and a barrister at the same time,' admitted Collins.

'Oh, he's very light on his feet,' rejoined Allard, turning the pages of his file.

Pilling looked at his fellow detective pityingly. Where had Collins been all his life? Half the House of Commons were barristers!

North did not hear this exchange. Leafing through her sheaf of papers, she had received a shock. Her eye caught one very familiar name.

'Right,' said Allard. 'The original investigation was led by Detective Superintendent Michael Walker, one of the Met's most experienced detectives and he—'

North raised a hand. 'Er, sorry to interrupt, sir, but before we go any further, I think you should know that Mike Walker is my, er, partner.'

Allard looked at her, taking a moment to appreciate what she had said. Then he was drumming his fingers on the table, thinking. 'Does this, let's see . . . Does it make your being on this investigation a problem, do you think?'

'Perhaps ethically it might, sir, if . . .'

If it came to a complaint against the arresting officer. But she did not need to spell this out – they all knew. Being in a relationship with that officer could make things complicated. Allard considered the question for a moment longer, his forehead creased. Then his doubts cleared and he said, decisively, 'Well, I think we should just push on for now. Obviously, you shouldn't discuss the case with him and if it does pan out that you feel unable to be part of the team, then you'll be replaced . . . unless by bringing it up you wish to step back now?'

North shook her head quickly. 'No, no, sir, on the contrary. I just felt that you should be made aware of my situation.'

Allard smiled. 'Thank you, but I know Mike Walker. He's a damned good officer and anyway, we're not investigating him. Our investigation is into the safety of McCready's conviction in the light of the fresh evidence which Mike didn't have access to. All right?' He looked hard at North.

'Fine,' she said. 'If you're happy, I am.'

'Right, page one, then. James McCready, aged forty-four, presently serving life. At the time of the murder in 1992, he was living in a relationship with Gary Meadows. Meadows' daughter, Fiona, also lived with them in a mobile home on an estate just outside Croydon. McCready has always maintained his innocence of murder, claiming that Meadows actually had the knife in his own hand and "fell" onto it.'

Pilling snorted in disbelief. Not *that* old story! But Allard held his hand up to stem any protests. 'I know, I know. Anyway, McCready never appealed because he had no grounds – no surprise there – but he is now trying to get his case back before the courts, which is why we are all gathered here. We've also been informed that there's one of those bloody TV documentaries in the offing and that'll stir things up, so we need to move as quickly as possible on this.'

* * *

When Rylands and Duffield next visited their client in Garton Prison, they were accompanied by a man on the young side of middle age, carefully dressed in the down-beat, would-be raffish clothing of the media man. This was Roger Barker, the television documentary producer. They went through the complicated security checks together, the media man's public-school voice booming through the security areas – some story about his recent overnight journey in a railway sleeping compartment.

'Then breakfast arrived. I said, "Is this continental?" The croissant looked as if it had swum the channel! Suppose it's better than the food they get in here, though!'

The metal detector buzzed as Barker went through the scanning arch. Rylands laughed. 'That's true! . . . You should take your keys out of your pocket, Roger.'

Barker stepped back through the arch and emptied his pockets into the bowl at the side. Then he stepped back through and was passed.

Duffield, while waiting in line, was rummaging through his briefcase. 'Right, now I've gathered together the new witness statements, I can give you copies . . .' He put his briefcase down on the conveyor belt and walked through the metal-detector arch. Ahead of him Barker was being checked over by a prison officer with a hand-held metal detector. Duffield went up and stood beside him. 'I've been Jimmy's solicitor for many years,' he volunteered, 'and I have to say, I've always been totally convinced of his innocence.'

Rylands emptied his pockets, put his briefcase and coat on the belt and walked through the metal detector arch. Although he knew how to conceal it, he did find Duffield irritating in the extreme. 'Mr Duffield has been most helpful,' he said crisply, 'in giving me details of the original investigation and trial.'

The prison officer was checking Duffield's waistband now, pulling on the leather belt looped through his trousers and twisting it. At one time, belts with zipped internal compartments were a favourite method of importing drugs into prisons. Duffield was pleased as Punch with Rylands' endorsement.

As the security checks ended and they were following a prison officer along the corridor, he tapped Barker's arm. 'And I will do anything in my power to help with your programme. This is just the sort of boost our campaign needs.'

'Well, I hope I can help, even if only by raising awareness of Mr McCready's story.'

Duffield nodded his head energetically, as if his neck were made of rubber. He was enormously gratified and could not prevent himself from showing it. 'Absolutely . . . and as I have been behind Jimmy from the start, I guess I'm probably the best person to talk to about the ins and outs of the case. I contacted Robert when Jimmy brought this newspaper article to my attention.'

Duffield was being too pushy. Barker had seen this behaviour hundreds of times – educated people who wanted, with every fibre of their being, *to be on television*. They generally kept very quiet about it, unlike talk-show and game-show guests, who gloried in their enthusiasm for tawdry public humiliation. To admit the desire openly, to be seen to be chasing after it too obviously, normally put a professional man to shame. But introduce him to a real-life TV producer and Duffield, like all the rest, haplessly showed his hand. The truth was he wanted to help Barker even more than he wanted Barker's help. This, as Barker believed, was what made television the ultimate power trip.

As they walked along the corridor, Duffield pulled out the newspaper article which he and McCready had already shown Rylands. He handed it to Barker.

'Ah yes,' said Rylands, striding along slightly ahead of them but turning to see the article. 'It's about a similar stabbing case. The same prosecution pathologist completely contradicts everything he argued at McCready's trial. I'd been interested in Mr McCready's case since he started writing to me a couple of years ago, but that article really spurred me on . . . with Mr Duffield's support, obviously.'

They arrived at the entrance to the visiting section. The prison officer stopped at the security door and buzzed an intercom. He looked up to the CCTV camera by the door. 'Visitation permits for prisoner McCready, prison number AC0047. Mr Robert Rylands, Mr Ben Duffield and . . .' The officer turned enquiringly towards Barker, who took a split moment to react.

'Roger Barker . . . Area Television.'

The intercom light bleeped, they were buzzed through the security door and escorted down another corridor with legal visits rooms on either side. They were shown into one of these and Rylands and Barker took their seats while Duffield hovered.

'Did you know,' Duffield said to Barker, 'that the Met Commissioner has already ordered an internal review of the case?'

Barker pulled out a notepad and clicked his pencil. 'Really? The Met Commissioner?' He jotted a note down and looked sidelong at Rylands.

'Yes,' Rylands confirmed. 'David Landauer's an old friend of mine, so I managed to pull a few strings. Ah! Here we are.'

The door sprang open again and Jimmy McCready walked in, a prison officer looming behind. McCready struck Barker immediately as ideally telegenic – steady eyes, good-looking in a boyish way, very healthy. He had the bony, chiselled face of the long-term prisoner, the hair short but not shaved and overall it was a neatly dressed, clean look. McCready would come over as a nice boy who took a hard knock and became a survivor. Not a nasty little thug or weaselly snout. He looked, in fact, exactly the kind of person that the *Miscarriage of Justice* programme would be proud to proclaim an innocent man wronged.

McCready held up his fist and knocked it against Duffield's. 'Good to see you, Ben.'

'Mr McCready,' said Rylands, 'this is Roger Barker, the TV producer I told you about. Roger, James McCready.'

The handshake was made more formally this time. 'Great to finally meet you,' said Barker enthusiastically, 'after reading so much about you.'

Rylands made a host's gesture and the four men sat down. 'Roger runs a company called Area Television,' Rylands began. 'And he—'

'And I'd just like to say,' interrupted Barker excitedly, 'I think your story is absolutely fascinating. It's perfect for our *Miscarriage of Justice* programme. We haven't actually got a green light on it yet, but the proposal is in with the network and I'm ninety-nine per cent sure they'll go for it.'

McCready looked a little hesitant. He nodded his head. 'That's fantastic. I really appreciate everything you're all doing. If there's anything I can do to help . . .'

'Well, I'm going to need all the help I can get,' said Barker, 'to make sure we get this right, obviously. We really want to pull the heartstrings on this one so if you can think of anyone we should be speaking to, any friends or family, then you must let me know.'

McCready smiled sadly, looking down at the table. 'Well, there's the irony. Gary and Fiona were my family and my best friends. I was far closer to them than any of my own family.'

At this, Barker's noisy, gung-ho manner changed, as if suddenly confronted by tragedy. He nodded sombrely, appropriately. From his days on the tabloids he well knew which emotional buttons to press, and when to press them. 'Of course. Well, naturally, we . . . we would like to try to interview Fiona, although I understand from Mr Duffield that her foster parents are very protective so we may have problems.'

'Yes,' chimed in Duffield. 'They don't want to cause any trouble for her at school.'

'I understand,' said McCready.

There was a moment's pause and then Barker started up again. 'But Robert tells me you still own the mobile home where it all happened?'

'Yes, unfortunately.'

'I tried for several years to sell it on Jimmy's behalf,' chipped in Duffield. 'But I think too many people believed all the press hype about a murder taking place there, so . . .'

'I see,' said Barker. 'Well, I'm sorry for you, Mr McCready – but it's good news for us in terms of a convincing reconstruction.'

McCready seemed surprised. 'You mean you want to film in it?'

'With your permission. I think it could be quite powerful.'

'So, this reconstruction . . . will you have an actor playing me?'

Duffield chortled. 'Well, I don't think they'll let you out to do it, Jimmy.' He paused a second and another thought hit him. 'Though they, er, won't have an actor playing me, will they?'

Barker gave Duffield a patronising smile. 'I shouldn't think so . . . not unless you were there the night it all happened?'

Duffield couldn't help showing his disappointment. 'Oh, no, I see. Just thought that as I was so involved in preparing Jimmy's defence . . .'

'I'm afraid legal paperwork doesn't make for very exciting television, Mr Duffield.'

Duffield nodded sadly. 'No, I suppose not.'

There was another pause, then McCready turned to Barker. 'I didn't kill Gary. I know at the time I said that I killed him, but I didn't mean it like that. My words were misinterpreted and taken out of context . . . To wake up and find the person you love lying dead beside you . . . It's just . . .' Barker was scribbling notes as McCready's voice wobbled. 'We didn't think the wound was that bad. I should've called an ambulance immediately, but I didn't. That's why I felt so guilty, but no one would believe me after.'

Rylands raised a finger. 'Correction, the police didn't believe you.'

'Nothing to do with the fact he's gay, of course,' said Duffield darkly.

Rylands switched to Barker. 'I know the Met like to pretend that they're all squeaky clean and PC, but no matter how hard they try to crack down on prejudice, they'll always be intrinsically homophobic.'

'Just tell him about Detective Superintendent Walker,' said Duffield. 'He made Jimmy's life hell. Am I right?'

McCready nodded. Barker leant towards him, even more interested. 'So you think the fact that you're gay played a part in you being convicted?'

'I'm sure of it.'

Barker's eyes flashed. 'Well, if that's the case, we could have a whole new angle.'

'Gay-bashing in the Met!' crowed Duffield. 'They're known for it.'

In contrast to the solicitor's enthusiasm for this new line of attack, Rylands was nervous. 'Now we have to tread very carefully on this issue . . .'

But Barker took no notice. He was in full cry now. He turned over a page on his notepad, writing furiously. 'What was the arresting officer's name again?'

'Walker,' said Duffield. 'Now Detective Superintendent Michael Walker.'

CHAPTER 3

MONDAY, 31 JANUARY, EVENING

NORTH AND Walker had met for a drink and then strolled over to eat at a favourite Chinese restaurant in Putney. Now they were perched on stools at the corner of the food bar, as the waiter laid the seven dishes Walker had ordered in front of them. Using chopsticks, North picked a morsel from each bowl in quick succession. 'I think we've ordered enough for four! Is this the prawn and ginger, yes? And chicken. Is this the sweet and sour chicken? Or this?'

Walker had already helped himself to the chicken and a mountain of egg *foo yong* which, never having mastered chopsticks, he was now shovelling voraciously into his mouth with a knife and fork. He stopped and looked at the food heaped on his fork. 'I think so.'

North chewed for a moment, swallowed and said, 'Mike, we need to talk.'

'I know, I know. I've been feeling bad about the way I behaved the other night.'

Piling some more food onto his plate he said, 'I want you to know that I'm behind you all the way. I'm really pleased you're finally getting the recognition you deserve.' He pointed to her plate. 'Eat, go on, eat.'

North dropped a prawn on her tongue and swallowed it. 'Thanks, Mike. I know it must be hard for you, but that's not the reason—'

'Why should it be hard for *me*? You're the one who's under pressure.' He pitched another forkful into his mouth. 'This isn't chicken, it's pork!'

'No, listen. This reinvestigation I'm working on . . . Mike, just give me a minute's concentration . . . you eat too fast. Mike! It's a case you headed up.'

Walker was laughing as he drank deeply from his wine glass.

'Mike, I am serious. James McCready, serving life for the murder of—'

Walker was suddenly more serious. 'What? Who?'

'McCready. He's trying to revive his case.'

Walker dropped his fork. 'James McCready? Sent down for killing his boyfriend?'

'That's the one, yes. There's some fresh evidence.'

Walker rolled his eyes upwards, incredulously. 'I don't bloody believe this!'

'I know. But George Allard's heading the investigation and he's a bit of a fan of yours. He didn't think my working on the case would be a problem.'

Walker reacted swiftly to this, pouncing on it like a cat. 'And why should it be? I've got nothing to hide.'

North shook her head. 'No, of course not.'

There was a moment of awkward silence, during which Walker seemed to be reflecting. 'You know McCready's boyfriend was married – before he suddenly decided he was actually a nancy boy. You had enough rice?'

'Yes, thanks.'

'Meadows got custody of his little girl when her mother topped herself . . . Probably when she found out she'd married a poofter.'

This was the side of Walker North found hardest to take. She decided not to react, saying only, 'Anyway, she's with foster parents now.'

'You meeting him?'

'Who? McCready? Possibly, eventually . . . depends.' She surveyed the seven dishes, all more or less cleaned up now by Walker's predatory eating. She couldn't understand it. The guy should be fat but he was as thin as a whippet. 'You still hungry?' she asked. 'I fancy banana fritters for dessert.'

Allard had told her not to discuss the McCready case with Walker, but she felt justified by her urgent need to know if there was anything dodgy about the case on the police side, and particularly in Walker's handling of it. If there was even the sniff of something wrong she'd have to jump out of the inquiry, though that would hardly make her the blue-eyed girl of the Home Office. But as they walked out of the restaurant and up the street she was none the wiser and a great deal more confused. Walker wouldn't let the subject of McCready go but he wouldn't answer a straight question either. He did what he always did, playing the hard-bitten, old-style copper, though tonight with even more than his usual bitter relish.

'Listen,' he was saying, 'when you see him, don't let McCready hoodwink you. He's very good at acting coy. But then they *all* are, aren't they?'

'Mike!' she warned. 'Can we give the homophobic remarks a miss?'

He was laughing.

'I didn't mean it like that. What I was going to say was, these bastards bleating for an appeal all turn it on. "Oooh, look at me, I'm innocent!" Hey! TAXI!'

But the taxi passed without stopping, the driver apparently not liking the look of Walker's slightly unsteady impression of a mincing gait. Walker swore, digging his hands into his pockets.

'You're doing it again,' said North, smiling in spite of herself. 'Now stop it, I'm not supposed even to discuss the case with you.'

'But you just can't *help* yourself, ducky!'

'Mike! Stop it!'

Walker slowed down and scanned the street for another cab. 'You telling me anyone with any intelligence is going to believe that bullshit about it being an accident? The knife was stuck right in the middle of his back, for God's sake!'

Walker put his hand behind him, as if trying to prod his own back with his hand.

'Yes, well, I have to draw my own conclusions on that.'

'Meaning what? TAXI!'

The second cab passed as contemptuously as the first and Walker was beginning to take it personally. He glared after it. 'You see that? He had his "for hire" sign lit up! Bastard!'

'Mike, we're looking at the new evidence, not you. Don't be so paranoid.'

'I'm not paranoid. What are you calling me paranoid for? You're the one getting your knickers in a twist.'

He went on a few paces then stopped again and turned round, looking back along the street.

'I should have got that cab's number. That bastard.'

'Why don't we just walk home? It's not that far.'

'Fine,' he said with grim humour. 'Whatever you want! You're the boss!'

North was shaking her head. 'I knew I should never have agreed to stay on this investigation, I just *knew* it.'

Walker took her arm and squeezed it. 'No, I'm glad you are. I'll be able to keep tabs on any dirt you dig up.'

She stopped and turned to him. It suddenly occurred to her that he had told her precisely nothing about his handling of McCready's case. But now he was talking about the digging up of dirt. 'Why, is there any?'

He kissed her on the cheek. 'Well, if there is, Miss Marple, I'm sure you'll find it.' Then he walked on ahead. North sighed, her mood coming down like a high-speed elevator. She made a face at his back. If only he would lose that habit of always getting the last word.

CHAPTER 4

WEDNESDAY, 2 FEBRUARY

THE ESSENTIAL starting point of Allard's reinvestigation, after he had spent two days absorbing the paperwork, was the scene of the crime, McCready and Meadows' old mobile home, which stood in a vast park – an estate of similar dwellings south of Croydon. Allard with Watkins and North were waiting for Ben Duffield, who had arranged to meet them there. He was late. They walked around the estate a little and North was surprised that these were not, as she was expecting, caravans – not on wheels. They were more like prefabricated houses, built in a factory somewhere and brought to the site on trucks. They varied greatly in appearance. At one end of the scale they were little more than huts. At the other, they were substantial homes, comfortably furnished, bright with paint and surrounded by well-kept gardens. The best of them had lace curtains and brass knockers, and climbing roses trailed up their walls.

Allard stood in the appointed place, tapping his foot impatiently. His two detective inspectors were also overdue. 'Now, where the hell are Pilling and Collins? And Ben Duffield?' It would be a nuisance to have Duffield breathing down their necks, but as the keyholder of the mobile home they couldn't enter without him. They *could* start without the two policemen.

Finally, in a worn beige raincoat and hauling, as ever, an overstuffed briefcase, Duffield hove into view. 'Sorry,' he said, panting as he joined them. 'Bloody cab driver dropped me off on the far side of the trailer park. Had to walk from right over there! I've got mud all over my shoes.'

He looked from face to face. They were unimpressed. 'I'm Ben Duffield, Mr McCready's solicitor.'

Allard shook his hand. 'DCI George Allard. This is DI Pat North and DC Watkins.'

There were handshakes all round.

'So, which one is McCready's?' asked Allard, gesturing up the road heavily lined with mobile homes.

'It's just along the first lane,' said Duffield. 'Shall we make a move?'

Allard glanced over Duffield's head. 'We're just waiting for two more, actually.'

Duffield swung round and scanned the middle distance. 'No problem,' he said.

Finally, Pilling and Collins pulled into the car park and Allard waved and pointed in the direction they were going. 'Right, let's go,' he said. 'They can follow us up.' They tagged along behind Duffield, all clutching identical folders containing the most important paperwork on the case.

'What kind of people live here, do you reckon?' wondered North aloud as Pilling and Collins panted up behind them.

'Poor people,' said Watkins. 'People who can't afford bricks and mortar.'

'Oh, there's probably plenty of money in some of these houses,' put in Allard. 'But the owners are not particularly comfortable with bricks and mortar, for whatever reason. They see themselves as basically unconventional.'

'Like shirt-lifters,' added Les.

'Thank you, Les,' warned Allard quietly. 'Ah! Here – this must be it.' They stood and looked at the place. 'Don't you think it's weird that McCready's kept the caravan all this time?'

'Apparently he did try to sell it,' said Watkins. 'But nobody wanted to buy a murder scene.'

'Well – when you put it like that!'

It was not unknown, as North was aware, for murder houses to remain unsaleable for years – the multiple murderer John Christie's happy home, 10 Rillington Place, had had to be demolished in the end – but it was an undeniable stroke of luck that the place had been left uninhabited and virtually untouched since Meadows' death more than eight years before. From the outside, the dwelling looked squalid. Eight years of nobody's tender loving care had left it heavily rust-stained, with the roofing-felt lifting off, the paintwork cracking and the window frames in a sadly dilapidated condition. Leaves, bits of paper and rubbish had collected around the steps and clogged the gap between the floor and the concrete plinth on which the whole thing stood.

'As you know,' Duffield told them as he fished out a set of keys and unlocked three separate locks on the front door, 'no one has been occupying the trailer since shortly after my client's arrest, so it'll probably be a bit dusty inside.' He swung the door open. 'I'm expecting Mr McCready's barrister for a viewing, so I'll let you in, then we'll look in after you.'

Allard looked at the others. Rylands was coming down, was he? 'Yes, thank you, Mr Duffield,' he said.

Duffield nodded and wandered off to rummage again in his briefcase.

'Be a bit of a crush in there,' said Allard. 'Perhaps we should look round in two separate groups.'

'Good idea,' said North brightly. 'Well, I'll go first, then, if no one minds.' She went in behind Allard. It was dark and he opened the curtains, revealing grimy nets. The light they let in was pale brown and depressing.

'God, it's musty,' Allard remarked. 'Leave the door open, for God's sake.'

North blinked to adjust to the dimness. 'Is the electricity on?' she asked.

Allard tried a switch. Nothing. ''Fraid not. Right, let's start in the bedroom, which would be' – he checked the ground plan provided in the file – 'through here and on the right.'

In addition to the living room, which gave onto a kitchen area and a tiny bathroom, the dwelling had two bedrooms. They now entered the larger of these and Allard again opened the curtains. The room was dusty but otherwise neat. The pictures and posters, a bedside clock radio, the child's drawings, the small ornaments that the little family had collected were all still here after all those years. There was something North found oddly moving about this time-warp element. She said nothing to Allard, who was busy comparing the space with crime-scene photos, taken before the police cleaners had been sent in. These prints clearly showed where the blood had splashed.

'So the fight, or argument, or whatever it was, supposedly started in here,' said North.

Allard looked from the photograph to the reality. 'The cleaners did a pretty comprehensive job.'

North started to check off items from her file. 'Glass top of dressing table broken, ditto mirror near the door. Clothes and colognes thrown to the floor. Forensic reports identify Meadows' blood all over the sheets and mattress to the left and dripping through to the floor, forming a pool on the carpet. A small amount of smearing from McCready, principally on the right side of the bed.'

Allard stood between the door and the bed, listening carefully to North's commentary. 'So how does Meadows get onto the bed?' he asked.

'Certainly not dragged – that would have left traces on the carpet. Carried is theoretically possible, but not easy within the confines of a caravan, as you can see. The defence, of course, said he walked there, assisted by McCready.'

'But however he got there, he actually died on the bed?'

'Well, the bleeding on the bed could mean that he was alive when he reached it.'

'How long between the stabbing and death?'

'That was the problem. Our pathologist said no more than five minutes, the defence expert said up to twenty minutes or even half an hour at a push.'

Allard was looking at the pathologist's notes. 'So, argument started in here and death occurred in here. What happened in between?'

'McCready says they continued arguing, moving into the hallway.' North walked out to the hallway herself, followed by Allard. 'At some point Meadows turns and runs into the kitchen, here, grabs a kitchen knife with an eight-inch blade from, I presume, the carving set . . . ah yes!' She was in the kitchen now, pointing to a set of knives hanging from the wall. One was missing. 'The argument then becomes heated as Meadows threatens McCready with the knife.'

'So they move back further into the hallway?' asked Allard.

North turned to look along the hall. She held up a crime-scene photograph taken from the same angle, which showed where the blood spots were marked on the walls. 'Most of the bloodstains out here were McCready's.'

Allard nodded, consulting another page in his file. 'Ah, yes, McCready says he received a slash to his left forearm and the palm of his hand, apparently while trying to defend himself – and struggling to get the knife off Meadows.'

'But now, according to McCready, he follows Meadows into the hall, still trying to get the knife, which he claims Meadows put behind his back so that he couldn't reach it.' North moved backwards down the corridor. In order to understand better what had occurred that night eight years ago, she was acting out the part of Meadows. 'Meadows backs towards this wall here and, so McCready claims, as he heads towards Meadows he trips on the rug . . .' She looked again at her notes. They contained a photograph of the loose rug. 'He trips, according to his story, making him seem to lunge towards Meadows, who subsequently lurches backwards straight onto the knife.'

Allard was studying the photographs of a half-naked Meadows that adorned the walls in this part of the house – posey, self-regarding shots.

'He then, says Meadows, withdraws the knife from his own back and tells McCready he's accidentally stabbed himself. McCready admits taking the knife and putting it back in the kitchen.' North now returned to the kitchen, making notes on the file, while Allard, himself a keen amateur photographer, continued to study the photographs of the handsome, narcissistic Meadows. 'Leaving the knife in the sink, he returns to help Meadows into the bedroom.'

Allard jabbed his finger towards the door of the small bedroom. 'And Meadows' daughter, Fiona, witnesses the incident from her bedroom doorway. As she claims in her recent statement, McCready tells her to go back to bed, that her daddy's feeling poorly. After assuring her everything's fine, she actually sees her father going into his bedroom.' He tapped on one of the shots of Meadows. 'By the way, you seen these photographs? Very good lighting!'

But North's mind was elsewhere. 'So she goes back into her room, and McCready then helps Meadows into their bedroom and into bed. McCready then takes a glass of brandy into the bedroom and gets into bed. Some time after that – not long, but long enough apparently for McCready to fall asleep – Meadows dies. That's McCready's version of events. He gave it at his trial and the jury didn't believe a word of it.'

Outside, Watkins was leaning against a wall, waiting for her chance to take a look at the McCready house. She was listening to Pilling talking about Mike Walker. 'He's on the mint murder, you read about it?'

'So?' said Watkins. 'I still don't see any reason why Pat shouldn't be on this.'

'Well, it could be a bit dodgy,' said Collins. 'If McCready's case *doesn't* get to appeal, and the press find out that one of the officers doing the reinvestigation was living with the detective who led the original inquiry.'

'Well, I'm sure if anything looks murky she'll step aside, sharpish. Pat's not stupid, nor is Walker.'

Pilling shook his head sagely. 'Very convenient for him, though, having her on this, isn't it? Must be a plus for him whichever way you look at it.'

Watkins sighed. 'What I meant was, neither Mike Walker nor Dave Satchell would be stupid enough to meddle with evidence and put the wrong man away.'

Pilling put his hands up, backing away apologetically. 'Excuse me. No offence meant!'

Somewhere nearby a car's wheels crunched and a door clunked.

'Then just stop stirring, OK?' warned Watkins. 'Pat's a very conscientious officer. No way would she want any dirt attached to her.'

Collins nudged Pilling. 'That MP has more than likely got the hots for McCready and this is all givin' him a hard-on, eh?' At this moment, he realised that Rylands himself, with Duffield in tow, was approaching the mobile home. Collins put his knuckles to his lips. 'Whoops!'

Behind Rylands and Duffield, a Porsche approached, pulling up ten yards short in a cloud of dust. Barker, with a trim, well-groomed girl beside him, lowered his window and reversed into a parking space. 'Robert!' he called out of the window. 'Came over as soon as I got the news. Show's been green lit, that's the good news. Bad news is they want it in the new season, so we'll be working to an impossibly tight schedule.' Barker sprang from the car, followed more slowly by the girl. 'This is my PA, Lucy. Lucy, this is Robert Rylands QC and MP, and Ben Duffield, Mr McCready's solicitor.'

'Hi. Pleased to meet you.' Lucy smiled and extended her hand to Rylands first. She was about to say something when Barker beckoned to her and they wandered away to look around the outside of the mobile home, Lucy carrying a clipboard for taking notes.

Meanwhile, Duffield smiled ingratiatingly at Rylands. 'Sorry to keep you waiting, Robert. Hopefully they won't be long and then we can have our *locus in quo*.'

After a reconnaissance that was abrupt even by TV standards, Barker rejoined the group. He was brisk and businesslike. 'As time is of the essence, we'd like to take some Polaroids inside the caravan and set up a storyboard.'

'That shouldn't be a problem,' Rylands assured him. 'We just have to wait until the investigation team leave.'

Barker brightened even more when he heard that detectives from the reinvestigation were on the scene. 'Hey, do you think I could get an interview from one of them?'

Duffield turned to Barker, eager to involve himself. 'You want *me* to talk to them?'

But Rylands moved swiftly to damp him down, smiling calmly. 'I'm sure Roger can handle it himself, Ben.'

CHAPTER 5

WEDNESDAY, 2 FEBRUARY

Walker was clawing laundry out of the dryer, looking for a sock. He had found one, but not the other. What the hell was it with socks? This morning, as had happened two or three times since he'd moved in with Pat, he'd left the house wearing odd ones – close, but not exactly the same. He couldn't understand why the pairs didn't stay together. Or what became of those delinquent ones that went missing. With Lynn it had never seemed to happen. She'd marshalled all his washing, and the kids', with a strictness that never, as far as he knew, let a single thing go astray. Socks in pairs, people in pairs. It was the same thing. Sometimes you thought there was a match until you looked at it in clear daylight. Sometimes a pair lasted together for years and then, unaccountably, one's gone . . . Where *was* that bastard blue sock? He started sifting through the heap of dry shirts, towels and sheets on the floor and he almost laughed. Look at him – the great detective searching for a sock. Instead he swore and kicked the tangled heap of washing, then started out of the kitchen. But at the door he stopped and returned to the washing with a sigh. Couldn't leave it here. He crouched and started folding up towels.

The front door banged and North came in from work. 'Hi!' she called. 'You're back early.'

'Yeah, got an early start tomorrow.' Walker carefully placed the last of the folded sheets on top of the pile, picked them all up and deposited them precariously on the kitchen worktop. Then he wandered into the living area, where she was sifting through the post. 'So, how'd it go today?' he asked.

'Fine, thanks. It's quite an interesting case.'

'Draw any conclusions yet?'

'Hardly! We're still getting our heads around the paperwork.' She was reading a decal-edged card showing the words 'Thank You' twined with summer flowers and mobbed by butterflies. 'Ah, sweet.' She handed it to Walker. 'Card from Satch and Catrina to say thanks for dinner.'

Walker hadn't bothered to look at the post when he'd come in. He was surprised. A thank-you card, especially one like this, didn't sound like Satch. This must be Catrina's doing. 'What? She's certainly got him under the thumb!' Walker tossed the card aside and perched on the edge of the sofa. North ripped open more envelopes. 'So, what exactly were you doing today?'

'Mike, I don't think I should discuss any details with you – just to be on the safe side, you know.'

Walker stood and held his hands up, fluttering them like those butterflies from Satchell's card. 'Fine, no absolutely. You're right . . . Cup of tea?'

'That'd be great!'

Walker retreated to the kitchen area to put the kettle on. He called out, 'You fancy seeing a movie tonight?'

'What's on?'

'Not sure.'

There was a letter about her tax return which she'd need to copy. She bent to tuck it into her briefcase and suddenly felt her stomach go into sharp cramps. She winced. Walker, having set the kettle to boil, was back in the lounge and he noticed.

'You OK?'

She hurried up the stairs and into the bathroom, calling out, 'No, been feeling a bit sickly, actually.'

Walker was at the foot of the stairs now. 'You think you've eaten something dodgy? Can't be the Chinese 'cause I'm fine.'

'No, probably the lukewarm pastie I had for lunch.'

'Ah, that'll be it, then.' Walker started to cross back to the kitchen but stopped on seeing North's open briefcase left by the side of the sofa. 'My mother always made a hot brandy toddy for wobbly stomachs,' he said, looking to the stairs and then down again at the briefcase. He hesitated, then gave way to temptation, swiftly stooping, lifting a file or two until he came to one marked *JAMES McCREADY*. He turned a couple of pages and started to read. After a moment he realised subliminally that it had gone quiet upstairs. She was probably lying down.

'Can I get you anything?' he called out.

But North's reply was just behind him. 'No, but you can tell me what the hell you're doing!'

Walker hurriedly put the papers down and disappeared into the kitchen. 'Just caught a glimpse of my name and was curious, that's all.'

North was closing her briefcase. Her face was white and tense with anger. 'That's not good enough, Mike, and you know it. How dare you go through my briefcase!'

'"Dare"? Oh, come on, Pat, I was hardly "going through" it.'

'That's not the point. You know how sensitive I am about working on this case as it is, without you snooping around behind my back.'

'For God's sake, calm down. I'm just naturally curious about what's going on, that's all.'

'And if I won't tell you, you'll search through my things until you find out! Is that it?'

'Oh, stop being so bloody dramatic. It's not like I've got anything to worry about.'

North placed the briefcase in the hall, beside the door. 'So you keep telling me, but the way you've been fishing for information, I'm beginning to wonder!'

Suddenly Walker, too, was seething. 'Oh, that's just great! And you're worried about being biased in my favour?' He passed her, crossing to where his coat was draped across the stair post. Suddenly he was pulling it on. 'I'm more worried you'll turn them against me! But *fine*, do it all your own way. Just don't come crying to me when you want answers.'

Answers? thought North. Walker's usual idea of an answer was to suggest another round of drinks. She watched him stride to the door. For a moment she felt nothing but rage. 'That's right, just run away like you always do!'

Walker stopped to straighten his collar. 'I won't even dignify that with a response,' he said. But he spoilt the effect by adding, 'I have *never* run away from anything – or anyone – in my life!'

Then he slammed the door.

He phoned Satchell from his car. 'Meet me for a drink, Satch. I want to talk and it's urgent.'

Satchell sighed. He'd just got in from a long day interviewing a bunch of suspects probably involved in a bullion fraud. Interviews at Fraud were always more taxing than most and he just wanted a hot shower and a quiet telly night. But Walker insisted. It was vital they should meet. 'OK,' agreed Satchell. 'But you come down here, Mike. You know my local? See you there in twenty minutes.'

Twenty minutes later they sat in the pub with pints of lager and a large packet of nuts. Walker was devouring the latter with his usual ferocity while he told Satchell about the reinvestigation of the McCready case. Until just over a year ago, Satchell had been his right-hand man – as well as his friend – on several major inquiries. McCready had been one of them.

'They're just checking out the safety of the conviction. Apparently there's no suggestion of any misconduct on our part.'

Satchell shook his head wearily. From the other bar, which had a big screen, the sound of the football commentary and the crowd noises washed through, rising and falling like the sea. 'Great!' he said. 'We're constantly put through the wringer and the bloody criminals get the red-carpet treatment.'

Walker nodded. 'Yes, and apparently McCready's got a hot-shot MP pushing it through.'

'And he'll be a shirt-lifter too, of course . . . That's right, finish the nuts!'

Walker had crumpled the empty nut bag in his fist and dropped it in the ashtray. 'Oh, sorry, you want some?' He half rose and cocked his head towards the bar.

Satchell shook his head with a narrow smile. 'Nah, forget it.'

Walker took a long sip of beer. He fished for a cigarette, snapped off the filter and lit up. 'Anyway, Pat's got all hot under the collar about being on the reinvestigation at the same time as us living together. You know how paranoid she gets. So we stay schtum about the Glasgow business, agreed? Not a word.'

At this Satchell's head snapped up from his own beer. 'Wait, wait! Hang on there, mate. That sounds like they're already sniffing out something.'

Walker shook his head. Satchell was as nervous as he was. 'They haven't started yet, but we'd both better be singing off the same song sheet when they do.'

Satchell resumed his sip, slowly this time, then replaced the glass with infinite care on the beer mat. He looked up and met Mike Walker's eyes, which were watching him, the lids narrowed almost to a slit. Satchell's throat felt parched. He picked up his glass and took another long gulp.

North lay curled up in the sitting room, clutching a mug of tea and reading from the McCready case file. Swallowing the last dregs of her tea, she looked up at the clock: it was after half past eleven. Sighing, she rolled off the sofa and crossed to the phone, rapidly punching out the number.

'Shit!' Walker's mobile was switched off. The answering service was requesting her sweetly to leave a message. She cursed silently and said, 'Mike, if you're not intending to come home tonight, you could at least have the decency to give me a call.' She slammed the phone down, looked to the clock again, then grabbed her coat and keys and pulled open the front door. She knew where he'd be holed up.

Fifteen minutes later she was ringing Satchell's doorbell. When Dave Satchell opened the door she said, 'Hi!' in a loud voice which echoed around the landing and stairs. 'Sorry to turn up so late but the pubs are closed. I knew he'd be here.'

Satchell shot a glance back over his shoulder. 'Er . . . I don't know . . .'

'Please, Satch, just let me in.'

'Look, Pat . . .' He stepped out into the corridor, drawing his front door almost closed behind him. 'He's well pissed. I think it's probably best if you leave it tonight, eh?'

'*Leave* it? Don't you two understand what I'm in the middle of? I mean, this is—'

Satchell held up his palm. 'Listen, don't drag me into this. Whatever's going down between you two has nothing to do with me, OK?'

North calmed herself. She swallowed, then started again. 'What is going down, Satch, is that I am on a team reinvestigating the murder of Gary Meadows. You worked on the case as well. So you are *both* in the middle of it, whether you like it or not.' She looked him straight in the eye. Satchell met her gaze steadily but said nothing. After a couple of silent beats, she turned and marched to the stairs. 'Tell him not to bother coming home.'

Satchell shut the front door behind him. He was just slotting home the security chain when Catrina appeared from the bedroom, her see-through dressing gown floating around her enticing body like a cloud. She slid her arm into his and tugged. Satchell caressed her shoulder. 'Be with you in a minute, babe. I'd just better check on him.'

'Dave, you said that half an hour ago!'

'Just go back to bed, eh? I won't be long.'

In the living room Walker was lying shoeless and sprawled on the sofa, watching a rerun of *Kind Hearts and Coronets* on television. Satchell stood in front of his friend, half blocking the screen. 'Well, you know who *that* was. You must have heard her. You're going to have to tell her about Glasgow, you know.' Satchell turned and switched off the TV just as another member of the D'Ascoyne family was being murdered by Dennis Price.

'Hey!' protested Walker. 'I was watching that.'

'Stop pissing around, Mike. You may not give a shit about your career but I care about mine and I'm not taking any flak for you. I mean it.'

Walker manoeuvred himself into a more upright posture. '*Your* career? I made your sodding career, sunshine. You were quite happy to bathe in the glory.'

'Maybe. But I'm not gonna wallow in your shit as well. It's all going to come out, Mike!'

Walker shook his head. 'No, it isn't. There's no records, there was no HOLMES database back then. Nothing's gonna turn up about me and McCready because there's nothing – absolutely nothing – either electronic or on paper.'

Satchell stayed silent as Walker heaved himself up and switched the television back on, saying, 'Go on, get back to Caroline, boy.'

'Catrina.'

Walker wafted a hand to and fro. 'Whatever. I'll just see the end of the film then let myself out.'

Satchell regarded Walker as he flopped back onto the sofa once more. 'Stay as long as you like. But if you want my advice, you really should come clean about Glasgow.'

When his host had gone, Walker lit up a cigarette and inhaled deeply. Soon, on screen, another contender for the D'Ascoyne inheritance bit the dust and Walker smiled, slowly clapping his hands. In difficult times, there was nothing like the simple pleasures, such as having a drink and watching members of the English aristocracy getting bumped off. Then he looked down at his stockinged feet and noticed he was still wearing odd socks.

CHAPTER 6

THURSDAY, 3 FEBRUARY

Marking Roger Barker's card, Duffield had told him he'd find the Frog and Ferret a well-kept, friendly neighbourhood pub, very lively in the evenings. It was less so at lunchtime, although reasonable food of the ploughman's variety was on offer across the bar. The place was also less than a hundred yards from the mobile-home park where McCready and Meadows had lived, and Barker had hopes of a few words with some regulars who might remember the death of Meadows.

He leant against the bar with a half pint of lager and his notebook open in front of him, eating a sausage sandwich. He'd already got a chat going with the barman, mentioning early on that he was in television. This information worked its usual magic. The chap was coming across with all sorts about McCready and Meadows. He'd been a fixture behind the bar at the Frog and Ferret on and off for years, so he knew a thing or two about local matters. His name was Keith and, if Barker was any judge, he, too, was gay.

'Keith what?'

'Tanner; two "n"s, like Elsie Tanner in *Coronation Street*.'

Barker wrote it down in his notebook. Keith moved away, dishing out lasagne and salad from the food counter. But he stayed within earshot.

'So, Mr Tanner, you were serving in the bar the night Gary Meadows died, that right?'

'Yes, the landlord threw a surprise party for me 'cause I was leaving the next morning for Marbella. I was out there for eighteen months, didn't know anything about the Gary Meadows thing until I got back.'

He clattered two plates of food down on the counter and shouted, 'Number nine – come and get it! . . . I told all this to some solicitor bloke . . . Duffield. You know him?'

'Yes, I do know him. But the *police* never questioned you?'

'Like I said, I was off to Spain. I moved around, working as a DJ, and by the time I got back, Jimmy was in prison. Anyway, I wouldn't have been able to tell the police anything worthwhile. I only knew the lads because this was their local.'

'That night, did you notice anything out of the ordinary about them?'

Keith was wiping glasses. He stopped and opened his eyes wide in mock surprise at the question. 'You *are* joking? I was off my face! Barely remembered my own name by the end of the evening! They were nice guys, though, very friendly to everyone. You know, you should probably talk to Eva. She claims she helped police with the investigation, but apparently she wasn't called for the trial.'

'Eva?'

'Eva Widelski . . . don't ask me to spell it, it's a Polish name. She lives on the same caravan site. She's some kind of mystic . . . well, when she's sober! Maybe she knows something, I don't know.'

A customer appeared at the far end of the bar and Keith acknowledged him with a nod. As he moved off, he fired a final shot. 'Jimmy would never have killed Gary, no way. Now I better go and serve that gentleman. Excuse me.'

Barker moved swiftly sideways to keep up with him. 'Would you be prepared to be interviewed for the programme?'

Keith replied over his shoulder. 'Oh, yeah. Love that. You know where to find me.'

After Keith had left him, Barker's fixed smile broadened and became genuine. This Eva What's-her-name sounded as if she might furnish him with some very promising material and, in the meantime, he'd found one man prepared to say sincerely and believably that there was no way McCready was a killer. His programme was looking better and better.

Allard had detailed North and Watkins to interview Meadows' daughter, Fiona. North, feeling a long way off the top of her form, had arranged for Watkins to pick her up at home.

'How's Mike?' asked the Detective Constable while she waited for North to get herself together.

North glanced at her elegant colleague, who wore a well-cut grey suit, her dark hair in a lustrous braid. North was not bad-looking but Watkins was beautiful. Unfair.

'Probably hung-over and feeling sorry for himself but, to be honest, I am starting not to care, Viv.'

'Sorry I asked.'

Hurriedly, North ran a brush through her fair hair. She didn't mind the colour but she'd always wished it was less lanky and fine. 'Everyone said it wouldn't work, with me and Mike. Well, maybe they were right. And if you don't mind, I don't want to talk about it.'

'Fine,' said Watkins, remaining diplomatically incurious. 'How's the tummy?'

'Better. I still feel a bit queasy, but under the circumstances, who wouldn't? OK, I'm all set. Let's go.'

The house was in Norwood and built in the 1920s, when it had been fashionable to give a supposedly Tudor look to the outside of any house, however mass-produced. In keeping with its period then, the walls of this house were painted white and criss-crossed by a few black planks to simulate half-timbering. The windows were casements and diamond-leaded.

Vivien pulled on the handbrake. 'Right,' she said. 'Her foster parents are Joan and Alister Plover. I spoke to Mrs Plover earlier on and apparently Fiona's quite nervy, but by all accounts an intelligent kid.'

'And no statement was taken from her after the murder?'

'Apparently not, she was very traumatised . . . couldn't speak. So she couldn't be interviewed.'

North reflected as she scanned the house carefully. 'Odd . . .' She snapped off her seat belt. 'OK, let's do it.'

* * *

It was a perfectly ordinary house, insofar as any house is ordinary. There was money here, not too much of it but enough. There was also care and there were standards. From the souvenirs around the place – fans, castanets, bullfighters and flamenco dancers – it looked as if there were Spanish holidays too.

Mrs Plover, forties, marginally overweight and wearing a grey cardigan, had dark red hair cropped in a 20s style, as if to match the era from which her house dated. She spoke with a slightly self-conscious gentility but her voice was mild as milk. If threatened, she looked as if she would be a complete pushover. But, from what she said next, North decided she might not be so easily forced from the fray.

'We've had the TV people bombarding us with phone calls,' she explained. 'One even turned up at the house yesterday, but I refused to let them see Fiona. This is all very nerve-racking for her. Mr McCready's solicitor, Mr Duffield, has talked to her a few times as well. Would you like a tea or coffee?'

North and Watkins refused. Mrs Plover led them towards the lounge but stopped at the door, grasping the handle. 'Fiona came to us straight after it all happened. It was not easy to begin with but she's settled down very well. She's a lovely girl . . .' Her voice had already been almost a whisper. Now she lowered it yet more. 'No one at her school knows, she doesn't like talking about it. Only the headmistress knows – we had to tell her, obviously.'

Watkins cleared her throat. 'And has Fiona had any contact at all with Mr McCready over the years?'

Mrs Plover shook her head, frowning slightly. 'Well, she has recently expressed an interest in going to see him, yes. But we've managed to put her off so far. Please, come on through.'

Ben Duffield, in his usual raincoat, was anchored to an armchair in the corner of the sitting room. As ever, his briefcase was open on his lap.

'Mr Duffield!' exclaimed North in surprise. 'What are you doing here?'

Duffield's mouth formed a momentary smile. 'Fiona is a defence witness.'

Mrs Plover gestured to where she wanted the police officers to sit. 'Mr Duffield's come to lend his support,' she said simply.

'I won't be any bother,' said the solicitor. 'I'll just sit quietly in the corner.'

North raised her eyebrows towards Vivien, who just smiled as they both sat down on one of two double sofas. At the same moment they heard the front door slam and a voice calling from the hall. 'Mum!

'Come on in, Fiona . . . Fiona?'

The door opened to reveal the fifteen-year-old Fiona, wearing a tracksuit and trainers. She looked shy and demure, her straight, shoulder-length brown hair falling forward to veil her face. Mrs Plover greeted her foster daughter with a smile that was a little strained. *None of this could be any fun for a foster mother*, thought North. She must want to have all this behind them, forgotten.

'Fiona, this is Pat and Vivien. They're from the police.'

Fiona reached for a strand of her hair and toyed with it. 'Hello.' She was very slightly out of breath.

'Do you want to sit down, Fiona?' said North. 'Have you been running?'

'No, skateboarding.'

'She's on it morning until night,' said Mrs Plover, sitting down on the double sofa beside North and Vivien. 'We've promised to take her to the skateboarding world championships in Miami. Sit down, darling.'

Fiona hesitated, then settled next to Mrs Plover. She clasped her hands round her knees, her head still lowered.

North turned a new page on her notebook. 'Now, I'm sorry to have to ask you this, Fiona, but would you tell me, in your own words and in your own time, what happened the night your father died? Everything you can remember, no matter how insignificant it might seem. And just before you start, we need to record this, OK?'

Fiona nodded. North pressed the record button on a small portable tape recorder and placed it on the table about halfway between them. 'OK, Fiona, in your own time.'

'Well, I was in bed, asleep. The music woke me up first, it was really loud. I heard Dad shouting, and then Jimmy – they often argued. Sometimes when they got angry with each other, I hid – you know, they used to scare me. I saw my dad running up and down the hallway. He had a knife and Jimmy was running after him.'

'And where were you at this point?'

'In my bedroom doorway.'

'OK, go on.'

'Well, I seem to remember Jimmy trying to get the knife and they started struggling with it.' She dried up.

North waited a moment and put in a prompt. 'Did you see Jimmy get cut?'

'I think so. I remember his arm bleeding.'

'So, after they struggled with the knife, what happened next?'

'Well, Dad put the knife behind his back to hide it from Jimmy and the next minute Jimmy fell against him and my dad hit the wall hard. Dad said not to worry, he was fine, and he went back into their bedroom.'

'Did he walk back or did Jimmy carry him?'

Fiona thought for a moment, frowning in concentration. 'I guess he must have walked on his own because I remember Jimmy coming over and kissing me. He said we were all friends again.'

'Then what happened?'

'Jimmy went into the kitchen looking for some bandages and I went back to bed.'

'When did you know something bad had happened?'

Now Fiona had started very quietly to cry. Mrs Plover had a tissue ready, which she passed across.

'Next morning,' the child snuffled, 'when Jimmy was crying . . . and the ambulance arrived. He'd been sobbing, well, and shouting, waiting for them to come.' Tears were wetting the child's dark hair now. She blew her nose. Duffield sat leaning forward, intent on Fiona's words.

'I'm sorry, Fiona,' North said softly. 'I know this is upsetting.' She waited a moment for the girl to compose herself. 'Now, I know this might be a difficult question, but why do you think you've remembered all this now?'

Fiona sat up and cleared the damp strands of hair from her cheeks. She seemed to square her shoulders, ready to face the truth, whatever it may be. 'Well, I'd totally blocked it out of my mind. All I knew was that it was such an awful time and . . . and I couldn't bear thinking about it.' She sniffed again and there seemed every sign that she might burst into tears once more. But she controlled herself. 'It wasn't until Mr Duffield came to see me that I forced myself to think back, and I realised I was the only one who could help Jimmy.'

'Thank you, Fiona,' said North. 'I think we can leave it there for today.'

Vivien reached and clicked off the tape recorder. North scribbled a final note and closed her notebook. She looked up in time to see Duffield clicking off a small Dictaphone of his own that he'd been holding in his hand. He slipped it into his pocket and favoured North with a bland smile.

As they drove away, North had one question for her colleague. 'Was she telling the truth, Viv?'

Watkins nodded. 'I reckon so. Anyway, the tears were genuine. What did you think?'

North closed her eyes. Her stomach felt tender, she was tired, she didn't want to think about it. 'I really don't know, Viv. She wasn't lying. But maybe she wasn't telling the truth either.'

'Is that possible?'

North nodded. 'Oh yes,' she said. 'It's possible.'

CHAPTER 7

THURSDAY, 3 FEBRUARY

In front of the McCready house was a line of vans, from which the film crew were unloading and setting up their lights, microphones and cameras. It was the first day of filming for the *Miscarriage of Justice* programme and, while the crew sorted itself out, Barker thought he would find out what the mysterious Widelski woman had to say. Dictating staccato production notes into his voice recorder, he walked beyond McCready's house and kept on past numerous similar dwellings. After making two turnings, he reached the home of the star of variety and clairvoyance – and also, perhaps, of his film on the innocence of Jimmy McCready.

Barker already had an idea of what she would be like. Following Keith Tanner's hint, he'd got Lucy, his PA and researcher, to phone Eva Widelski yesterday afternoon to get her story.

'She drinks,' Lucy had warned him. 'But she's perfectly clear and never stops talking. You wait till you meet her – she's had some weird but wonderful experiences with the police. She wouldn't tell me the details over the phone but I think she's a gift.'

That bode well, because Lucy was ambitious and had often surprised Roger with her intuitions. She could be a pain in the neck, but stupid she wasn't.

'It's got everything, Roger,' she'd finished by saying. 'It's colourful, it's convincing, it may tip the balance in the programme's credibility and it's completely bizarre! Go for it.'

He went through the Widelski front gate, checking the number before going up the path, and noticed a woman, presumably the old girl herself, peeking out through the curtains. As he reached the door, it opened. She was a striking figure: at least sixty, with unruly chestnut hair and vivid makeup, thick enough for the stage which she had so often graced.

'Are you with the TV people?' she demanded boldly.

He whipped out his Area Television business card. 'I am. I'm the producer from Area Television, Roger Barker. I wonder if I could come in and talk to you?'

'About the murder? Oh yes, come on in.'

The tiny lounge contained moth-eaten chairs and a small sofa draped in shawls. But before she invited him to sit, Eva treated him to a conducted tour of her memorabilia. The walls were arrayed with black-and-white production stills and theatrical posters, signed programmes and sheet music. Eva had evidently based much of her career around old-time music-hall shows. Pride of place was given to the 'Ever Popular' Eva Widelski's famous 'Those Were The Days' impersonation of the male impersonator Vesta Tilley. On one poster Eva did a soft shoe shuffle in front of the footlights, wearing top hat and tails, twirling a silver-knobbed cane. On another, she leant against a grand piano, and a third had her linking her arms with a long, feather-waving, high-kicking chorus line. At last he persuaded her to get down to the business at hand. Yes, Eva told him, she did remember that awful night.

'The two lads, Gary and Jimmy, came into the pub, the Frog and Ferret. It was late – you know, a party after hours. I sang "My Old Man". Gary was playing the piano and I danced with Jimmy. Of course, Keith was behind the bar. Like I said, that's everybody. I was on the stage for thirty years, you know. Musical comedy. Did you ever go down the Old Tivoli Music Hall by The Strand? I had a regular spot . . .' She started singing, gently, '*Swing me just a little bit higher Obadiah do* . . . I never did the TV shows, but those really *were* the good old days. Would you like a sherry?'

Hurriedly, Barker shook his head. 'Thank you, no. Tell me, were you interviewed by the police at the time of the murder?'

Eva was helping herself to the bottle of dark sherry. She winked. 'Kind of. I had an officer come round. Do you remember "A Little of What You Fancy Does You Good"?' She pointed to a poster of the Old Tivoli Music Hall, with herself in top hat and tails. 'I worked there as Vesta Tilley . . .' And again she was singing. '*I'm following in Father's footsteps, I'm following the dear old dad.*'

Barker took a deep breath and counted to five. 'This officer who came round, do you recall his name?'

'No, he was shortish, well-built, though, dark-haired. Nice young fellow.'

'Was he Scottish?'

'Oh, I can't remember that, dear.'

'What did he ask you about?'

'Well, as a matter of fact it was in my other professional capacity – as a clairvoyant. I've helped out on quite a few cases in the past, you know. In fact, I've got a scrapbook.'

Barker didn't quite know how to take Eva. She was virtually auditioning for him. She now plonked a big scrapbook down in front of him and turned the pages.

'So what exactly did this officer want you to do?' he asked.

'He had a glass with him, in a plastic bag. He wanted to know if I could get anything from it.'

Barker sat forward. 'What do you mean?'

Eva dropped her voice to a dramatic murmur. 'Well, sometimes I can get mental images from touching certain objects. I do drawings. I also do seances. I charge twenty-five pound for tarot, twenty-five for palm and fifty for an astrology chart. All complimentary to the police, of course.'

Barker was finding her circuitous conversational style difficult to handle. He tried to steer her back to the subject. 'Were you able to give the officer any information with regard to this . . . glass, you said?'

'It was a brandy glass and I got a very clear picture from it so I made a drawing for the officer.'

'What was it of?'

'Well, that's the strange thing. It was a fireplace.'

'Fireplace?'

'Yes, but not a very special one. Old, cheap tiles, square, 40s style. It came through very clearly.'

Barker was sitting tensely on the tasselled edge of his chair. He framed his next question carefully, as if afraid it would break. 'I don't suppose you still . . . er, have the drawing?'

Eva giggled. 'Of course, I never give away the original. Always make a copy for the client.' She indicated a very small, old photocopier in one corner and then turned her attention back to the scrapbook, flicking the pages until she found a square of drawing paper which she unfolded, examined and passed to Barker. 'There you go.'

As she had said, it was certainly a fireplace: columns at each side supporting a mantelpiece, the firegrate, the tiled surround. 'So where is this fireplace?'

Eva shrugged extravagantly, rolling her eyes heavenward. 'No idea! The images are just sent through me. Maybe it was somebody else's fireplace, you know, someone else broke into my mind.'

Barker stood up. His head was spinning. The dim light, the oppressive decor and Eva's pungent scent were making him claustrophobic. He was becoming anxious to get out. 'Thank you very much, Miss Widelski. We're very interested, very interested indeed in this. Especially about the glass. May we contact you in a day or two when I've got a shape for the final programme?'

'Of course, dear. Don't forget I'm an old trouper. Call me anytime. I'll still be here.'

Back in McCready's house, two lookalike actors were rehearsing the stabbing sequence while a young girl, playing Fiona, watched the proceedings with her chaperone. The small crew, including Lucy, were huddled together in the narrow space. Barker, as both the producer and presenter, stood in front of the camera with Phil, the handsome, fit-looking actor playing Meadows. Duffield hovered around, getting in the way. The makeup girl was touching up the wound in the left forearm of Derek, the actor cast as McCready – a two-inch artificial gash.

'Good, looks good,' said Barker. 'Now, before we do a take, let's just walk it through. Derek?' Derek stepped forward and took up his position. 'And props . . . we want the mock knife for the rehearsal.' The props manager handed Phil a convincing-looking stage knife which he tested out, making to stab himself and watching the retractable blade apparently disappearing into his belly. 'OK, let's just walk it,' called Barker. 'You start, Phil. Back down the hall. Rehearsal, quiet please! And cue . . . smoke.'

A smoke machine pumped out a burst of smoke and a runner wafted it around the mobile home. Duffield, peering in at the door, coughed and whispered to Lucy, 'Why do they need smoke?'

'Atmosphere,' she said crisply.

The reconstruction began. Derek clutched his arm. Phil crouched in readiness opposite him, jabbing the air with the knife. 'Gary, give me the knife . . . Gary, stop this, look what you've done to me. GARY!'

'Stay away from me! I'm warning you or I'll do a lot worse!'

'Hey! You've had too much to drink, Gary, give me the knife.'

Phil was now backing away, switching the knife teasingly from his right to his left hand. 'Come and get it, come on! You bastard!'

'Gary, give it to me NOW!'

Phil hid the knife behind his back to keep it from McCready's reach. Barker was very pleased. 'Good, good! Keep well to your left. Derek, don't block Phil from the camera! Now go for the lunge. Go for it!'

Derek glanced down to locate the rug, then tripped forward towards Phil, who toppled backwards, still holding the knife behind him in his left hand, and hit the wall. As Phil fell heavily against him, there was a clatter as the knife fell to the floor.

'Good, good. All right, Phil?'

Phil was retrieving the knife. 'I dropped the knife! I can't get it in the right position to stab myself, no way!'

Barker frowned. 'Try again. Take it from . . . Phil, take it from your line "Come and get it", OK?'

Phil and Derek resumed their positions. Duffield hovered behind Lucy, still peering through the door. He tapped Lucy's arm, whispering, 'Will they interview me in here?'

'I doubt it,' she said. Lucy was sick of having to cope with Duffield's inane questions. Why couldn't he go away and bother some other member of the crew? Impatiently, she turned a page of her shooting script.

'And . . . action!' said Barker.

Once more, Phil backed down the corridor, wielding the knife as Derek advanced on him. 'Come and get it, come on!' he snarled.

'Gary, give it to me NOW!'

Again, the knife went behind Meadows' back, again McCready tripped forward, forcing him back to the wall and onto the knife.

'OK this time, Phil?' asked Barker.

'No.'

Duffield turned again to Lucy. 'Looked good to me!' She ignored him.

'It's impossible to hold onto the knife,' Phil was saying. 'It's natural for me to drop it to stop myself falling.'

Barker stepped forward and turned round, waving his hands in the air. 'Just hold the smoke for a minute.' He turned back. 'Try again. Just pace it, don't rush it. No smoke!'

'I'm not, but I have to hold it in my left hand and I'm right-handed.'

'So was Gary Meadows,' said Lucy under her breath.

But Barker heard. He shot a quick glance of irritation at the PA then returned to the task at hand. 'Listen, no problem,' he said to the actors. 'We do a close-up of you, Derek, then cut back to Phil with the knife in his back.'

Lucy stepped forward. 'Should we really do that? I mean, it's supposed to be as it happened and, if he can't do it, how did Gary Meadows do it?'

There was a silence, and an uneasy feeling, as Phil picked up the retractable knife. Duffield looked unhappily from Lucy to Barker, who clicked his tongue impatiently. He wished the girl would try to be more helpful and positive instead of trotting out these quibbles. He shut his eyes, settled himself and returned to the task in hand. 'Try again. Just see if you can get it on the pad on the left side of your back.'

They ran through the scene again. Phil backed off, Derek lurched forward, Phil hit the wall and, this time, managed to 'stab' himself in the right spot. He turned around, holding the knife, now apparently sticking into his left lower back. 'I did it!'

Barker turned back to Lucy and said, a touch sarcastically, 'All right, Lucy? He did it!'

'Yeah,' she said sceptically. 'Third time lucky!'

CHAPTER 8

THURSDAY, 3 FEBRUARY

An important witness in the McCready/Meadows case had been an elderly lady living, at the time of the murder, next door to the two men. This was Vera Collingwood. Whenever McCready and Meadows went out in the evening – which they often did – Vera would babysit Fiona, putting her to bed and calling in to check on her during the evening. And that is what she had done on the night Gary Meadows died.

Allard's reinvestigation team, checking through those who had made statements eight years ago, had Vera Collingwood marked high on the list of those for reinterview. Now North and Watkins stood on the doorstep of the address where she had moved in the meantime. North rang the bell.

'Smart place,' whispered Watkins. 'Everything looks new.'

It was true. Vera Collingwood's place was essentially the same as the others in the park, but it had been professionally patched and painted so that, now, it looked almost as new. The garden was well maintained, the neatly leaded windows were clean and the slated roof looked as if it had been recently renewed.

After more than half a minute the door was opened by Vera herself who, according to the date of birth given in her statement, would be sixty-seven. She had once been a pretty woman but had long let herself go, the impression of physical decline emphasised by her gasping, which North attributed to smoking. A luxury-sized cigarette, the tip pinked with her lipstick, smouldered now in her fingers and she had a smoker's wrinkles across her upper lip. She looked at them steadily, taking a quick, staccato drag on the cigarette. 'Yes?'

'Mrs Collingwood?'

'That's right.'

North showed her warrant card. 'Hi, I'm Detective Inspector Pat North and this is Detective Constable Vivien Watkins. We'd like to ask you some questions about the Gary Meadows murder.'

'I was wondering if someone would come and talk to me.'

'Oh yes?'

'I know you were over at Jimmy's place. Mr Duffield said to expect you.' She spoke huskily, breathing with difficulty, her shoulders heaving up and down.

North exchanged a glance with Watkins. 'Mr Duffield certainly gets around!'

Vera stood aside to admit them. 'Please wipe your feet. This is new carpet, shag pile! Still fluffing up, terrible for my asthma, it's chronic. I do nothing but hoover!'

Vera's lounge was very plush, with an expensive three-piece suite, an apparently new nest of side tables, a gleaming sideboard, brass lamps with tasselled shades and many garish porcelain ornaments on every surface. North sat on the sofa with Vivien in the armchair opposite. Vera plumped up the cushions of the other chair, her breath still coming in short gasps, and collapsed into it.

North explained that they would like to tape-record the interview. She also showed she had Vera's original statement with her, and handed over a copy for her to read through. Then she activated the tape recorder and flipped open her notebook. 'According to your original statement, you were one of the last people to see Gary Meadows alive.'

'I suppose so. It was after midnight' – *gasp* – 'I'd been babysitting Fiona, well, not at their place, I used to pop in and out when I lived next door. I moved here a few months back' – *gasp* – 'but that night, I came out of my place 'cause I heard them coming home. Both a bit tipsy, they were' – *gasp* – 'fooling around and—'

North interrupted. 'I'm sorry, could I just go back on that? You say you actually came out of your caravan?'

'Yes, yes, I did. They were such lovely boys, very friendly and good fathers to that little girl' – *gasp* – 'and they gave me a few quid for looking in. I'm a pensioner now, but even then I'd not been able to work for a while because of my' – *gasp* – 'asthma. Anyway, I said good night and went back inside and they went into their place. I heard loud music. I could see them silhouetted at the window. Then I heard' – *gasp* – 'some shouting and I looked out. The loud music was still playing and I saw both of them passing to and fro. I thought they were dancing. Then I saw them in the bedroom, looked as if' – *gasp* – 'they were drinking, then the lights went out. Next morning I heard this howling, then the ambulance. Poor Gary was dead; shocking, terrible. But Jimmy'd never have harmed him, he' – *gasp* – 'loved him.'

North jotted a note. The gasping was frightful. Would she ever make it into the witness box? 'Sorry, Vera, but it's very important we get this straight because in your original statement there is no reference to your seeing Jimmy and Gary at their bedroom window.'

Vera hesitated, as if remembering. Then, when she spoke, she was definite. 'But I did see them in the bedroom . . . then the lights went out.'

'Originally you only referred to seeing them return home, not seeing them at the window.'

Vera heaved in another breath. 'Well, I did tell them. Are you going to be on the TV show?'

'No, we're not.'

'Well, Eva Widelski told me she is and she didn't even know the boys.'

North was puzzled. The name hadn't come up before. 'I'm sorry – Eva Widelski?'

'She lives over on the west side. Says she's a clairvoyant . . . truth be told, she's an alcoholic, that's what *she* is!'

North wrote 'Eva Widelski ???' in her notebook and, after asking a few more questions about how long Vera had known the two men, details of the payment she received for babysitting and what she knew in general about their relationship, she turned off the tape recorder.

* * *

Afterwards, North and Watkins strolled back to Vera's old mobile home, which, like McCready's, now stood deserted and dilapidated, though it had quite obviously never been up to much. North walked all around it, peering in the windows and taking sightlines from various places towards the windows of the McCready house about twenty-five yards away.

Vivien looked at her watch. 'So this is where Vera lived at the time?'

'Yes. She must have good eyesight.'

'As well as a good memory!'

North looked at her notes. 'She's a widow, isn't she? Pensioner . . . Does she have any family, I wonder? Must know someone with some cash.' She nodded towards the house that was now occupied by Vera, fifty yards along the lane. 'That's a very expensively kitted out caravan – well, compared to this one.' Looking back again along the lane, she caught a glimpse of Vera, peering towards them through the window of her lavish new home.

Later, at the office, North went in to tell Allard about Vera Collingwood's additional information. 'She says she saw them dancing in their house *after* they got back from the pub, after they'd paid her for babysitting. Saw it through the window, apparently. Only it wasn't in the original signed statement – *or* on the tapes, I've checked. According to what she says now, she did tell the investigating officers what she saw – though it must have been off the tape, if true.'

Allard rubbed his chin. 'Well, it would have been a bloody good point for the defence, wouldn't it? If they were dancing instead of having a murderous argument . . .' He looked at the transcript of the interview and her statement of eight years ago, scratching his head. 'What's she like?'

'Crumbling. Only sixty-seven but might be ten years older. Terrible bronchial problems – asthma plus ciggies. Lives in a very nice house, though. Somebody's providing for her, though there's nothing in the file about any immediate family.'

'That doesn't necessarily signify. There could be a brother, nephew or niece – someone like that, in Canada, say.' He slapped the file shut.

'OK, Pat. Thanks. Good work. We must all get home for a good night's sleep. Steel ourselves for Dr John Foster tomorrow – right?'

North smiled. She knew John Foster of old. 'Right, sir.'

CHAPTER 9

FRIDAY, 4 FEBRUARY

Foster's laboratory adjoined one of central London's largest mortuaries. As he sometimes said, it gave him a smart metropolitan address and exceptionally quiet neighbours. Foster's sense of humour was lugubrious.

Allard and North were met in reception by the great man himself. On the way back to the lab, Foster was telling them how he'd met Duffield and Barker. 'Did you know about this? They're doing a documentary on the McCready case. McCready's solicitor came to see me, clutching a newspaper cutting. Appalling bloke. Accompanied by some television producer. I doubt I'll be making my screen debut, though. I don't think I passed the audition. My interpretation of the script didn't suit them. This way.' They followed him into the lab itself. 'I've had these made up.'

He indicated a display board on which were two large outline diagrams of the male torso, one clearly labelled 'Thompson' and the other 'Meadows'. Both showed the position of the heart, coloured red, and in each case a dotted line aiming towards the heart from somewhere below the ribs.

'This is Thompson,' said Foster, 'and this is your case, Meadows.'

Allard looked closely. To his eye the two drawings looked remarkably similar. 'Well, our problem is the defence are saying that comparisons with the Thompson case do suggest you have shifted your ground, doctor.'

Foster whipped off his glasses impatiently. 'No, no, no. Absolutely not. That's the trouble with laymen, they think they understand it all, and they don't. You're not comparing like with like here.'

Allard bristled. The bottomless pomposity of experts was something that never surprised him, but he still couldn't get used to it. 'Well, it doesn't look like that to me. The description of damage to the heart inflicted by the knife in each case reads exactly the same . . . but then I am only a layman.'

'But they were different wounds entirely!' The pathologist was raising his voice both in volume and pitch. 'Look at the angle the knife went in . . .' He produced a straight-edge from his pocket and, pointing to the diagrams, first of Thompson and then of Meadows, traced the direction of the two knife wounds. 'Here, in Thompson, it was thirty-five degrees, making an eighteen-centimetre wound, as against here in the Meadows case, where the angle was fifty-three degrees and the wound was only seventeen centimetres.'

'Well, that's all very well,' said Allard, holding up a sheaf of statements. 'But it says here that the two cardiac surgeons consulted by the defence describe the damage in each case as virtually identical.'

Foster took the statements and put his glasses back on. 'What's this?'

'They're the surgeons' statements.'

Foster quickly skimmed the printed pages, noting especially the signatures at the bottom, and the letters after the names – LDS,

MRAcS. 'Well, you know, we medical folk are notorious for contradicting each other.'

'Yes, but not for contradicting yourself,' put in North. Foster now looked again at the last page of the first report, studying the paragraph headed 'Summary of conclusions'. He looked suddenly tense, tight-lipped, as North continued. 'If Thompson, and I quote from your evidence in that case, "could well have survived for twenty minutes to half an hour after sustaining his injury" why couldn't Meadows have done?'

'Well . . . I . . . I was deducing from the medical evidence that . . .'

Allard said, 'You dismissed any question of twenty minutes at McCready's trial, saying, I quote, "he'd have been dead within five minutes".'

Foster whipped the page over, turning to the second surgeon's summary of conclusions. When he'd finished his reading he briskly handed the statements back to Allard. 'Yes I did, and I stand by that.'

North turned back to the display boards. 'So, Dr Foster, bearing in mind your views on Thompson's life expectancy, after being wounded like this, can you really rule out the possibility that Meadows, with his wound like this, might also have been alive for twenty minutes to half an hour?'

Foster looked again at the diagrams. Like with like? The angles were different. The wounds were of different sizes. And yet . . . 'Well . . . er . . . no . . . No, I don't suppose I can.'

Allard jumped in. 'But you said at trial—'

'I suppose you could say that what I said at trial may have been misunderstood, if you follow me.'

'Well, I'm not sure I do,' came back Allard. 'Surely the issue at trial was how long a man who had suffered such a wound might be expected to live without treatment?'

'Yes.' Foster was a little hangdog now. Not happy about being put on the spot, either. There were so many grey areas in pathology, that was what the police never seemed to understand. It became a minefield if you made statements that were too definite.

'You see, Dr Foster,' continued North, 'our problem is that Meadows had to have been alive for at least fifteen to twenty minutes to make the defence account feasible. Helping Meadows into the bedroom, getting bandages, drinking brandy and making up after their quarrel. All this was ruled out by your insistence that there was such a short period between the stabbing and death.'

'But for my money, none of that happened.'

'Yes,' retorted Allard, 'but you see, some uncharitable counsel in the Court of Appeal might suggest that the distinguishing feature between the two cases was that, in Meadows, you were for the Crown, whereas in Thompson you were retained by the defence.'

Foster bristled. 'That's completely preposterous. I . . .'

'I'm sure it is, Dr Foster, but at least you'll be ready for it, if it is suggested. Forewarned is forearmed.'

North was expecting Foster to erupt at any moment. She said, in a placatory tone, 'Well, if it comes to it, you could give a little ground on the point. And then they won't need to call you, but just read a statement from you which says you may have expressed yourself badly at trial.'

Foster was calming down, but he had been rattled. He considered the position and nodded. 'Yes, yes, I can see that. Perhaps that's the best way of resolving this.'

Walker was going to Bristol to interview a key witness in the mint murder case. Unable to face the M4, he'd ordered a minicab to take him to Paddington, but was surprised when the doorbell rang ten minutes before the time he requested. He picked up his coat and went out, to be greeted by a fortyish man in a suede jacket. He did not look like the average minicab driver. 'You're early but OK, let's go.'

The man seemed slightly taken aback. 'Detective Superintendent Walker?'

Walker pulled on his coat. 'Yes.'

The man levelled his hand for shaking. 'Hi, I'm Roger Barker, Area Television.' He groped for a card. Walker ignored it. A television guy? He didn't think the mint murder was that big already. 'I asked at your station and they said you were not due in until—'

Walker stopped him. 'Wait, wait! You say you got my address from my station?'

'Well, not exactly, we have a research department but I phoned you—'

Walker rarely liked any TV people he'd met and he didn't like the man in front of him. 'What's this about?' He moved on towards the gate which led into the road. He might intercept his cab, get away from this parasite.

Barker hurried after him, surprised by this abruptness. 'Surely you want to defend the decisions you made?'

'Right now I haven't made any decisions,' Walker told him. 'No one has been charged and you know I can't discuss an ongoing case.'

'But this case isn't exactly ongoing—'

He touched Walker's shoulder and the policeman spun round. 'Wait a minute, pal. This isn't about the mint murder, is it?'

'No, we're making a documentary about the James McCready case.' Walker's features darkened: a storm warning. But Barker ploughed on. 'If you'd just answer a few questions, preferably on camera if you would. You originally arrested James McCready yourself, correct?'

Abruptly, Walker snatched the business card from Barker's fingers. He read the name with a curling lip. 'Roger Barker. Right, Roger, you take my advice and get out of my face.'

Barker started to bluster. 'Look, Superintendent, this is your opportunity to . . .'

Walker pulled out the flap of Barker's breast pocket and slotted the card into place. Then, as if to pat the pocket flat, he gave Barker a push so that he staggered backwards. 'Get the hell out of here!'

CHAPTER 10

MONDAY, 7 FEBRUARY

LOOKING CLEAN and eager, McCready sat in the legal visits room opposite North and Watkins. He was certainly good-looking in his close-fitting and immaculately white T-shirt and navy trousers. His manner was sweet, even shy, but beneath this he displayed an ease and a self-assurance that was remarkable in a man who had served eight years of a life sentence among some of the most violent criminals in the system. Just now he was smiling. It was the first time he'd found anything like a sympathetic ear in the police force and he could hardly believe it.

'Thank you very much for coming to see me. I'm sorry I kept you waiting but it was lunch. They don't let us out for anyone if they're serving up the nosh. I think it's because it's the officers' lunch break and one of them has to walk me from my wing.'

North had already shown him the recorder. Now she pressed the record button and clicked her pencil. 'We'd like to ask you some questions for the purposes of the reinvestigation.'

'Ask me anything you want, I've nothing to hide, all I want is the chance to appeal.'

'I would like you to describe, in your own words, the events that led up to the death of Gary Meadows.'

McCready straightened his back and looked over their heads, trying to visualise what he was describing. 'OK, right. My lover,

Gary Meadows, and I had lived together for four years. We looked after his daughter, Fiona, between us; shared the school runs, cooked and washed, kept house together. We were a family, I loved him a great deal. Before Gary, I'd never had a long-term relationship.'

North, as she always did, kept a close eye on McCready's body language: his delicate hands, those slight feminine gestures to his hair, the soft speech and the little gestures towards the lips that seemed almost intentionally sensual. Finally, his eyes, which had quickly slid back from the middle distance, engaged those of both the women questioning him. Some would call his manner almost seductive.

'That isn't to say we were all lovey-dovey, we had our ups and downs, like any couple. Usually we only argued if Gary had been drinking. He was the kind of person who could get a bit punchy. No, that's not the right word. It was more like he only ever got angry about things when he'd had a few drinks. Liked to pick arguments, you know? I think he sometimes got a bit edgy about his sexuality. I've always known I was gay but he, you know, he was married before we met, worked on a building site. Er, just a second.' He thrust his hand into his trouser pocket and dragged out a plastic photo-wallet. 'This is Gary, it was taken a few months before he died. I always carry it.' The snapshot showed a grinning Gary Meadows, blond, blue-eyed and muscular, swinging from a scaffold bar beside some building site.

North looked at the picture for a moment and placed it on the table between them. 'Could you tell me about the night he died?'

'Well, we'd been to Butterflies in Soho. It's a gay club. It was cabaret night and I did my Blondie rip-off. Impromptu act. I got up on the stage. Anyway, we left quite early. We didn't want to be too late because of Fiona, but as we passed our local, we remembered there was a lock-in that night for Keith, the barman. He was off to Marbella, doing a DJ job. Pub's not far from the caravan site.' He looked from North's face to Watkins' and back again. He seemed completely guileless and utterly truthful. 'We'd had quite a skinful and didn't leave the pub until about midnight.'

'Did you have a babysitter? Gary's daughter was only what, seven?'

'No, but the woman next door, Vera Collingwood, would check on her from time to time. Fiona knew her well. It wasn't as if we'd left her alone.'

'Go on.'

'We got in and Gary wanted to carry on drinking, but I asked him not to, he'd had enough. He started playing music really loud – you know, he'd have woken up the whole site, never mind Fiona. Then we started bickering. I tried to calm him down but he was in a real rage and he ran into the kitchen. Next minute he's dancing around in front of me waving a knife. I tried to get it from him but caught my hand on the blade, here.'

McCready held out his left hand, where a white scar could be seen across a corner of the palm. 'I was annoyed and upset, you know, it was bleeding and I begged for him to give me the knife, but he wouldn't. I managed to get hold of it but Gary wouldn't let go and in the struggle, he slashed my arm.' He tilted his arm in the light so that they could see the mark of the eight-year-old knife slash. 'By this time I was really distressed, well, quite angry to be honest, and I chased him up the hall. Can I show you?'

He got up, pretending to be Meadows with the knife, dancing backwards from foot to foot, juggling an imaginary weapon in his hands. Concerned at this sudden activity, the prison officer outside the door approached the glass and glanced into the room but North gestured that it was OK. 'He swishes the knife in front of him like this,' McCready continued. 'Then when I try to get it from him, he switches it from his right hand into his left and puts his arm behind his back. He was laughing, goading me. I said, "Give me the knife, Gary, give it to me, please." And as I moved towards him, I tripped.'

'Why did you trip?' asked North.

'I just tripped on the rug and fell against him, really hard.' McCready lowered his head and was quiet for a moment. Briefly his shoulders came up in a hunch and then dropped again and he straightened. This time his smile was bleak. 'I'm sorry, where was I? He sort of moaned. I said I was sorry, I didn't mean to hurt him and then . . . and then he says, "Oh my God, Jimmy, I've stabbed myself!"'

McCready moved to his seat and sat down. His eyes were filled with tears, his whole body shook. 'We shared a glass of brandy. I checked Gary's cut but it didn't even look deep and then . . .' He took a deep breath to show he had composed himself. 'You see I was cut bad, I was tending to myself as well, and—'

'You mind if I just interrupt here, Mr McCready?' asked Watkins. 'At what point did Fiona come out of her bedroom?'

'While I was helping Gary into the bedroom. He turned and saw her in her bedroom doorway. She must have seen everything that had happened. Gary told her to go back to bed. She was a bit upset, what with us shouting and carrying on. So I kissed her and said we were all friends again.'

North was writing furiously. The phrase rang a bell. 'We were all friends again?'

'Yes. Fiona was like my own kid. We were a proper family. I really miss her. Eight years we should have been together, eight years. But no one would listen to me. Walker had me down as a murderer from day one. He wouldn't listen to the truth.'

Watkins was looking at him hard. 'It's understandable in a way, Mr McCready. When you called the ambulance, you said . . .' Watkins picked from the case file a transcript of the emergency service's recording of the call. She read aloud. '"I've killed him, he's dead, I think he's dead." That is what you said, Mr McCready, isn't it?'

'Yes, I know, but my words were taken out of context. At the time I thought I had killed him. It was me who tripped and fell against him. It was me who'd caused the accident and I'd gone to sleep next to him. I'd believed him when he said he wasn't badly injured so I didn't call an ambulance after our argument. That was all I could think of at the time, that it was my fault. I still live with that guilt. But after that, Walker wouldn't listen to me, he kept saying. "You killed him", kept on, "You killed him, you killed him." Then he got crude, making disgusting remarks about me and Gary. He was always making nasty remarks about me being gay, calling me a queen. It was horrible, disgusting the way he treated me.'

'True, or too good to be true?' North asked Watkins as they walked to the car. 'Did you notice how similar their descriptions were?'

'Whose?'

'McCready's and Fiona's. I mean, don't you think it's strange that eight years on, they both remember word for word the exact phrase McCready used after he kissed her good night?'

'I didn't notice. What was it?'

'They both remember McCready saying, "we're all friends again".'

'Yes, I suppose it is.' But less so if it actually *was* said, she was thinking.

'What time do we meet tomorrow?' asked North.

'Nine, conference room, assess findings to date. What about Mike?'

'What about him?'

'Come on, I know him, you know him. You think he overstepped the mark?'

'Well, there's only one way to find out. Review the interview tapes. We'll have to look into it.'

'I'll get on to it first thing in the morning.'

North bleeped the car locks and half opened the driver's door. In that instant her legs gave way and she clutched at the door for support, her eyes closing. Watkins saw it and raced round to North's side of the car.

'Pat . . . PAT! What's the matter?'

North shuffled cautiously past the door and was holding herself up on the bonnet of the car as she clutched her stomach. 'I'm going to faint. I feel terrible.'

'You OK? Do you want me to drive?'

'Yeah, do you mind?' As Watkins helped her into the car, she said, 'Sorry about this. I'm really sorry.'

Roger Barker had been invited to call on Robert Rylands at the House of Commons, to discuss the McCready documentary. Walking his guest back to his office from the lobby, along the sumptuously carpeted neo-gothic corridors, the MP was treated to a full account of the strange reception Barker had been given when visiting Detective Superintendent Michael Walker the previous day.

'He became bloody abusive and threatened to throw me off the premises. So it looks like there'll be no Walker interview on the show . . . unlike Mr Duffield. We had enough footage of him for a four-hour miniseries!'

Rylands smiled at this picture of Duffield's bid for fame. 'Yes, Walker is a very abrasive character and I have just been told we may have even more reason to get the Police Complaints Authority to open an external investigation. I've found out that one of the officers investigating our case is actually living with him.'

Barker, when he appreciated the full import of what Rylands had said, was at first dumbfounded and then he laughed. 'That'll make explosive coverage. Good, good. And I've got something else. A clairvoyant! How worthwhile it'll be to put her in the documentary is questionable, but . . .'

'What? A *clairvoyant*, did you say?'

'Yes. It never came out at trial but apparently one of the investigating officers went round to see her. It might have been Walker, we don't know. She can't remember a name. But whoever it was took her a glass to see if she could get any spiritual vibes from it!'

This time it was Rylands' turn to be almost dumbfounded. 'You're not serious?'

'Oh, but I am! I'm sure the PCA will be interested to hear that the Met is so in touch with its spiritual side – what do you say, Robert?'

North sat in the car, parked outside a chemist shop. She watched Watkins walking out of the shop with a bulging paper bag full of her purchases. As soon as she was in the car she dropped the bag on North's lap. North peered into it. 'I got Tums, Bisodol and . . .'

'I can see what else you got.' She reached in and pulled out a proprietary pregnancy test. She looked at Watkins in disbelief. 'Come on, Vivien – at my age?'

Watkins nodded like a schoolmistress. 'You don't have to be a teenager to get caught out, you know. You've been showing all the right symptoms recently. At least that'll put your mind at rest.'

'It's not *my* mind, it's yours. I know I'm not, it was that pastie or it could have been the corned-beef hash yesterday. I am *not* pregnant.'

'So test yourself and prove it! That's a simple one; if you get a pink dot, you are, and if you don't, you're not, and for nine ninety-nine you might as well . . .'

North hit her gently on the upper arm. 'Nine ninety-nine? Nine ninety-nine! What a waste of money!'

CHAPTER 11

TUESDAY, 8 FEBRUARY

ALLARD WAS late for the morning meeting. North, Collins, Pilling and Watkins, having gathered in the conference room at nine o'clock, were talking among themselves, though North was quiet. She was thinking about the testing kit Watkins had bought for her yesterday. Tonight, she had vowed, she would do it. She could have done it last night, but they'd gone out for an Italian meal. It had been a short date in the end, but on recent form one of their better ones. She had felt tired and Walker's unrelenting flippancy about the mint murder made her more so. She hid her mood as best she could, glad at least that he could make jokes. They got home without an argument, which in itself had felt like an achievement. Later they made love – an even greater one.

She dragged her attention back to today and her colleagues. All seemed relatively pleased with the way things were coming along, although no one thought they could yet see the whole picture. The inquiry was still at the stage of examining the broken pieces of the puzzle. North, for her own part, had tried as little as possible to dwell on Walker's role in the case and, tactfully, the others had tiptoed round the subject, at least in her presence. But last night, lying in his arms in the dark, she had been troubled. She had the feeling there was something not quite right. North well knew how ruthless and single-minded Walker could be on certain cases. Had he really browbeaten McCready? Had he let his old-fashioned view of homosexuality warp his judgement? And – the most anxious question of all – would their relationship survive the outcome of this investigation?

Suddenly the four seated around the conference table heard the swing doors from the corridor bursting open. A moment later Allard tore into the room and violently slapped his file down on the table. He was not trying very hard to contain his anger. They all looked up apprehensively. Allard leant on the table, resting on his knuckles, breathing heavily. He held their attention for a moment of suspense, then hit them with the news.

'I have just been informed that the Police Complaints Authority have taken over the investigation. As such, they will gather their own team from outside the Met. So . . . we're all off the case. The external force begins this afternoon. I suggest we give them every cooperation.'

There were murmurs of disappointment from all four of his team. Collins said, 'Why, sir?'

Allard flashed him a tense, cynical smile. 'Mr Rylands obviously has friends in high places.'

In an elegant Whitehall building, Rylands took the lift to the floor where the Police Complaints Authority was based. He was in very good humour. The McCready case made him feel both virtuous and tough, a true hunter for justice. When were the police ever going to learn? Not, he would guess, until a lot more of these maverick officers like Walker were rounded up and corralled. And Rylands enjoyed leading the chase so much he might almost have done it for nothing. With hardly a wheeze, the lift braked at the sixth floor and he stepped through the opening doors to find a tall, elegant black woman, with a mass of hair, waiting to greet him.

'Hello. Mr Rylands, I presume? Zita Sallinger.' They shook hands.

'Good afternoon, Miss Sallinger.'

'This way.' She ushered him along a short corridor past glass-walled offices, packed with desktop computers and lined with files. He thought, unless one had an exceptionally broad mind, this work must leave behind an indelibly jaundiced view of the police. It was all here, in the records of hundreds of investigations into police conduct – bribery, careless use of firearms, abuse of procedure, intimidation of suspects, prejudice, deaths in custody – many of them supervised by the Authority and all of them reviewed by it. Case worker Sallinger's office was slightly larger than those they had passed. It had law books on the shelves and smelt pleasantly of fresh coffee.

'Please, take a seat.' Rylands did so, snapping open his well-polished briefcase. 'I read your letter, Mr Rylands, and have familiarised myself with the Meadows case.'

'Yes. As you know, I am very unhappy with the way the reinvestigation is being carried out. I was stunned to discover that a Detective Inspector Pat North, common-law wife of Michael Walker, the original SIO on the case, is actually on the investigating team.'

'Yes, I can quite understand your insistence on our meeting.'

'As you can imagine, this cohabitation is a matter of considerable concern for myself and Mr McCready. I find it difficult to believe that DI North could remain impartial.'

She nodded. 'Absolutely. We will be interviewing DCI Allard and DI North. Now, let me outline PCA procedure in this case. I have already organised an external investigating team to take over, led by Assistant Chief Constable John Stanley from Sussex Police. He and his team will review all the statements and re-interview all the relevant witnesses in order to determine whether police procedure was followed correctly. I will personally oversee the investigation and keep you informed of any major developments.'

'Thank you. Now, there is another major concern which my client has voiced. It is that Detective Superintendent Walker was extremely hostile towards him in the original investigation. He strongly believes that Walker's homophobic attitude and aggressive nature had a strong bearing on his initial interviews and his conviction. Of course, Walker was very careful to behave correctly while the interviews were being recorded, but when the tape was stopped he became highly abusive.'

'That's according to McCready,' Sallinger pointed out pertinently. A barrister herself, she did not allow herself to be intimidated by Rylands' reputation. She was – and she knew it – a formidable personality in her own right. 'We will consider all the issues, Mr Rylands. The two main areas we will be investigating are: one, was any evidence suppressed or abused in any way?; and, two, was the investigation run properly by Detective Superintendent Walker? Any factors that may have led to an inappropriate conviction will come out in the wash, believe me.'

'Good, good. Thank you for giving this your immediate attention. I appreciate it.'

She gave Rylands a sidelong look. '*Every* case is given our attention, Mr Rylands. Few can jump the queue, but as McCready's appeal is looking likely . . .'

'As is the television documentary.'

'I hear you loud and clear, Mr Rylands. So . . .' She turned the pages of the file, coming to a handwritten list of bullet points. 'In the meantime, may I just clarify a few more things?'

North walked into the flat, let the door slam, chucked her briefcase aside and took off her coat. She'd thought the flat was empty but Walker surprised her, coming out of the kitchen. He noted her tired expression. 'You look as if you had a good day!'

'Yeah. The PCA have taken over the case. We've all had our marching orders.' She flopped down onto the sofa and closed her eyes. Walker got a bottle of wine from the kitchen and was ripping off the foil. 'They used me and our relationship as one of the main reasons that the inquiry should now be handled externally. I knew I should have stood down.'

'Ah well, sod 'em. Bloody idiots.' Walker uncorked the bottle and poured drinks. He passed one to North, who took the smallest sip and put the glass down on the low table beside her.

'The PCA are not idiots, Mike, and they've got one of their top members overseeing it, Zita Sallinger. You heard of her?'

'Nope. Sounds like a tennis racket!'

'She's a trained barrister, very clever and has quite a reputation. They call her The Piranha.'

He slid onto the adjoining bar stool. 'Fine,' he said lightly. 'If that's how you want to play it. You remember the McCready case?'

'How could I forget?'

He lit a cigarette. 'Well, somehow the bastard's managed to get the PCA involved and it's looking like he might get an appeal.'

'So?'

'I need that video, Barbara.' At last she looked at him and he could see there was still anger and hurt in her eyes – after all the years that had passed. 'I see. So you act like you don't know me whenever our paths cross. But, now you need my help, it's all "you look great" and "can I get you a drink?". You've got a lot of nerve, you know that?'

'Listen, it was you that wanted to meet up! I was quite happy to do this over the phone.'

'Do what exactly?'

'Look, Barbara, can't we just call a truce? I know I behaved badly but it was a long time ago.'

'I heard you left Lynn.'

His reply was tentative. 'Ye-es.'

'So what happened to "I couldn't do it to the kids?"'

'Things change, Barbara.'

She shook her head, not angrily this time but sadly. 'Yeah, well, I hope Pat knows what she's let herself in for.'

Walker would not be drawn down this blind alley. He let a moment of uneasy silence go by, drawing on his cigarette. 'So are you going to help? I wouldn't be bothering you if it wasn't really important.'

Barbara's mood changed. She almost laughed. 'I warned you. I warned you it could all blow up in your face.'

'Well, you're right there. I've a feeling it's just about to.'

'Well, don't expect me to cry when it does, Mike.'

North, wearing a dressing gown, read the instruction leaflet for Watkins' pregnancy test a third and fourth time, checking on how long she should wait. Now, alone in the house, she had the test tube in her left hand and was gently waving it around, as if that would speed things up. She studied her watch, waiting impatiently for the right time to lift off the concealment-strip. Four minutes.

She paced restlessly around the house, following the second hand round the dial. Two minutes ... one minute ... thirty seconds. Then, having timed the moment so that it happened in the bedroom, she was ripping away the strip with clumsy fingers. She looked.

'Oh no! No. Oh dear God, please, no.' The shock took the strength from her knees and she sank into a sitting position on the bed. Quite unable to believe, she looked at the tester again. But the colour of the dot was still pink.

CHAPTER 12

WEDNESDAY, 9 FEBRUARY, MORNING

When a complaint about a serious matter has been lodged with the Police Complaints Authority, a senior officer from a force other than the one being investigated is always brought in to lead the inquiry. For the McCready case, PCA case worker Zita Sallinger had asked the Assistant Chief Constable of the Sussex Police, John Stanley, to come in. Stanley lost no time in assembling his team of experienced officers, whose first task was to become fully conversant with the case file before going out to test the weight of the complaint. Stanley's next priority was to interview Jimmy McCready at Garton.

Sallinger and Stanley were waiting in the legal visits room when McCready was brought in. The PCA case worker shook hands with the lifer. 'Hello, Mr McCready. I'm Zita Sallinger, from the Police Complaints Authority, and this is Assistant Chief Constable John Stanley from Sussex Police, who is now leading the reinvestigation into your case.'

'Pleased to meet you,' said McCready. His tone was cautious, not knowing quite what to expect from these visitors and wondering how best to make his impression. Stanley simply nodded to him.

Sallinger sat down and invited the prisoner to do the same. 'Now, let me explain a little background,' she began. 'The

Police Complaints Authority is an independent organisation, not connected to the police in any way. It is our job to hear your complaint. Furthermore, a new external team, lead by Assistant Chief Constable Stanley here, will look into the handling of the original investigation. All the officers connected to your case will be questioned, as will all the witnesses. If we find any irregularities or any form of wrongdoing, this will be recorded.'

Throughout this, McCready maintained eye contact with Sallinger. Stanley in turn was studying McCready intently. 'Will this affect my appeal?'

'That depends on what we find. Now, take me through exactly what happened the night Mr Meadows died, if you would.'

McCready lowered his eyes and felt in his pocket. Slowly, almost reverently, he took out the photograph wallet, opened it and laid it down with a certain theatricality on the table in front of his visitors. 'This is Gary,' he began.

At Area Television, Barker was polishing his voice-over script for the *Miscarriage of Justice* film on Jimmy McCready. He had drafted out what he hoped was a reasonable first go and he was sitting in his office, reading it through aloud in front of a mirror. 'James McCready was sentenced to life imprisonment for the murder of his partner, Gary Meadows . . .' He noticed that Lucy was hovering nearby. He snatched off his reading glasses and called out, 'Hey, Lucy. Did the prison Governor get back to us about filming at the prison?'

'Er, I think Tom was sorting it out, but he's gone up to Glasgow for something or other. Do you want me to check?'

Barker closed his eyes and fetched a heavy sigh. 'Well, somebody bloody well should, we're scheduled to shoot there on Tuesday.'

He put on his reading glasses and redirected his attention to the script. So important to get this right. All hung on it, really. He rubbed his hands together. 'Right, where was I?'

'Facing camera,' said Lucy as she drifted away.

That girl, he thought. Bloody pretty but as his mother always used to say, so sharp you'd cut yourself. 'You're getting just a *touch* overconfident, young Lucy!' he murmured to himself as he turned back to the mirror. 'OK. This is Roger Barker, Area Television, presenting *Miscarriage of Justice* . . . no . . . presenting another *Miscarriage of Justice*. Today I am outside Garton Prison, where James McCready is serving a life sentence for the murder of his partner, Gary Meadows.'

He scrawled a pencil note in the margin and continued. 'James McCready, brought up in Hornchurch, Essex—'

He was utterly caught up in his anchorman role and it was a moment before he realised the phone had rung. Impatiently, he snatched it up. 'Roger Barker, *Miscarriage of Justice* . . . Tom? Hang on, you're cutting out . . . Tom? . . . OK, I got you, what? . . . Say that again . . . I got that. But this is brilliant, Tom. Are you sure about it? . . . For God's sake, double-check, we can't afford mistakes.'

Lucy had returned to drop off a memo. He held the phone away from his head, his eyes sparkling. 'Get this, Lucy. We just struck gold! Our Detective Superintendent Walker more than knew McCready. He tried to charge him for a murder in Glasgow!'

Lucy smiled. 'Another murder? Is that necessarily a *positive* thing, Roger?'

Silly girl, was she moralising? Or just trying to throw him? He returned to Tom on the phone. 'Hello, yeah, yeah, I'm still here. Give me all the details later. Did we get permission to film outside Garton Prison by the way, or not?'

Walker had overslept. North had gone to work without waking him. Still angry with him, then. He draped his tie around his neck, pushed his feet into yesterday's shoes and picked up his phone. After keying in the incident-room number he trapped the phone between his shoulder and ear and began knotting the tie.

'Walker!' he said. 'Any messages? OK, I'll be with you in about an hour or so . . . Yeah, yeah, we're going to charge him. So it's roast lamb and mint sauce all round, eh?' He laughed. 'Well, I'll see you. Bye.'

Humming tunelessly to himself, he began emptying his pockets of receipts, an old fag packet, chewing-gum wrappers. He crossed to the waste-bin to chuck away the rubbish. Something inside caught his attention. He bent to fish it out: the crumpled box of a pregnancy-testing kit. He studied the box, reading the small print. He looked again into the bin, stirring the contents with his hand until he found what he was looking for – the tester itself. He picked it out and at once saw the pink spot.

Rylands was sitting at his desk reading *The Times* when the phone rang. It was his secretary, Jane.

'Mr Rylands, I have Roger Barker, Area Television, for you on line one.'

'Thank you.' He flipped the switch on his board. 'Hello.'

'Hi, Robert. It's Roger. You've got to hear this! One of my researchers has come up with some pretty fantastic stuff on Walker . . .'

Rylands listened attentively as Barker told him what young Tom had just uncovered. He had been ready to be underwhelmed, since he considered that Barker, like all media men he'd ever met, was much too easily excited by trivialities and side issues. But in this instance, he could see at once that there was more than a little reason for excitement. 'And Walker was on the case, you say?'

'Yes, but not just that. He was there.'

'He what?'

'He sustained an injury himself. He was a victim, Robert!'

'You sure these details are correct, Roger? Because they give Walker every reason to want McCready put away. Mind you, at the same time, it doesn't do much for James's character.'

'Well, nothing happened to McCready in the end. He wasn't charged.'

'Ah! No charges brought, well that's something. OK, thanks, I'll pass this on to the PCA.' For a few moments Rylands thought the information through, drumming his fingers on the desk. Seeming to come to a conclusion, he buzzed Jane. 'Jane – could you get Ben Duffield on the phone? It's urgent.'

CHAPTER 13

WEDNESDAY, 9 FEBRUARY, AFTERNOON

Each year 10,000 complaints float across the desks of Police Complaints Authority case workers. One in ten is serious enough to merit close PCA involvement, when the Authority supervises the investigation by an outside force and reviews the findings to determine any further action. Procedural slip-ups by police officers are not enough to bring the PCA in, unless the case itself is very high-profile. But gross incompetence or, even more so, the attempt to cover up incompetence, is very likely to bring them in. Deliberate malpractice, on the other hand, is meat and drink to the Authority. Intimidation of suspects, mishandling of witnesses, suppression of evidence, bribery, prejudice – these are their daily fare.

Stanley and Sallinger had spent the morning going over the McCready house and spent half an hour with Vera Collingwood. They learnt nothing that had not been in Allard's report. But their next stop would, they were sure, lead them into fresh terrain.

'Now for the mysterious Eva Widelski,' announced Stanley, setting off to walk to the surprise witness's home.

From the start, both Stanley and Sallinger had been especially intrigued by the business about Eva Widelski. Allard's team had never even got a sniff of it: until now Rylands had kept it safely up his capacious sleeve. A brandy glass from the crime scene handed to a mystic – the same brandy glass that had figured in McCready's account of Meadows' death, possibly with relevant fingerprints? Maybe – just maybe – some important piece of evidence was being manipulated here.

'I went back to the exhibits' log to check for the brandy glass,' said Stanley as they approached the Widelski house. 'But there's no mention of any glass being bagged or sent to the forensic labs for testing. But, look at this crime-scene photo . . . on the floor by the bed?' He flipped open his file at one of the shots, where a small balloon glass was clearly to be seen. Sallinger took the file in her hands and looked closely. She hadn't noticed this before.

'Good grief. It doesn't make sense. Why take it to a psychic?'

Stanley laughed with a touch of derision. 'It's a mystery to me.'

They had reached Eva's front step. Sallinger rapped her knuckles loudly on the door.

A few minutes later Sallinger and Stanley were sitting together on the sofa. Eva stood in the corner, rummaging through her scrapbook and humming to herself. She pulled out a piece of paper and placed it under the lid of her old photocopier, then pressed the copy button. They listened to the machine clunking and churning until a green light flashed under the lid. Eva picked out the original and the copy and handed the latter to Stanley.

He looked at it closely, then held it at arm's length. 'A fireplace?'

'Yes. Like I told the TV producer, I am not just psychic, I also read tarot cards. I have a good reputation for palm reading, ask anyone round here.'

Stanley put the picture aside. He was temperamentally suspicious of anything that smacked of mysticism and the New Age. 'Yes, yes, I am sure you do. But if I could just take you back again to when the officer came to see you. Was it definitely a brandy glass?'

'Oh yes, I remember holding it in my hands—'

Sallinger butted in sharply. 'You held it? Was it not in a sealed plastic bag?'

'Um, I think it was, yes.'

'And did the officer take it out of the bag?' asked Stanley.

Eva reflected, putting a finger to her lips. 'Now did he? No, no, I don't think he did.'

'Are you sure?' asked Sallinger.

'No . . . yes! Yes, I remember. I was worried it might confuse the vibes but he wouldn't take it out. He said it had been held by someone who might have killed somebody. Anyway, it didn't matter and I was able to draw him the picture.'

'This fireplace?' asked Stanley, completely lost.

'Correct. My skills have been used in a number of police inquiries. If you look through my scrapbook again—'

'Miss Widelski,' interrupted Sallinger. 'Why did you draw a fireplace?'

Eva leant towards them and lowered her voice, aiming to pitch it on the spooky side of mysterious. 'I am psychic, dear, the forces come to me. I can't direct them, I'm just a vessel. I showed it to the television producer. Nobody seems that interested in it once they see it, but it must have come from somewhere.' She smiled broadly and the pair of investigators smiled uncomfortably back.

Toys littered the carpet around Detective Inspector Barbara MacKenzie as she knelt on the floor of her office, picking them up and stowing them in a storage box. Files and open file boxes were strewn around the room. Crude crayon drawings by tiny hands were pinned to the walls. Barbara had made the deliberate choice to specialise in the work of the Metropolitan Police Child Protection Unit for the last decade, not only taking on crimes committed against children but dealing with the sensitive cases of juveniles who happened to be caught up as witnesses in adult cases. Barbara had conducted the videotaped interview with seven-year-old Fiona Meadows, after her father had been killed by, as Mike Walker was convinced, Jimmy McCready. It was this that had first brought her into contact with the man who, she liked to think, had ruined her life.

Their on-off affair had lasted two or three years but its effect on Barbara had been considerably more long-lasting. Walker's refusal to leave his horrible wife, and then his sudden abandonment of Barbara, had badly crushed her self-confidence. She had not been able to sustain a lengthy relationship since, though recently things had begun to loosen up at last. She'd dated one or two men, though it was nothing serious. Then, just like a bad conscience, he'd popped back into her life as if to remind her just how unworthy she really was. She still found herself thinking about him, though she would rather think about absolutely anything else.

She heard a tap on the door. 'Come in, it's open.'

A tall woman with straight fair hair slipped through the door and Barbara knew her at once. They'd never been more than formally introduced, but Barbara knew her all right. It was Pat North – the love of Walker's life.

'Hi, I don't know if you remember me, we met on a case led by Mike Walker.' She seemed hesitant and embarrassed, as well she might.

Barbara looked away from North. She studied the floor, taking a couple of deliberate breaths. 'I don't believe this,' she said after a moment. 'God, he's a gutless bastard. I can't believe he's got you doing his dirty work.'

'I'm sorry?'

Instead of replying, Barbara rose and carried the toybox to the side of the room. She returned to her desk, clearing it of children's books and playthings. 'Listen, I told him, the tape is gone. There are no other copies. There's nothing else I can do!'

North was bewildered. 'I'm not sure I understand what you're getting at—'

'He's got some *nerve* sending you over here!'

North took a step further into the room. 'Hey, hold on! Mike hasn't sent me to do anything. He doesn't even know I'm here.'

This stopped Barbara in her tracks. 'Oh. I see . . .'

'I know he called you.'

'Listen, if this is to do with me and Mike then I can assure you it was over a long time ago.'

'What? What do you mean?'

Barbara softened suddenly. 'You didn't know, did you?'

'No,' said Pat, shaking her head sorrowfully. 'No, I didn't know.'

'Well, like I said, you've got nothing to worry about. It was over before it started anyway.'

'Right.' North didn't know what to look at. The pictures on display, the toys, Barbara's face. There was no good reason to feel threatened by this woman and her long-dead relationship with Walker. But she couldn't help it. She couldn't understand why Walker hadn't told her.

'So, why *are* you here?' asked Barbara.

North took a deep breath. She should just ask her questions and get out. 'Well, I know you worked with Mike on the McCready case . . .'

'Yes, he told me about the reinvestigation.'

'I understood that you tried to interview Fiona Meadows at the time but she was too traumatised.'

'Yes, she was completely terrified, scared rigid. She could hardly speak.'

'So what was this tape you mentioned?'

Barbara swept a pile of children's books from her desk and carried them to the bookshelf. 'Look, I don't want to get caught up in the middle of all this.'

'Of what?'

Barbara, slotting the books into place, said nothing.

'Barbara?'

Barbara turned. She shrugged. 'I'm sorry, but I really think you should talk to Mike. Not me.'

North hurled her coat onto the stair post. 'Mike? You home, Mike?' In the lounge, in the large vase, was a huge bouquet of flowers. Beside it stood a bottle of champagne.

Walker thundered down the stairs, wearing one of his best suits. 'Hi! Come here, you.' He attempted to enfold her in his arms but she stood stiff and unresponsive.

Backing off, she gestured at the flowers and bubbly. 'What's all this in aid of?'

'A celebration, I hope. Don't you have something to tell me? The pregnancy-testing kit?'

North took another step back. 'How did you find out?'

'I'm a detective!' North didn't laugh. His cheerfulness was having no effect. 'Ach, I was just throwing some stuff out and saw it in the bin. Why didn't you tell me?'

'I wanted to be sure. This flowers-and-champagne bit's all a bit premature!'

'So? What was the result? I tried to figure it out but . . .'

'Well, it reads positive but we can't be one hundred per cent sure.'

'It's positive?'

'Yes, it was.'

Walker made a sort of convulsive movement, almost hopping in the air. 'It was? It *was*? You mean you could be?'

'Yes, I could be.'

He took her in his arms again, hugged her hard and stood back and punched the air. 'Fantastic! I don't believe it. That's bloody marvellous!'

North looked at him in disbelief. 'Are you crazy? You're not even divorced! Besides you've got two kids and . . .'

'What? What difference does that make?'

'A lot, we've only just moved in together, for God's sake.'

'Hardly. It'll be a year next month. Anyway, shouldn't that be my speech?'

'Just be realistic, Mike, for heaven's sake.'

Walker suddenly sobered up. He looked pained and confused. 'You don't want it, do you?'

'It's not a question of that.'

'Of course it is. Come on, come clean. If you are pregnant, do you want it?'

North almost screamed at him. 'It, it, *it*! It's a *child*, Mike. Think of the responsibility. Think just for a second what it'll mean, to me, to you, to us. We're not ready for it. Oh shit! I need a drink.' Heading for the kitchen she began searching through a cupboard. 'I just feel I'm not ready, not prepared, and right now is not the right time.' She found the bottle and a tall glass and poured herself a vodka and Coke.

'For you?'

'And you, Mike. Be sensible, you already have two kids.'

'But they're not yours.' North took her drink and made for the stairs. Walker followed her up and into the bedroom. 'I love you, Pat. I'll push the divorce through, we'll get married if that's what you want. It's up to you, what do *you* want?'

She wanted to lie down. She kicked off her shoes and fell onto the bed. 'I've not had time to think it through, well, not properly. But, as you know, my career's going really well right now.'

'Don't tell me, they've made you Commissioner!'

'Come on, Mike, be realistic. If I was to have the baby, that'd mean about six months on maternity leave and I'd miss out on all the new developments and training prospects. I've been given a great opportunity with this Home Office scheme.'

Walker sat beside her. He was crestfallen, but trying to keep up appearances. 'You *have* thought it out, haven't you? Nice of you to talk it through with me. Well, if it's not what you want, then you do what you have to do. Whatever. I'm here for you.'

'Sometimes it doesn't feel that way, Mike. You say I've been unreasonable the past few days, but you've not been exactly easy to live with.'

Walker stared at the floor, thinking already of what might have been. 'I've had a lot on my plate.'

'And I haven't? That's what's constantly tugging us apart, you know. We're just not communicating. I know you're holding things back and it hurts. If we can't talk to each other, be honest with each other, then what's the point?'

'So tell me what you want.'

'I want you to talk to me.'

'I meant it – about the baby.'

North let that hang in the air for a moment then took a deep breath. 'I think I should have an abortion.'

She looked up at Walker but he hung his head, refusing to meet her eye. She rolled off the bed and shut herself in the bathroom. Walker wandered across and sat at North's dressing table. He felt a widening void between them and didn't know how to bridge it. He stared at his reflection in the mirror, lifting a finger to touch the scar across his right eye.

CHAPTER 14

THURSDAY, 10 FEBRUARY

On the morning after the bizarre interview with Eva Widelski, John Stanley and Zita Sallinger were back at the PCA offices, reviewing the previous day's work. John Stanley, with his moustache and close-cropped chin-beard, had an unusually continental look for a British copper. Zita Sallinger had worked with him before, on an appeal in an assault case, and trusted his judgement. But Stanley was also cautious. New ideas had to pass stringent tests in his mind before he admitted them. However, as even the younger and more imaginative Sallinger had to admit, Eva's story needed pondering.

'It seems to me this brandy glass could have been a vital piece of evidence,' she told him in her office. 'Bearing in mind that McCready claims they went to bed *after* the stabbing incident, where they both drank from the same brandy glass, what if the glass had fingerprints or saliva from each of them to show that they'd both drunk from it and blood was present? Wouldn't that confirm McCready's account?'

'Well, I thought that initially, but now . . . I don't see how. I don't think Forensics could determine exactly *when* they both drank from the glass.'

'If Meadows had blood on his hands, it could prove he was still alive when he accepted the brandy . . .'

Stanley had to concede that. 'But that still doesn't prove McCready didn't stab him,' he pointed out.

Sallinger spread her hands and her eyes wide. 'Nevertheless, a piece of evidence vanished or was lost by someone. And as Detective Superintendent Walker led the team he must have been aware of the possible importance of the glass.'

Stanley heaved a sigh. Truth be told he could become wearied by poking around trying to find dirt on excellent fellow officers. Everyone hated the PCA but someone had to do the job, of course. 'Well, it'll certainly be interesting to hear what Walker has to say for himself. I'd hate to see such a good cop go down.'

Sallinger's voice was smooth but her look was full of warning. 'Not if he tampered with evidence to ensure a guilty verdict for an innocent man.'

'See, I knew I was right!'

In the small coffee shop where they'd arranged to meet, Watkins bubbled with delight for her friend. North sipped her cappuccino experimentally, and was pleased to find that pregnancy had not deprived her of the taste for it. 'It's not definite yet.'

'Pretty damned likely, though! Pat, that's wonderful! Is Mike pleased?'

'Viv, I'd appreciate it if you kept it quiet.'

'Absolutely, first few months are crucial.'

North put down her cup. 'No, you don't understand. I'm not going to keep it. It's just not the right time, for me or for Mike.'

Watkins' face fell. 'Oh, I'm sorry.'

'Don't be. It was my decision, actually. Mike was buying flowers and champagne ready to celebrate, but, like I said, wrong time . . . well, for me.'

Watkins reached out and gave her a small squeeze on the shoulder. Then she said, 'Funny, isn't it? Life. Here's me, been trying for five years, lost two, haven't given up yet. But time's running out. And there's *you* . . . I'd give anything to be in your position. I want a child so badly. It doesn't seem fair, does it?'

Suddenly it was North who was all concern. How could she have been so stupid? But she hadn't known. 'Why didn't you say something?'

Watkins shrugged. 'It's not something I feel comfortable talking about and, to be honest, working gets me over it, or it got me over the miscarriages. But a word of advice . . .' She made North meet her intent gaze. 'Now don't take this the wrong way, but your clock is ticking. You should think hard about this. You might not get a second chance and you could regret it for the rest of your life. Careers can wait, babies can't.'

North held the eye contact for several seconds, which was as long as she could bear. Then she broke away. 'Can we change the subject, please?'

'Sure!' Watkins smiled and took a sip of coffee. 'Hey,' she said suddenly. 'You know the alcoholic psychic that the old lady on the caravan site mentioned?'

'Yeah?'

'Well, apparently one of the investigating officers took a key piece of evidence to her, but she can't remember his name.'

North thought about it for a second and then almost laughed. 'Oh, come on, Viv. You don't seriously think Mike would take a valuable piece of evidence to a *psychic*?'

'Exhibits' documents were altered, Pat. That's what I've heard on the grapevine. Anyway, I've got to go.'

After Watkins had left her, North looked at her hardly-touched coffee and suddenly felt nauseous. Images of babies flashed in front of her mind, and the face of Walker. He hadn't told her. But what was he covering up? She lowered her head into her hands until the sickness passed.

'Er, let me think, brandy glass . . .'

Dave Satchell had hardly seen it coming. At a pinch he thought they might have got hold of the Glasgow thing, but not the glass. So when Assistant Chief Constable Stanley and Zita Sallinger hit him with these questions about the glass, he was caught without a prepared answer.

He was in an unaccustomed situation. The room was familiar enough. He'd spent thousands of hours in interview rooms like this, but always on the other side of the table.

'Come on, Detective Sergeant Satchell!' said Sallinger with the exaggerated impatience of the interrogator. 'It's here on the crime-scene photograph.'

Satchell groped for the knot of his tie and loosened it. His palms were sweating. 'You've got to remember this was a long time ago, eight years or more, and, er . . .' He couldn't help a nervous laugh. 'I *was* still a bit wet behind the ears back then.'

'And being "wet behind the ears" makes your memory faulty?'

'No, no, it doesn't.'

'So what is the problem? Do you recall seeing a brandy glass or not?'

'I wasn't scene of crime officer. I don't know.'

'It really *is* there on the photograph.' She passed a crime-scene photograph across and Satchell examined it miserably.

'Yes, well, er, I'd have to look at my old notebook. You know how easy it is to forget stuff . . .'

'Stuff? It sounds to me as if you chose to forget about a vital piece of evidence.'

Satchell held up his hand, a stopping gesture. 'No, hold on, you're putting words into my mouth!'

'Am I? Or did you hope this missing piece of evidence would just go away? It wasn't disclosed to the prosecution or defence, was it?'

'No. At the time it simply didn't seem important.'

For a moment, it looked as if Stanley was going to interject, but Sallinger was unstoppable. 'That was not your decision to make, Detective Sergeant Satchell. What you have just admitted to me is nothing short of a conspiracy to pervert the course of justice.'

'No, that's not the way it was at all. I just didn't think it was important.'

Sallinger's tone was acid now. 'McCready could be an innocent man and you chose to ignore a potentially vital piece of evidence. First you ask me to believe you couldn't remember the incident, then you say you didn't think it was important. Isn't it more realistic to say you did not "think it was important" because that is what suited you?'

Satchell was squirming. He just hoped it didn't show. 'You're twisting what I'm saying.'

'Am I really? If you're protecting someone, it really isn't worth it.'

'I'm not. I'm not protecting anyone.'

'Not even Detective Superintendent Walker?'

Grimly, Satchell knew he would now have to give ground. With Walker's name coming up, the stakes had been raised. But also he felt on firmer ground here, because the glass had been his cock-up. If they were out to get Walker, they were chasing the wrong rabbit. 'It was just an accident, that's all. A complete accident!'

Sallinger leant slightly towards him, as if closing in on her prey. 'What was an accident, Mr Satchell?'

Satchell sighed, breathed in deeply and straightened his back. He was cornered. The Piranha had got him and it was time for the truth. 'Right. We'd bagged up all the exhibits, and started logging them, getting them ready to go to the forensic labs. She had been hovering, getting in the way, especially at lunchtime when she'd had a skinful.'

'Who's "she"?'

'This psychic woman, asking if we wanted palms read, crystal-ball stuff. Anyway, Detective Constable Frank Dailey, the exhibits officer . . . It was just a bit of a joke, but he got all stroppy, you know. He believed in it all: tarot cards and stuff. I said I'd prove that it was crap.'

'So, what are you telling me? That Detective Superintendent Walker let you take this glass to the clairvoyant?'

Satchell laughed. 'No. I didn't tell him I was going. I just took the brandy glass and went over to her caravan. Frank and I had got a twenty quid bet on that she was no more psychic than

Gypsy Rose Lee. I showed her the glass to see if she could get any . . . you know . . . vibes from it.'

Sallinger seemed to have trouble taking in this information. She knew that plenty of people believed in the paranormal – but a modern police officer, using it in a case? 'So you – you personally – took a vital piece of evidence to Miss Widelski?'

'Is that her name? Well, I didn't know. Anyway, I showed her the glass . . .'

'Did you take it out of the exhibits' bag?'

Satchell shook his head firmly. 'Oh no, I wouldn't do that. I just showed it to her and she did this big act, rolling her eyes around and saying she was getting a strong message.'

'Did *she* take it out of the bag?'

'No, she drew a picture.' He laughed again. 'It was ridiculous. It was a fireplace. It had nothing to do with anything. So I went back to Frank and said he owed me twenty quid. He was a bit pissed off, well more than that, he was annoyed that he'd lost the bet, said he'd got to take it to the labs and went to grab the evidence bag off me. I fooled about and – well – it dropped.'

Sallinger looked at him in stunned amazement. 'It *dropped*, you say?'

'Yes. It got smashed. The pair of us got into hot water with the Governor.'

'Walker?'

'Yeah. He gave us a right bollocking, but he said it wasn't much use as a piece of evidence because you can't put a time on fingerprints or blood, so it was never added to the exhibits' log.'

Sallinger was nodding her head and writing on her pad. 'I see.' There was a pause while she turned the page. 'All right,

Mr Satchell, moving on to one last matter. Would you describe Detective Superintendent Walker as homophobic?'

Satchell swallowed hard. It was the question he had been dreading. 'Pardon?'

'We have listened to the interview tapes and of course Walker's interviewing technique seems above board, on tape, but McCready has accused Walker of being extremely homophobic and aggressive.'

Satchell shook his head. 'That's nonsense.'

'Not according to this detailed statement from Mr McCready.' She held up a sheet of paper which Satchell could see was a typed statement. 'As you were present during his initial interviews I would like you to tell me if any of these disparaging terms were used by you or Walker, when addressing McCready. You ready?'

Satchell nodded.

'Queer, poof, arse bandit, shirtlifter and one I had not heard before, sausage jockey.' She raised her eyebrows. 'It continues with some exceptionally crude remarks McCready claims were used when the tape was switched off and—'

'Come on,' cried Satchell, unable to listen to any more. 'This is all his lies. If he was treated badly in any way, then why didn't he bring it up at trial? When Walker stopped the tape, the interview stopped, simple as that. Walker is not homophobic and nor am I.'

On the whole, Satchell felt the interview had gone better towards the end. But, when they let him go on his way at last, he found himself thinking back over his answers and of little ways in which he could have given better answers. It was going to be a long time before he forgot the grilling he'd had from Zita

Sallinger. And the Assistant Chief Constable hadn't got in with a single word.

North went straight from the coffee shop to her doctor's, where she had made an appointment to confirm the pregnancy. Sitting among the waiting patients, all of them thumbing through months-out-of-date magazines, she was conscious of a young, heavily pregnant girl and her boyfriend entering the waiting room. He attended her at every step with courtly concern, sitting her down comfortably, finding her reading matter. They sat and waited close together, his arm around her shoulders.

'That's nice, isn't it?' she was saying. 'Do you like that? What do you think of this buggy?'

'Oh, I like *that*. Do you like that colour?'

The boyfriend was still agreeing lovingly with everything she said when the surgery door opened and another pregnant girl – she didn't look much older than seventeen – waddled out of the consulting room. She carried a plump little boy in her arms. Unfolding a pushchair she sat the toddler in it and fastened the straps. Then she rubbed his cheek with her fingers, planted a dummy in his mouth and wheeled him away.

North must have seen little bits of business like this – mother-and-child business – countless thousands of times. But it was as if she'd never seen it before. *This is what it's like*, she thought. *Motherhood.*

The doctor's door opened and a young person looked out into the waiting area. It took North a moment to realise that it was the doctor herself. 'Pat North?' she inquired.

CHAPTER 15

THURSDAY, 10 FEBRUARY

WALKER LEFT work early. In the morning he'd finally charged the husband in the mint murder, so now he should be feeling it had been a good day. He didn't. His mind was unruly. He'd drugged himself since lunch with paperwork, but the thought kept coming back to him. The baby. Their baby. His baby. Somehow, without even thinking about it much, he'd started to love it already. And, as it was hardly more than a blob of jelly at this stage, this was unreasonable. And it was quite *reasonable* for her to choose to dispose of it. That was her choice, her right. He just didn't happen to agree.

He started to drive towards home but saw a parking space outside a pub and pulled in. It was still early. She wouldn't be expecting him home and what was the hurry? At the bar he ordered a pint and a whisky chaser and sat down at a corner table.

In the abstract he wasn't against abortion. His Catholic boyhood was a long time ago. He knew, God knows he knew, the misery of young teenage mothers surviving on shit-hole estates, blowing their benefit on scag, falling into the clutches of loan sharks. He'd seen it over and over as a young copper in Glasgow. Those babies, screaming for attention in their filth, while their mothers nodded away. It would have been better if they'd never been born. But this baby was different. It was their baby. His baby.

He hit her mobile number on the phone. She answered, sounding tired. He could hear the sounds of traffic behind her. 'Hi, it's me. Shouldn't be too long, just having a drink with a few of the lads. Do you want me to bring back something to eat?'

'No, I'm at the supermarket now. I'll get it.'

'OK. Everything all right? You all right?'

'Yes, I'm fine. Went to the doctor. Everything's good. What about you?'

'Me? I'm fine. See you later, then.' He had lied to her. There were no lads. Just himself and two glasses – was that sad, or what? He drained the chaser just as the barman came past for empties. Walker caught his eye and pointed to the tumbler for a refill.

Roger Barker already had a Visiting Order for Garton Prison and now he used it. Tom had come back from Glasgow this morning and Barker was itching to get McCready's reaction to his researcher's dramatic discovery.

Barker knew the basics of McCready's biography. He was born into poverty in Glasgow, but his parents had had enough energy and talent to get away to England. In the Thatcherite phrase they 'got on their bikes'. It worked. Old man McCready qualified as a telecom engineer. His missus was a hairdresser, ending up with her own salon. By the time little Jimmy was five they were living at Hornchurch, Essex. They had a comfortable purpose-built home in a new development, a Ford Granada, nice neighbours. They also worked every waking hour, terrified of slipping backwards. Jimmy's father worked every scrap of available overtime. His mother kept the shop open till nine every night. And guess who felt neglected? Guess who eventually became more at home visiting his nan back in Glasgow than he did living on the pseudo-suburban development? To his parents, Hornchurch represented paradise, but to Jimmy, heaven was in the pubs and clubs of the city of Glasgow. It was a classic path to criminality. All his friends were unemployed young men with not enough money and too much time on their hands.

'James,' said Barker in the visits room, after they had sat down opposite McCready. 'You told us you used to go back up to Glasgow quite often when you were younger. So we sent one of our researchers up there to do some digging. Unearthed some pretty explosive stuff.'

McCready hesitated and, as Barker saw, involuntarily narrowed his eyes. 'I've never hidden the fact that I was no choirboy,' he said guardedly. 'But I didn't have a record. I've admitted to Mr Rylands I used to get pretty out of it, mixed with a rough crowd. Not that I can remember much, I was always stoned.'

'You've said you did not recall ever meeting Detective Superintendent Walker prior to the murder investigation?'

'Correct.'

'I see.' Barker reached into his briefcase and produced a photocopy of a newspaper cutting. He placed it with a flourish in front of McCready. 'Do you remember this?' It was the *Daily Record*, dated 17 June 1977, and the headline read 'PC Murdered in Pub Brawl'.

McCready was confused. He merely glanced at Barker's photocopy and said, 'No, no, what's this about?'

'Read the article, Jimmy.'

McCready read. Possibly he grew paler. His face certainly registered stunned surprise. He dropped the paper and it slid across the plastic-veneered tabletop to be trapped by Barker's hand. 'Oh my God! It all makes sense now . . . why he had it in for me.'

'Yes, the PC that died was Walker's friend. Don't you remember being there?'

McCready put his head into his hands. 'Yes, but I didn't remember him. I'd forgotten all about this.'

North opened the front door, weighed down by bulging supermarket bags and with a large teddy bear under her arm. She put the groceries on the floor. 'Mike?' she called out. 'You home yet, Mike?'

Silence. She shut the door with her heel, hoisted the teddy bear and looked around. She then sat the soft toy directly in line with the front door and carried the groceries into the kitchen.

Walker fumbled for his keys. He felt tired more than drunk. And in all the thinking time he'd given himself in the pub, he hadn't worked out how he should talk with North. Argue, try to persuade or just give in and say it was her choice? He straightened his jacket and tie before inserting the key in the lock.

What the hell was this? The big teddy bear sat dead centre in the hall, staring glassy-eyed at the door. It looked like a brand-new bear. He shut the door with his shoulder and frowned. He picked up the bear and tucked it under his arm. She was chopping vegetables.

'Is this for me?' asked Walker, holding out the bear.

Her laugh sounded nervous. 'No, it's a clue, though. I've been to the doctor's, and I was surrounded by baby posters and pregnant women and . . .' She turned round to face him. 'The doctor looked like a teenager, and, well . . .' She spread her hands, a gesture saying, *How could I help it?*

'And?'

'And we need to talk it through, obviously, because it shouldn't be something that's just my decision but . . .'

'But?'

North shook her head slowly. Blast Walker! He would never meet her halfway. 'You must have an idea of what I'm trying to say.'

Walker came closer to her. 'My heart's jumping out of my chest right now – if what you're going to say is what I think you're going to say. What this little fella's about . . .' He held up the soft toy hopefully. 'Tell me, go on.'

'I want the baby, Mike.'

Walker flung the bear up in the air with a whoop and it landed behind him, in the lounge doorway. Then he flung his arms open wide and they were clinging onto each other, turning round and round in the narrow space and he thought, *there must be a God.*

The phone rang. Walker kissed her with a big, smooching kiss and broke away to go for the phone. He was beaming as he answered. 'Good evening – and a very good evening it is too,' he said jauntily. It was Satchell. 'Hi, Satch.'

North felt much lighter. He hadn't been lying, he'd wanted the baby too, really wanted it. There was still a doubt lodged in her mind, like a seed trapped between teeth. Walker's whoop of joy had dislodged it. She knew she was doing the right thing.

She watched him. But the smile had gone from his face, the good humour had evaporated. His face had switched from registering sunshine to storms in a matter of seconds. 'Well, thanks,' he was saying. 'Thanks a bundle . . . No, forget it. Bye.' He hung up the phone.

'What's wrong?'

Walker forced a smile, unconvincingly. 'Nothing. Everything's going to be fine. Now you come here and give me a hug.'

She wrapped her arms around him and she could feel the tension. 'Tell me, Mike, what was that?'

Walker half detached himself and looked at her. The strained smile was still there. 'Nothing I can't take care of!'

'Don't do this, please,' she pleaded. 'Stop shutting me out.'

'I'm not.'

'Yes you are! Talk to me, Mike, please.'

Walker shrugged and said, in a low, reluctant voice, 'Well, I think Satch might have landed me in it with the PCA.'

North laid her head against his shoulder. 'Mike, what went on with that case? You've got to be honest with me. I can't handle this anymore, it's affecting our relationship. This is you and me now. I'm not working on the reinvestigation anymore and whatever happened, we have to work it out together.' She felt him hesitating. She went on, reckless now. 'I talked to Barbara.'

Walker stepped back from her, as if he'd been stung by a hornet. 'What? Still checking up on me, are we?'

'Well, you wouldn't talk to me and I needed some answers. I was worried about you. I am still.'

Walker bent and picked up the teddy bear, sitting it on the kitchen table. 'You want to know how I know McCready's a killer, Pat? I've got the scar to prove it. I see the evidence every day.' Walker ran his finger up and down the almost vertical scar that crossed his eyebrow. 'He did this to me! And I got off lightly. The officer with me died!' He lowered his voice to a growl. 'McCready got away with murder once. I wasn't going to let him get away with it again.'

When Rylands, accompanied by Ben Duffield, visited McCready a few days later at Garton Prison, he had the look of a great benefactor, a bearer of tremendous news. 'So Mr McCready . . .' he said as they all sat down. 'Are you free on July the 3rd?'

McCready was puzzled. Free? He was in jail, for Christ's sake! 'What do you mean?'

Rylands smiled. And before he could speak again, Duffield butted in. 'We've got an appeal date!'

Rylands hid his irritation at Duffield's lack of finesse in timing. He smiled warmly. 'You will be moved from here to Brixton Prison for the hearing. Congratulations, Jimmy. I am very confident.'

McCready sat stock-still for a moment. Suddenly he reached out to touch Rylands' hand. 'Hey! That's . . .' McCready looked only at Rylands. Duffield might not have existed for him. It had been Rylands, not Duffield, who had opened this window of hope. McCready felt he was standing on the sill of that window, preparing to fly away. 'Thank you, thank you.' He held Rylands' steady gaze. Then he remembered the other man and flicked him a glance, a small incline of the head.

CHAPTER 16

SUNDAY, 25 JUNE

It was four months later and Walker was decorating: hanging teddy-bear wallpaper in the little spare room, now designated the Baby's Room. He was cackhanded at all DIY tasks, though not in his own mind. In fact, at this moment he was congratulating himself. 'I could've been on *Changing Rooms* if I'd not joined the force,' he told himself, pasting a new sheet. He lifted it and walked quickly towards the stepladder. He walked too quickly. The paper crumpled inwards, with the pasted side getting stuck together. 'Pat! Pat, will you come in here? PAT!'

'What?' She wandered in, now visibly though not extravagantly pregnant, to find him halfway up the ladder, struggling to straighten the length of paper. But this had now become impossibly twisted.

'Can you get hold of the other end? It's stuck together.'

'Hang on, I don't want to get paste on my top.' While she was looking for something old to change into, Walker lost patience and suddenly gathered the sticky wallpaper into a soggy ball. He squashed it so hard that wet paste oozed out over his hands and wrists.

'Don't bother, don't bother,' he said tetchily. 'I'll do a fresh piece.'

'What you should do is fold each end in, and then hang a bit at a time.'

'All right, all right.' Walker didn't consider she could teach him anything about paperhanging. 'What's the time?' he asked.

'You've got another half an hour before it's on.' She went round and tapped her finger on the join between two of the five strips of paper he had spent most of the afternoon hanging.

'They're supposed to match on the join, you know. You've got a teddy with two heads and one with no arms!'

'It's all right, he won't notice. Go on, get out of here. I reckon I'll have this finished tonight.'

'Not at the rate you're going!'

He measured the next sheet, cut it and laid it on the pasting table. He plunged the brush into the bucket of paste and came up with a dripping dollop of the stuff which, when he started to spread it on the paper, poured over the edge and onto his shoes. 'Shit!'

Miscarriage of Justice started at nine. North and Walker sat together on the sofa, their dinners on trays on their laps. The music began in long, doomy chords, the bass end rumbling, the top end interjecting eerie stabs. On screen they saw a montage of news stills and footage from eight or nine years ago. McCready was led from a prison van into court by a uniformed officer. The mobile home was seen from the outside. A newspaper headline read: 'Gay Slaying Suspect in Custody' with a shot of McCready, Meadows and young Fiona in a family snap. The white-overalled scene-of-crime officers unpacked their gear outside McCready's house. Police officers came and went.

The voice of an unseen Roger Barker, his diction almost pedantically precise, was heard over the pictures. 'In September

1992, James McCready was convicted of the murder of his lover, Gary Meadows. At the trial, McCready's defence team argued that Gary's wound was in fact self-inflicted, the result of a bizarre and tragic accident. To this day, eight years on, McCready maintains his innocence and continues to fight for an appeal. On tonight's programme we examine evidence never brought to trial and identify manifest irregularities in the police investigation which may just point to another miscarriage of justice.'

Cue the title sequence. The foreboding music gave way to a bright, garish pulse while the main credits flashed up, with Barker's own name appearing no less than three times as writer, producer and presenter. As the title music died, an overhead establishing shot of McCready and Meadows' mobile-home estate at sunrise faded in. The camera closed in slowly on the Meadows/McCready home. 'Croydon mobile-home estate, once home to James McCready, his partner of four years, Gary Meadows, and Meadows' seven-year-old daughter, Fiona. This was to become the setting for an extraordinary investigation.'

Cut to more old news footage from 1992 of the murder scene: the cordoned-off mobile home, police officers and forensic experts coming and going. At the same time the soundtrack played snatches of news reports from the time. 'McCready lived on the estate with his gay lover . . . bled to death during the night . . . died from a fatal stab wound in the centre of his back . . . police were alerted to the scene by a hysterical 999 call from McCready, who told the operator, "I've killed him, he's dead."'

The word 'dead' reverberated and Barker's voice was back. 'This is the telephone call recorded by the emergency services on the morning James McCready discovered his partner was dead. "*Please help me. I've killed him, he's dead!*"'

The voice was woolly from the heavy compression of the telephone signal. '*I think he's dead. Come quickly, I need an ambulance. I've killed him, he's dead, somebody help me, please.*'

Cut to Barker, on screen, standing in front of the mobile home. 'That was the voice of James McCready, who awoke to find the man he loved lying dead beside him. He was evidently in deep shock. That telephone call proved to be an important piece of evidence in McCready's conviction. The police inquiry was led by the then Detective Inspector Michael Walker. He declined to be interviewed for this programme.'

An old still shot of Walker appeared, with hair long enough to touch the top of his ears. North hooted. 'Yay hey! Where did they rake that up from? It's you with hair, Mike.'

Walker was squirming. 'Very funny.'

Barker's commentary resumed. 'We have reconstructed the events of that night, filmed in the same mobile home that saw these tragic events unfold more than eight years ago . . .'

Dave Satchell, too, was watching tensely with Catrina. They saw the actors playing McCready and Meadows – both fair lookalikes – walking arm in arm towards the mobile home. It was dark and the lights were on. Vera's impersonator stood in the driveway as the caption 'RECONSTRUCTION' flashed onto the screen.

'She's been ever so good,' said Vera. 'Did you have a nice evening?'

'Yes thanks, love,' said Meadows. 'Sure she wasn't any trouble?'

Vera shook her head comfortably. All was right with the world. 'No, she went off to bed at nine. I've looked in a couple of times, she's fast asleep.'

'Want some ice cream?' asked Catrina.

Satchell tipped his beer can vertically and drained it. 'No thanks, I wouldn't mind another beer, though, ta. It's all bullshit, making them out to be so angelic. According to her statement, and the barman's, they were pissed as newts, the pair of them, legless. This is totally biased crap.'

'Well,' said Catrina tartly, 'you're the ones being scrutinised, so you're bound to say that, being on the defensive.'

Satchell waved her down. What did she know? 'Oh, forget it. Shush.'

'Shush yourself.'

'I can't wait to see how they film the murder, probably set it to wind chimes and choral music! Where's my mobile?'

Walker was concentrating hard on the TV, now showing Barker's interview with a very nervous Vera. 'Well, we had a nice conversation, just about Fiona, you know, but I could tell they were a bit merry. They liked a drink, no more than any of the young chaps around here and, er . . . a bit later I heard loud rock music, but I don't like to complain, so I went about my business for a while.'

Walker's mobile phone trilled. He ignored it.

'It's yours, Mike,' said North.

He ignored her. He wanted to listen to Barker's next question. 'What happened then?'

'Well, then I heard them shouting, quite loud, so I looked over, but by then they seemed to be drinking and chatting in the bedroom.'

'Mike,' said North. 'It's your *phone*.'

He fished around for the phone in the sofa, didn't find it, got up and tried to locate the phone by ear, his eyes all the time on the screen.

'It'd all settled down, so I went back to bed,' said Vera.

'Why didn't you mention all this in your original statement to the police?'

'Oh, I did. Can't think why they didn't take it down, but I told them everything I saw.'

Walker found the mobile and retreated to the bathroom. 'Hi, Satch.'

'You watching this, Mike? What a load of crap.'

'Of course it's crap, but that business with the clairvoyant – if that comes out tonight, it'll have repercussions for me.'

'What about me? Who dropped the bloody glass?'

'Quit panicking, Satch, and get off the phone, I'm missing it.'

'You not recording it?'

'Course I'm recording it! I'll talk to you later.'

He went back to the sofa in time to hear Barker lay out the case his programme wanted to make.

'Who has the answers? Was an innocent man, so consumed by grief and guilt, misinterpreted, making his words look like an admission to a murder that had not taken place? Did James McCready stab his lover to death and then make up a story claiming it was an accident? Or is that in fact the truth? It was, without doubt, not premeditated, not planned in any way. Was this, then, a terrible miscarriage of justice or a domestic argument that got tragically out of hand? After the break we will disclose details of a past connection between Detective Superintendent Walker and James McCready of which the defence at trial were unaware . . .'

As the commercial break started, North turned round to Walker, who was standing behind her. 'They're more than pointing the finger at police misconduct, Mike. They've already brought up that missing brandy glass, shown crime-scene photos, plus forensic logs. Are you listening?'

Walker slid over the back of the sofa and landed beside her, nuzzling her shoulder.

'Who was that on the phone?'

'Satch getting his knickers in a twist. They've got nothing, this is all crap.'

They watched the first commercial in silence.

Satchell went off to get another beer and seconds later the commercial break ended. Catrina shouted, 'Dave, DAVE! It's started again.'

Satchell was still doing up his flies as he walked in. He picked up a change in Barker's voice now, switching into what he heard as a self-congratulatory bark. The man's surname was apt. 'Our team of researchers recently unearthed a dramatic new twist to this tragic story. A newspaper article, dated 17 June 1977, reports an incident in Glasgow fifteen years prior to the murder of Gary Meadows which proves that Detective Superintendent Michael Walker and James McCready had met before.'

On screen were pictures of the Glasgow pub, the Brown Tavern. Satchell frowned.

The sight of the pub made Walker's mouth fall open. It dropped even further as Barker's commentary continued. 'Walker, then starting out on his career as a police constable in the City of Glasgow Police, had been called in to break up a brawl at the Brown Tavern, along with colleague and friend PC Colin Hood.'

On screen, a picture of Colin Hood, looking incredibly young and raw in his constable's uniform, appeared. Walker said, 'Jesus Christ! This is bad. Where'd they get all this?'

Barker continued in full spate. 'In the ensuing fracas, Hood was stabbed and later died in hospital from his wounds. We talked to Colin's sister, Elizabeth Hood.'

Walker whispered, 'Liz! That's Colin's sister!' Liz Hood! He remembered her well, as a very stylish, very intelligent girl. Way out of his league at that time, though it hadn't stopped him wondering. Of course, she was more than twenty years older now, but in his opinion no less bonny and slim.

'My brother was only nineteen when he died,' she said. 'He was the kindest, sweetest person and totally dedicated to his job.' Cut away to a shot of McCready as a young man. Liz's voice broke off and started again – the edit palpable. 'James McCready often stayed with a relative on the estate we lived on. He always seemed like a pleasant young man.' The voice cut off as abruptly as before. Walker could have sworn he heard a 'but' on the end of Liz's sentence before it was overwhelmed by Barker's returning voice-over.

He turned to North, outraged. 'Hear that! Hey! Did you hear that? They've cut something out!'

North slapped him on the arm, not entirely playfully. 'Would you shut up and let me listen.'

'McCready,' Barker continued, 'was in the pub at the time and was arrested, but later released following a statement from local drug addict George Connelly, who was involved in the brawl.' Cut to a family photograph, and then a police mugshot, of a handsome young man, George Connelly. In the first he looked happy and normal. In the second he looked guilty as hell.

'Connelly admitted that he, and he alone, had killed PC Hood and vehemently denied suggestions of McCready's involvement. But could it be that fifteen years later, Michael Walker still had a grudge against McCready and held him in some way responsible for the murder of Colin Hood? If this is the case, could this have influenced how the Meadows case was handled? Was James McCready *framed* for a murder he did not commit?'

North stared at Walker but said nothing.

Satchell was sitting there, his beer completely forgotten, his face in his hands. 'Aw shite! And we were worried about a sodding *brandy* glass!' He just knew the phone would ring. His colleagues would be switching off the telly and getting on the blower, just to gloat over his discomfort. A few seconds later it did.

After the programme, North went to bed with the teddy bear while Walker made tea. As he brought it into the bedroom, the house phone rang by the bed. Getting there before North, he lifted up the receiver, dropped it down again and then left it off the hook. 'I'm not taking any calls.' This sounded self-important and to make amends he sat by the bed and touched her face. 'You know what, from now on, I'm really going to look after you. You don't go lifting or carrying anything.'

She frowned, thinking back over what she had learnt tonight. ‘Mike, don’t you think we should talk about what went on in the programme?’

Walker smiled and shook his head. ‘No, sweetheart, I don’t.’

He placed his hand on the mound of her stomach. ‘I don’t want you worrying about any of this, stress isn’t good for you or the baby.’

She laughed out loud at this. ‘Don’t you worry about me, I’m as strong as an ox!’

But Walker was serious. ‘I know that, but it’s not as if you’re in the first flush of youth—’

‘Hey!’ she shouted, giving him a side-swipe with the bear. ‘Enough of that, thank you!’

Walker lay down beside her and closed his eyes. ‘I still think David, if it’s a boy and if it’s a girl—’

‘No,’ she interrupted. ‘We are *not* calling her Violet!’

Walker propped himself up on one arm. ‘Why? What’s wrong with Violet?’

North yawned sleepily. ‘You *are* joking?’

‘What? Of course not. It’s a beautiful name. Wait until you *meet* my mother.’

That would be an interesting day, thought North. From what she’d heard, where son Michael was concerned, Violet Walker was an entire police force all on her own.

CHAPTER 17

MONDAY, 26 JUNE

McCready stood in the prison phone queue, impatiently fanning the air with his phone card. As the man in front of him finished, he pounced on the receiver, hunching himself around it as all the prison inmates instinctively did. He slotted in the card and pressed the numbers of the Glasgow STD code. 'Sean, it's me, Jimmy. Did you see it? . . . Yeah, it's looking good, but the guy they used to play me wasn't as good-looking . . . Yeah, you can. I'll sort it for you when I'm out.' His voice went quiet, almost to a murmur, and he looked to right and left. 'George Connelly – you found him? . . . Yeah, I hear you, Sean . . . OK, OK . . . Well, when you do, the going price: double it! Right? Right – my man!' He hung up.

Walker had often been in trouble in the past, and not solely before he joined the police force. He had many times broken the spirit of the procedural rules and, on one or two occasions, the letter of them too. But he had got away with it, mainly because he almost always produced results, helped by the fact that he kept a low public profile. Give or take the odd *Crime Night* appearance, he'd never been one of those media-friendly detectives, swarmed all over by politicians and hacks. If he had been, the top brass would have cut his legs off years ago.

So he'd known there would be trouble when he turned up for work this morning and he'd been ready to give his side of the story as best he could. He never got the chance. As soon as he walked into the Chief Superintendent's office, a sixty-kiloton air-blast of fury hit him square in the face.

He left the building feeling dazed. Satchell's car, the passenger door open, awaited him. He climbed in thankfully. 'The bastards have just suspended me from duty.'

Satchell rocked back in the car seat. 'Aw shit! I'm sorry, Mike.'

'So am I, Satch. I'm sick of the sodding media dictating police procedure. McCready must be creaming himself. I'm going to be pushing paper around for at least the next six months, thanks to him and that bullshit documentary! How the hell did they dig up all that stuff about Glasgow?'

'Researchers, at a guess.'

'Well, I'm going to do some research of my own. I'm going to find George Connelly and get the truth once and for all.'

'Connelly's the guy that took the rap for McCready for the Glasgow murder, right?'

'Yep. He must be out of prison by now.'

'And how are you going to find him? The TV lot obviously couldn't, otherwise they'd have had him on the bloody documentary as well.'

Walker smiled grimly. 'Don't worry. I've got friends up there. His dad Jock for starters. Connelly and I used to live on the same estate in Glasgow when we were growing up.'

'No kidding?'

'I'll take Pat up to meet my mother while I'm at it. Kill two birds with one stone.' He chuckled.

Satchell was glad he could see the funny side. 'I thought you had an interview with the PCA woman coming up?'

Walker checked his watch. 'I do, in half an hour.'

'Watch out for her, Mike. She's cracking-looking. Comes across at first like butter wouldn't melt, but they don't call her The Piranha for nothing.'

Walker scowled at Satchell. 'I can always depend on you to make me feel good. Piranha! Well, I'm a bloody Great White Shark, mate.'

'So what do you think you're going to find in Glasgow?. It must be more than twenty years ago.'

Walker shook his head conspiratorially. 'I was only a young copper in the inquiry. Connelly and McCready were both suspects, but the case against them was paper-thin, until Connelly suddenly held up his hands and made a statement saying he had the knife, not McCready. Of course, both men were involved in the fight but it was a big, big ruckus. Colin and I piled in to try to stop it and, next thing, I'd been slashed and Colin was stabbed. With blood in my eye I never saw what actually happened to him. I thought it was McCready but I couldn't swear to it. Everyone else kept schtum. So we had no clear eyewitness, no motive, no forensics – never even found the murder weapon. We reckoned someone else in the pub thought they'd do him a favour by picking it up off the floor and throwing it in the Clyde. And what does that tell you, Satch?'

'At least one person saw what really happened?'

'Exactly. And I'm going to find out who.'

In the interview room, Sallinger sat coolly turning the pages of her thick case file. Stanley sat beside her with his own bulging file. Nervous and resentful, Walker sat opposite, thinking the man looked not too bad for an assistant chief constable. Might be old school, might see his point. The female, on the other hand, looked deadlier than the male.

Stanley activated the tape, cleared his throat and for ten minutes they discussed the brandy glass. Walker put his hands up to everything – a ploy he'd seen used by old lags time and time again: own up to any minor misdemeanour, whatever it was, when you knew a major charge was coming along behind.

'So,' said Stanley summing up. 'You do admit to not recording the breakage of the glass and simply leaving it off the exhibits' log?'

'Yes, but as I said, only because it was broken as the result of an unfortunate accident and I didn't think it was an important piece of evidence.'

Zita Sallinger had said very little so far. But now, without warning, she cut in. 'The court decides what is important and what is not, Detective Superintendent.'

'Look, everyone had access to the crime-scene photos and McCready's statement. Had anyone queried it, I would have told them the truth. As it was, I didn't think it was necessary to draw attention to the fact that one of my officers was a bit cack-handed!'

'I see,' she said smoothly. 'So you go on the assumption that unless evidence is asked for by counsel you have no reason to produce or submit it?'

Walker knew he was sweating. He pulled at his collar. 'That's unfair. Like I said, we had enough to press charges and the brandy glass seemed irrelevant to me.'

Stanley suddenly started thumbing through his file. 'Let's move on, shall we? This previous incident when you were involved with McCready, the murder of PC Colin Hood in Glasgow . . .'

Walker steadied himself. He nodded. 'Right. I saw no reason to mention the Glasgow business as McCready was released without charge. McCready may have implied I had something personal against him but I don't. If I had, at any time, given him reason to believe that I or my investigation was prejudiced, then why didn't he bring it up at the time?'

Stanley remained expressionless but Walker noticed that Sallinger pursed her lips sceptically. 'How close were you to Colin Hood?' she asked, her voice as smooth as silk.

Walker shrugged. 'Not very, like they said on the documentary, we worked together now and again. About the only thing they did get right. Apart from that it was all lies. Eight years later and people suddenly start recalling facts they didn't mention at the time. All a bit convenient, isn't it? But I suppose back then there wasn't a television documentary being paid, er, made.'

Sallinger smiled icily at Walker's none-too-clever slip of the tongue. 'So you're happy that the right man was convicted for the murder of Colin Hood?'

'I did my job. It's not my business to comment on the outcome.'

Stanley had been studying his file. He looked up. 'Why was Fiona Meadows not called to give evidence at McCready's trial?'

'She was only seven years old. She was so traumatised, she couldn't speak.' He looked from Stanley to Sallinger. 'We did . . . Well, we did have a videotaped interview done by a Child Protection officer. But I was advised by the prosecution barrister at the time that it was inadmissible evidence because she couldn't be cross-examined.'

'And what did she say on this video?'

Walker looked down at the table. He would never forget the child's horrified expression, but he couldn't find the words to describe it. 'It wasn't exactly what she said – she barely spoke. She was dumb with terror, but made it pretty clear McCready stabbed her father.'

'So where is this video now?'

Walker hesitated. Then looked up, risking a rueful smile. 'Seems to have disappeared without trace. It was eight years ago, after all.'

Sallinger made a rapid jotting. 'Mmm. Well, we'll definitely look into that.'

Stanley was still flicking through his paperwork. 'What about McCready's accusations that you are homophobic and bullied him while he was in police custody?'

Walker held up his hands as if to put a stop to this. 'Oh, please! I work with gay people, I have gay friends; their sexual preference is none of my business. Perhaps if McCready had had a gay MP championing his cause at his trial he might have tried it on with these accusations then, but he didn't. It's all fabrication.'

Sallinger tipped her head to one side, eyes narrowed. 'So these accusations of police misconduct are, what?'

'Completely unfounded,' said Walker firmly. 'The jury concluded that McCready killed his partner in cold blood. I am certain any appeal will produce the same verdict.'

Sallinger glanced at her watch and smiled more sweetly this time. 'We just have a few more questions, Detective Superintendent Walker. Sorry to keep you so long.'

'Take as long as you want,' he said grimly. 'As you know, I have been suspended from duty.'

Stanley went on to ask about Satchell and the rest of the team who'd worked on the Meadows murder. Walker answered calmly but Zita Sallinger noticed how, apparently unaware of what he was doing, he kept massaging the scar over his eye.

When he got home, Walker found North in the baby's room. True to his word he had finished the nursery wallpaper. The cot was also in place and above it, North was fixing up a hand-made cot mobile with cartoon policemen dangling from it.

'Pat,' Walker began. 'I've just been speaking to Mum and— Hey! What's that?'

'I know it's a bit naff but Viv and some of the girls at the station made it.'

Walker twirled the mobile. 'Very inventive . . . it'll give him bloody nightmares.'

'Sorry, you were speaking to your mum and . . . ?'

'Oh yes. Well, she's invited us both up to Glasgow this weekend. It's the perfect chance to tell her our news. What d'you think?'

North cocked her head to one side suspiciously. 'Yeah! Good idea. I can't believe you still haven't told her!' She rubbed the bump on her stomach. 'Just so long as this doesn't mean we have to call her Violet if she's a girl.'

Walker made the mobile spin once more. 'Tell you one thing, Pat. If it's a boy, he ain't going to be a copper.'

Before a criminal trial, the media is not allowed to comment. Appeals are different. The cases for the prosecution and the defence have been previously aired, the arguments rehearsed. Naturally, the Appeal judges deem themselves to be unlike a jury of common men and women and incapable of being adversely influenced and so comment is freely permitted. And yet Rylands and Duffield both felt that Barker's documentary would not only boost the case for McCready, but be invaluable in marshalling public opinion. They knew that the stronger the public thought in one direction, the harder it would be for the Appeal Court to move in another.

McCready was certainly on a high, sitting once again at the legal visits table with his defence team.

'There was a tremendous reaction to the documentary,' said Rylands.

'All positive feedback!' chimed in Duffield.

'Yeah,' McCready said excitedly. 'I've had loads of letters – like fan-mail!'

'Well, it won't all be plain sailing,' warned Rylands. 'Apparently Fiona Meadows was video interviewed by a Child Protection officer shortly after your arrest. Did you know about this?'

McCready thought for a moment. Suddenly he was aghast. 'But . . . she couldn't speak.'

Duffield had not heard of this either and was quickly spluttering with indignation. 'Nobody ever mentioned anything about a video. It's impossible, she was in complete shock after her father's death. If they'd made a video, surely they'd have used it in the trial?'

'Well, I don't know,' continued Rylands calmly. 'But apparently a video interview *was* done.'

McCready was shaking his head. 'No, no, that can't be true. I mean, I mean, where has this tape suddenly come from?'

Rylands smiled reassuringly. 'Ah! Well, the police don't actually have a copy of it. Apparently all CPT videos are sent to a property store in Chalk Farm, where they're kept until the child turns eighteen. But they have no record of Fiona's interview ever being sent to them.'

'I see.' McCready was ashamed of his moment of panic. 'Are they likely to find it?'

Rylands was looking at him closely. 'Well, eight years after your trial, I seriously doubt it. But, well, could there be anything contradictory on the video? In other words, could Fiona have said anything, do you think, that might incriminate you – anything that differs from her present useful statement?'

McCready shook his head vehemently. 'No, no, of course not. Even if some Child Protection officer is put up to say more lies about me, that's all it is . . . *lies*. I only want Fiona to tell the court the truth.'

'You are sure? Only I was hesitating about calling her.'

McCready smashed the table with his fist. 'No! Call her. She's my most valuable witness. I want Fiona called. I have nothing to hide.' He looked defiantly from one lawyer to the other and Rylands was reassured. 'Let them do their worst, then,' he said.

CHAPTER 18

WEDNESDAY 28 JUNE

Walker and North were standing on the concourse of Glasgow Central Station. She had chosen a very loose dress which hardly revealed her pregnancy but Walker was not going to let her forget it as easily as that. He had become a fanatic on the subject. 'Just give me the bag. You're not to carry anything!' He took the bag with one hand and, with the other, flipped open his phone.

She said, 'Shall I get some flowers?'

'Yeah, yeah. You do that, I'll give Ma a call.'

She walked over to a flower stall. Walker put the bag down, punched in a number and waited patiently while his mother allowed the telephone to ring exactly twelve times. He knew all her superstitions. 'Hello? It's Mike.'

'Did you say Mark?'

'No, no – your son! Can you hear me?'

'Yes, I hear you.'

'OK, we're at the station.'

'Already? I thought—'

'Yes, Glasgow, we're here.'

'You've such an English accent these days, Michael, I can hardly recognise you. Have you that woman with you?'

'Yes, she's with me.'

'What's her name again?'

'Pat.'

'Pat?'

Walker began to pace the concourse as he talked. 'Yes, Pat, and I don't want any nonsense from you, do you hear me? You be nice to her.' He stopped walking and looked back across the concourse, to where North stood at the flower stall. Instinctively, he lowered his voice. 'Listen, Ma, has anyone called for me? Any messages?'

'No, no messages at all.'

'OK, well if anyone does, can you take their number and tell them I'll call back?'

'Are you in Glasgow, did you say?'

'Yeah. Train's just got in. We'll get a cab. OK, bye.'

North returned, carrying a huge bunch of flowers. Walker rubbed his hands together. 'She's well pleased she's finally going to meet you.'

North was looking curiously around their feet. 'Where's the overnight bag?'

Walker looked down. 'Shit! It's all right. Don't panic!' He spotted the bag fifty feet away and sprinted off to retrieve it.

On the way, Walker explained that his mother lived in recently converted sheltered accommodation: a large Victorian house, split up into self-contained flats for elderly people. On the ground floor lived a warden; a meals-on-wheels service came every day; the Mobility Bus called regularly with its shopping service; the toilets were adapted for the disabled. 'It's supposed to help them to feel independent. The flats are even big enough for them to have family to stay, like us. But there's this big safety net. There's alarm bells hooked up to the warden in every room.'

'Your mother must be delighted, isn't she?'

'It's me who's delighted. Saves a lot of worry. But she hates it. She's always been a tough cookie, and she likes her independence. But she's got a heart of gold – you'll see!'

On the steps Walker squinted at the row of bells and then rang one. There was no answer. He rang again.

'Did you tell her what time we'd be arriving?'

'Yes, yes.' He rang a third time. He didn't bother to explain that his mother never answered the door before the third ring. 'She's expecting us.'

A crackling voice was heard on the intercom panel. 'Hello?'

'It's Mike, we're outside. Can you buzz us in?' The buzzer did not last long enough or Walker didn't react fast enough to open the door. He pressed the buzzer again. 'Ma! Keep your hand on the buzzer a bit longer, we're still outside.' The door buzzed again, he pushed and in a moment they were heading up the stairs. The place was in reasonable order, though the carpet was a bit threadbare. The staircase was old, and wide, with a stairlift at the bottom.

'Big place,' commented North. 'It must have been lovely at one time. Look at the cornicing.'

As they arrived at the first floor and flat 2B, Walker walked ahead and rang the doorbell. North hung back slightly. He rang again and then a third time. At last the door opened slightly. But the chain was still on.

'Hi there.' Walker's mother, Violet, fumbled with the chain. 'Can you manage all right?'

'Be in trouble if I couldn't. I've been on my own long enough!' Violet finally got the chain off the door and opened it wider. She was a neat, diminutive woman with white, permed hair, wearing a pink twinset, pearl necklace and pink slippers. North put her age in the mid-seventies. Walker kissed and hugged her and turned, making a gesture towards North.

'This is Pat. Pat, my mum, Vi, Violet.'

'Hello,' said North as cheerily as she could manage. 'Nice to meet you finally.' She handed over the flowers. 'These are for you.'

Violet took them coolly. 'Thank you. You'd better come in. It was such short notice I've no had time to do any housework and my help only comes in once a week.'

Walker shut the front door and Violet led North and Walker along a small narrow hallway. 'Will you be staying overnight or is this like your usual, ten minutes and off again?'

'We'll stay over . . .'

'Oh, I *am* flattered. It'll be more than a cup of tea, then? Makes a change!' Violet still had not actually looked at North, she gestured to a door. 'There's the spare room. Will you be sharing a bedroom?'

Walker stopped and looked hard at his mother. 'We will, and don't you start.' He turned to North. 'I'll put our bag in the bedroom. You go on through.'

North followed Violet into the lounge. The room was immaculate, but it had a peculiar deadness to it. Each piece of furniture looked hardly used. The chairs had lace antimacassars. A dining table stood in one corner and a rug was placed in front of the electric fire. Odd ornaments sat on the dresser alongside a gilt mirror. The room contained no other personal items except for framed photographs of Violet's grandchildren and a wedding photo of Walker and Lynn.

North stood uneasily as Violet busied herself fetching a vase, filling it with water and depositing the flowers in it. North's offer to help was ignored and she wished Walker would come back. She could hear him washing his hands in the spare room. Violet meanwhile crossed to the coffee table, where a tea tray was set with three cups, a pot of tea and a plate of biscuits.

'You'll have a cup of tea,' said Violet.

At last Walker rejoined them. 'Yes, please. Sit down, Pat. Here, Ma, let me help.'

'No, you sit down. Do you take milk and sugar, miss?'

'Pat, please. No sugar, just a drop of milk.'

'Place looks nice,' said Walker.

'Could do with a dust.' North looked round. There was not a speck of dust anywhere. Violet handed North's tea to Walker. 'Give this to your friend and there're biscuits too.'

Walker winked at North as he passed the tea across. As he returned to collect his own he impulsively kissed Violet on the cheek. 'It's good to see you.'

'How are my grandchildren?'

'They're fine.'

'And Lynn?' she asked pointedly. 'Is she well?'

'She is, they're all fine.' Walker kept his voice level during this exchange. He returned and sat with his cup of tea, as Violet sat down with hers.

'I sent your birthday card to your home.'

'Lynn sent it on to me, at my *new* home.'

'I might go and stay with Lynn,' she said without inflection. 'She's asked, and it'll be nice to see the grandchildren.'

The phone rang and Walker stood up. 'I'll get that. It might be Jock Connelly, he called earlier.'

He dodged out to the hallway, where the phone was. *Connelly?* What was he up to? North shut her eyes in weariness then opened them again, remembering she had to keep up appearances with Walker's mother. Violet Walker was staring into her cup. All this time, since she'd first walked into the flat, she had still not looked at North.

'So, how long have you lived here, Violet?' she asked patiently.

'It's part of a rehousing scheme for the elderly. They moved me in with a lot of old women I don't know. I hate it. Biscuit?' She passed the plate, looking only at the biscuits.

'No, thank you,' said North. 'What lovely photos.' She gestured towards the array of photographs on the mantelpiece and chimney breast – Mike's kids in snapshots and formal school portraits.

'Yes,' said Violet. 'They're my grandchildren. Lynn's such a wonderful mother.'

North was still reeling from this sideswipe when Walker returned. He leant down and put his mouth near her ear. 'I've got to go out for a while.'

North's face must have registered a mild degree of panic. 'But we only just got here! I'll come with you.'

Walker shook his head. 'You won't. That was George Connelly's father. He's going to show me where to find George. Apparently he's dossing down with some drunks in a squat!'

North touched his arm. 'Mike, you promised. Just leave it alone!'

But he took no notice, simply kissed her on the cheek and spoke loudly to his mother, who had been looking on impassively. 'We've got some news, Ma.'

North looked at him wildly. 'Mike, I don't think now's the right time.'

Again he ignored her, driving cheerfully on. 'We're having a baby, you'll have another grandchild.'

There was a clatter as Violet almost dropped her raised cup into its saucer. She looked from one to the other, almost horror-struck. 'It'll be illegitimate! You should both be ashamed of yourselves, at your age. And you've already *got* two wee children.'

'But not one by the woman I'm in love with and intend to marry!'

'Well, you'd better get a divorce first!'

Walker sat forward and touched Violet's shoulder. 'Listen, Ma, let's talk about this later. I've got to nip out for a while. You take care of Pat for me?'

He stood up and beckoned to North. 'Sorry about this. But I really don't think it'd be wise for you to come. It's a really rough area, full of winos.'

North was resigned. 'I'll be fine, don't worry,' she said, without conviction. She followed him into the narrow hall and he put his arms around her.

'I'm sorry, she's got a right mouth on her. I won't be long, I promise.' He kissed and dodged out of the front door.

As North turned she almost bumped into Violet, carrying the tea tray and heading carefully towards the kitchen. Violet put down the tray on the worktop and turned deliberately towards her guest, though keeping her eyes directed towards North's shoes. 'I have every right to feel the way I do. He should never have left his wife, worse his two children. He's always been too much the one for the ladies.'

North was thinking, *Change the subject!* 'Can I help wash up?'

'No, thank you.'

The response was so cold it made North shudder. But she was not going to lie down silently, and suffer. 'Look,' she began, firmly, 'it's obvious I'm not welcome here. I'm sorry, but Mike led me to believe—'

And at last Violet looked up and met North's gaze, looking at her ferociously, as if it were some reckless, life-endangering act. '*What* has he told you? Never believe a word he says. He always was a liar. His father was the same, couldn't tell the truth about a thing. I was always surprised he left Lynn. When his da went off it broke his heart, so he knows what divorce can do to a family.'

Violet now began running water into the sink. North edged into the kitchen behind her; at least, they were communicating now. Violet squirted washing-up liquid and methodically began to wash the cups. 'So what work do you do?'

'Has he not told you?'

'He's not, but then he keeps everything to himself.'

'I'm a police officer.'

'Ah I see, you work for him, do you? And did you not know he was married when you started up with him? Married and with two bairns! But then I suppose when you get to your age, and you're not married, you take what you can.'

This was too much. 'Violet, I had *nothing* to do with his separation.' She paused, waiting for some softening, some sign that the fret had blown itself out. But Violet continued unmoved, silently washing the saucers. Summoning her dignity, feeling tears not far below the surface, North decided on a tactical withdrawal. 'I think I'll go and wait for him in the bedroom.'

But backing out into the hall, she was pursued by Violet's parting shot. 'I don't approve of him bringing you here.'

'No,' said North. 'You've made that *very* clear. Excuse me now.'

She shut herself in the spare room and, without turning on the light, lay on the bed. In other circumstances, North might have found the situation grimly funny. It was like being carpeted by a vengeful headmistress. But she could also appreciate that Violet's attempts at cruel sarcasm hid a desperately sad personal truth. She was truly a bitter and disappointed woman. Her own marriage had been a disaster, her son's the same. And what of her grandson's and great-grandsons'? Would it be so for generation after generation? Violet was one of those old-fashioned enough to think that, if your marriage failed, it was the failure of your life. For Violet to have to confront North here, in her own home – and, worse, *pregnant* – was in that way a confrontation with her own failure. North tried hard to make herself sympathise but she couldn't, not even for Walker's sake. She was overwhelmed instead by a sense of her own isolation in this bleak, uncompromising home. It was all right for him: he had obviously found his own way of coping with Violet. But what about her – and the unborn one? She must keep thinking about the baby. All this anxiety wasn't good for it.

The trip hadn't been entirely wasted. If nothing else, she'd learnt where Walker had got his appalling manners from. But this was enough now. She had taken a week's leave for the occasion but now she'd go back to London in the morning.

CHAPTER 19

WEDNESDAY, 28 JUNE, EVENING

IT WAS raining in sluices when Walker met Jock Connelly. Connelly took him to a run-down section of the city that had been partially demolished and then left for years, while developers, residents and the council fought over the rebuilding plans like cats in a bag. The result was planning blight: broken waste ground, derelict buildings, patches of unruly vegetation, piles of dumped waste. Walker almost didn't know Jock. He hadn't seen him for more than ten years, in which time, never a big man, he had shrunk even further. There was also a new frailty about him, when once there was firmness and humour. His voice had a tremor and his breath whistled.

They put up their collars and crossed a brick- and rubbish-strewn waste ground. 'How are George's kids?' asked Walker.

'Doing well. They live in America now. Sheila took 'em over there after he got sent down. I sometimes get postcards. Once I even got a home video, the grandkiddies at Disneyland! Wonderful! Real little Americans, they are.'

'That's good. Poor Sheila, hey? Getting out was probably the best move to make.'

'Ay! You know he's been in and out of rehab like a yo-yo, can't keep off the drugs. Always saying he was gonna go to see her, but he never got straight enough to find his way to the airport. He's still a crazy bastard, always was, now worse than ever. He thinks someone's trying to kill him! Drink and drugs, bane of his life. Mine too.'

They continued to pick their way across the rough ground towards a tall block of flats. The windows of the first two floors were boarded over with thick plywood; higher up the glass was broken. No one had lived in these flats – not as settled, civilised homes – for years. But people still used them for shelter, wrecked and cut off from services though they were.

They came to the swing doors of the flats' entrance. One of these had long swung into oblivion while the other hung half detached from its hinges. Beyond them a corrugated-iron sheet was nailed to the door frame. Walker and Jock peered around, then Walker spotted a broken window to one side, with a bank of broken bricks and earth piled up to it. He started towards this but Jock pulled at his sleeve. 'This is where I love you and leave you, Mike. I've had too many run-ins with him. I might be his father but I can't take no more, you ken?'

Walker found a fiver in his wallet and handed it across. 'Appreciate this, Jock, thanks a lot. This is for a pint, now.'

Jock pocketed the note and smiled warmly but without humour. 'There's nothing you can do for him. It's too late!'

Jock Connelly stumbled off into the rain while Walker squinted through the window and into the darkness, wishing he had brought a torch. But gradually his eyes adjusted. Somewhere he heard the crash of a breaking bottle and then a guitar being strummed. He mounted the bank of builders' waste and climbed through the window, following the sound.

Walker had never read Dante's *Inferno*, but he fancied this was like one of its scenes. It certainly looked like hell on earth. He was in a fair-sized room with bare concrete walls. The floor was strewn with slag and rubble, and pooled with oily water. At the far end, some kind of fire was burning, giving off the only light. He moved on towards it.

Suddenly a young girl appeared in front of him. She looked no more than sixteen although he knew, with drug addicts, such appearances could be deceptive. She was staggering around, hardly noticing Walker except as some impersonal feature of the outside world. She herself clearly wasn't engaged with the outside world, being completely stoned and reeling. She continued to stagger away from Walker until she came to a stop against the wall, where she suddenly vomited.

Connelly, a man of Walker's exact age, but looking ten years older, was sitting by a small fire, singing and strumming a broken guitar. They had grown up together but the forty-year-old man now looked nothing like the youth Walker remembered. The hair was long and greasy, the unshaven face was reddened by booze and scabbed by falls, the clothes filthy and stinking. George was singing the 'The Skye Boat Song'. '*Speed Bonnie boat, like a bird on the wing . . .*'

Incredibly, the voice had somehow survived the wreckage of George Connelly's life. Even though he was violently drunk and the words merged into a slurry of meaning, his singing had a soft kind of innocence to it. Walker thought George a lost soul. He was damned, yes, but was it all through his own fault? Walker watched and listened for a moment, filled with pity for this wreck of a man whom he'd known in the larky strength of boyhood. But his sadness was tinged with frustration. Connelly could open the door to McCready for him, but it was like having a key made of rotten wood, a key liable to break itself in the lock and jam up the mechanism. He moved nearer. '*Burned are our homes, exile and death, scatter the loyal men . . .*'

'Long time no see, George!'

Connelly slowly placed his guitar aside and turned his head up towards the man standing over him. His eyes were sunk deep into their sockets, his hair hung down in filthy rats' tails. 'Who are you?'

'Mike Walker.'

Connelly squinted. 'Do I know you?'

As his eyes grew accustomed to the half light, Walker realised there were people lying all around the room, wrapped in sleeping bags or simply curled up wherever they had laid down. There were cans of Special Brew and empty Thunderbird wine and cider bottles everywhere. In a few places a small attempt had been made to set up camp. He saw the wreck of a poolside sunbed, a half-collapsed picnic chair. Graffiti was scrawled over the dripping walls.

Connelly groped around on the floor and found a handful of twigs, which he tossed into the flames.

'You did, a long time ago!' Connelly picked up a bottle and drank from it. Walker went on, 'You were always going to join a band, back in the old days.'

Connelly was interested in this. A memory stirred. 'What did you say your name was?'

'Mike, Mike Walker.' Still Connelly stared, then drank. The name did not appear to mean much to him. Walker tried again. 'I need to talk to you.'

'Oh yeah, what about? Come on, you, what do you want?' He drank again, then dropped his chin to his chest, burping.

'It's about Jimmy McCready.' Walker leant forwards, which was a mistake because now, without warning, Connelly roused himself. He lifted his arm and hurled the bottle at Walker. It missed, but gouts of rough liquor spilled on Walker's face and clothes. Connelly was scrambling to his feet so that he stood unsteadily at bay.

'You don't scare me, mister.' He swung a wild punch, which by chance connected, almost knocking Walker off his feet and giving him a bloody nose. Before he could protect himself, Connelly grabbed him, caught hold of his lapels and tried a head butt. But it was not a fair fight. Alcohol had sapped Connelly's strength and destroyed his coordination. Walker, recovering from his surprise, kicked the other man's legs out from under him. Connelly crashed down like a felled tree, grabbing at Walker's legs and dragging him down also. For a few seconds they grappled together among the muck and half bricks, thrashing around while Connelly grunted and gouged at Walker's face.

'You don't scare me, I'll smash your son-of-a-bitch face in. Come on, McCready, fight me. You owe me, you bastard. Come on, you don't scare me none. I'll fuckin' kill yer first.' From his prone position he flailed wildly at Walker again and was met by a shuddering punch to the side of the head that sent him rolling away into a stagnant puddle.

'I'm not McCready!' panted Walker. 'He didn't send me.'

Connelly was rolling over, laughing and flailing his arms. 'Go on! Get on with the kicks! You can't hurt me, I feel no pain.'

Walker heaved himself up and found a handkerchief to wipe his bleeding nose. 'I'd call twelve years a lot of pain for something you never did.' He extended a hand. 'Come on, let me look at you. Can you get up? You all right?'

Connelly waved away Walker's helping hand, pushing himself into a kneeling position from where he was able to totter to his feet. He began to look around for his bottle.

'It's Mike, Mike Walker – remember? Look at me, George. Don't you remember me?'

Connelly found the bottle, miraculously unbroken and still with some liquor inside. He started to pour more of it down his throat. 'The wee police officer, right?' he said thickly. 'Oi, here you go.' Pathetically, he was holding out his fists for Walker's handcuffs, the bottle still in one hand.

'You offering me a drink now?' asked Walker. This confused Connelly but he let Walker take the bottle and watched closely as he raised it to his lips. Walker found it was some very rough spirit, possibly rum.

'You got a fag on you?' begged Connelly.

Walker passed over his pack and Connelly fumbled one out. He looked up as Walker struck up a light, suddenly resembling a dog awaiting a reward. Connelly cupped his hands around the flame, trying to keep steady, and momentarily his wrecked face was fully illuminated, bruised, scabbed and grimy.

'So you know McCready?' he asked after he had inhaled.

'Aw come on, Georgie, I was there. That stabbing – you were so drugged up, you could hardly walk, let alone kill someone. Who used the knife, George? Because I know it wasn't you.'

Now Connelly was wandering away from Walker but only in order to do a small circle, returning to the fire and slumping down beside it. He looked up and pointed at Walker. 'You had blood all down your face, right? That's right, you got cut!'

'Yeah, that's right, I got cut. But who is it has Colin Hood's blood on his hands? Not you! Not you, George! Tell me it wasn't you.'

Connelly suddenly seemed to focus for a brief moment and was about to say something. But now the young druggie girl reappeared, her eyes red-rimmed and vomit on her chin. 'I'm sick, George, I feel real sick. Can I have a smoke?' She slumped to the ground and, by the light of the fire, started to sort out some heroin for a smoke, shaking it from a twist of plastic into a strip of tin foil. Her hands shook and her nose dripped. Connelly suddenly staggered to his feet, enraged, grabbing her by the hair.

'You want to know why I took the rap for that murder?' he shouted at Walker. 'It wasn't for McCready's sake. I didn't give a shit about that bastard. I did it so my wee daughters wouldn't end up dripping at the nose by the age of fourteen. All right? Good enough for you?' Contemptuously, he pushed the girl aside, leaving her scrabbling to save some of her smack. He swayed and leant against the wall to steady himself.

His mood switched and he became again a maudlin drunk. 'Yeah, I did some bad things. But the moments I'll die happy with are my wee girls being born, coming home to them. Dada . . . sweetest sound on earth . . .' He leant forward, his hands on his knees, swaying and weeping, drifting back to the past, forgetting Walker entirely. 'Dada, Dada!'

Walker touched his shoulder. 'George, look . . .'

Connelly shrugged him off angrily. 'I did it for my *kids*, right? They held my wee girl over the railings, they'd have let her drop. But I got them out, far away from here. You wanna fight, you bastard? McCready can send who he likes. Come on, yer bastard!'

Walker stared at Connelly shambling belligerently towards him once again. He made no more than two yards before he fell face down at Walker's feet. Walker crouched and turned him over but he was out cold. Walker rose and made for the open air. As he climbed through the window, he realised the young addict had followed him. She was holding out her hand. 'You wanna have some fun? Hey, mister. Give us a tenner.' Walker's lip curled in disgust and horror. He turned and strode as fast as he could away across the waste ground. Her voice came after him, pleading and then accusing. 'Give us a fiver! Oi! Sod off, then, you shite!'

Violet's spare room was little different from a bedroom in a cheap but well-kept bed-and-breakfast place. Candlewick bedspreads, a wardrobe, a bedside table and a small dressing table, and not one personal item. This was at least consistent with the rest of the flat.

North sat up in bed watching Walker as he paced around in front of her, with a piece of cotton wool staunching the blood from his nostril. 'This is how I see what happened in the Brown Tavern, OK? They were both drugged up, right? Connelly and

McCready. But it was McCready who had the knife. I know because he slashed me and even though I didn't see it happen, I know it was McCready that stabbed Hood and then persuaded Connelly to say he'd done it.'

'But why would Connelly agree to that?'

Walker shook his head. 'God knows. Connelly was just nineteen and already had two kids. He married Sheila at sixteen because she was pregnant and no sooner was one born than she had another. By that time she was as drugged up as George . . .' He shrugged. 'Anyway, George got a life sentence and McCready walked free, simple as that.'

'It's hard to believe, Mike. Are you sure?'

'He said they'd threatened his kids, held one over some railings or something. I would guess he was up to his eyes in debt to half the drug barons in Glasgow, as well as to McCready.'

'Under those circumstances I guess prison doesn't seem like such a bad option.'

'What?' snapped Walker. 'A life sentence? Your wife and kids in Florida? Not exactly easy for prison visits.'

'So you think McCready paid off Connelly's debts, that's why he went along with it?'

'Probably.'

She shook her head. 'I don't believe it, I'm sorry. How long has Connelly been out of prison?'

'For the murder? Well, he served twelve years before being released on licence, but he's been back in and out of rehabs and various institutions for drugs ever since. He might be an addict, Pat, but he's not a killer.'

'What if you're wrong?'

Walker shook his head. 'I'm not. He thought McCready had sent me! Bloody attacked me, he was so paranoid.'

'Mike, McCready's in prison.'

Walker stopped pacing for a moment, arrested in motion. He frowned. 'But his *punks* aren't . . . Shit, no wonder Connelly was so paranoid.' He thought for a moment and seemed to make up his mind. He patted his pockets, then went to his bag for a fresh packet of cigarettes. 'Pat, I'm going back.' He found the smokes and she looked on helplessly as he headed for the door.

As soon as Walker's taxi pulled up, he feared he was too late. The block was surrounded by patrol cars, their lights flashing garishly in the rain. Two fire engines were also in attendance, with yellow-helmeted firemen busy recoiling their hoses. Uniformed officers went about their business and from the number of them Walker knew it was a serious incident. Nearby an ambulance, with lights flashing, stood with its back doors open.

A uniformed sergeant was talking into his radio while a group of pale, thin people, like a bunch of refugees from some war, were being ushered past him away from the scene. Many carried filthy bedding, almost all had beer cans. When the sergeant lowered his handset, Walker approached him, showing his ID. 'What happened?' he asked.

'There's been a fire at the back of the building. It's under control now. You should stay back, sir.'

'Do you know how it started?'

'One of the kids said something about petrol being poured over someone. Drug-related, I imagine.'

CHAPTER 20

THURSDAY, 29 JUNE

North stood at the door of the standing train, clutching a newspaper and a bottle of water. Walker, down on the platform, passed the overnight bag up to her. 'I'll be straight back after the funeral,' he said.

'You don't mind me leaving, do you?' she asked. 'I just can't take much more of your mother.'

'No, no, it's all right. She just takes a bit of getting used to, that's all.'

Someone blew a whistle way down the platform and Walker slammed the carriage door. North opened the window and leant out to kiss Walker. As their lips touched, his mobile rang. Walker jumped back in surprise. He answered the phone, just as the train started to trundle out of the platform. North, wanting to wave, had no one to wave at as Walker's attention was taken by his conversation.

'Hello?'

'Mike?'

'Yes, this is him.'

'It's Liz, Liz Hood.'

Walker's face lit up.

'Oh hi, Liz. Thanks for getting back to me.'

'I wasn't surprised to get your message. I saw *Miscarriage of Justice*. What was a miscarriage of justice was the way they cut

The sergeant's radio squawked again and Walker took the chance to give him the slip, walking on towards the smoking building. He entered by the main door, whose corrugated iron had been ripped away by police.

Inside, the fire damage was minimal but the place had been drenched in the fire brigade's hoses. Police officers with high-power torches stood around the pitiful, charred corpse of a man. It was hardly recognisable as human except for one blackened, outstretched arm, beside which lay the partly burnt remains of a guitar.

Walker stood for a moment, meditating on George Connelly's horrible death. In one way George had finally achieved what he'd been aiming at. Inside himself, he'd been dead for months, even years. But then Walker remembered the skittish young kid from his own estate, who he'd played football with and messed about in the park with, and he was sorry.

He heard a high-pitched voice behind him and turned. The little teenage druggie, still stoned and her legs wobbling, was being interviewed by two more uniforms. 'One of 'em pointed at him and said, "Is that George Connelly?" I nodded and then they started pouring petrol over him. I was in ma sleeping bag. I yelled at them but they threw a match on him.' The kid was crying now. 'He never did nothing to stop them. He was lying there, all his clothes on fire and . . . and . . . I ran over, shouting for help, but they just walked away, laughing.'

'Did he know them?' asked Walker, coming at them out of the darkness. They turned towards him, surprised. He showed his warrant card again.

my interview to shreds. I agreed to go on the show to talk about Colin and they made it look like I was supporting McCready!'

'I knew it! I knew it must have been something like that.'

'I was so angry about it that I decided to do a bit of digging of my own. I think you might be interested in what I found out.'

'Look, I'm at the station, seeing someone off. It's noisy. Why don't we meet somewhere?'

'OK,' said Liz. 'George Square, in fifteen minutes?'

'I'm on my way.' He snapped the phone shut and looked down the track. But the rear end of the train had already disappeared in the direction of London.

Walker and Liz had kept in desultory touch over the years – a few Christmas cards, a chance meeting or two when Walker had visited his family. But strolling with her now around George Square, the largest patch of green in the centre of Glasgow, he realised how little he knew about her life over the last twenty years. She gave him a concise autobiography: St Andrew's University and then qualification and practice as a solicitor. She specialised in family law. Walker decided not to bring up his impending divorce. He mentioned his ex-wife, the kids, his work. He didn't talk about North.

They moved on to the business in hand. Walker told her about McCready's chances of a successful appeal – not promising, unless the appellant's team could hang Walker out to dry first. 'They're aiming to prove I had it in for McCready and deliberately concealed evidence.'

'Because of what happened with Colin?'

He nodded. 'Right.'

'Watching that documentary brought it all back.'

'Connelly didn't kill your brother, I'm sure of it.'

'I know. A friend of mine works in the same firm of solicitors as a guy called Ben Duffield. Recognise the name?'

'That piece of scum who represents McCready.'

'The very same. Well, you know that, back in the 70s and 80s, it was a well-known fact that Duffield was bent. Took back-handers left, right and centre. All the druggies used him.'

'Yeah, if there was a bust, Duffield was there before the cops!'

'Exactly! Well, supposedly he's cleaned up his act. Very respectable now, no whisper of his past. But when I found out he was executor of Gary Meadows' estate as *well* as representing McCready . . .'

Walker stopped and patted the air. 'Whoa, wait, you're going too fast. What estate are you talking about?'

'It's one hell of a conflict of interest, Mike. Duffield is handling Fiona Meadows' inheritance *and* representing the man convicted of killing her father!'

'Is that legal?'

'Afraid so. I got so angry that he was up for appeal that I got my friend to do some digging. Now this is totally off the record, Mike, because she could lose her job over this.'

'What have you got?'

'Apparently Gary Meadows was completely broke when he died, hardly left a thing to Fiona. But, a year ago, Gary's sister died very suddenly of a brain tumour. She had a life insurance policy for £150,000, plus about £50,000 in cash.'

'Who gets it?'

'That's the tricky bit. She hadn't changed her will since Gary's death. She left everything to her brother and his heirs – Fiona, that is – with the money to go into a trust fund for her if she died before Fiona was twenty-one.'

'And dirty Duffield is handling the trust fund!'

Liz Hood suddenly pulled a file from her shoulder bag and opened it, showing him a set of photocopied papers. 'You got it! Two hundred grand's a lot of money. I'd like to know if it's all still there.'

She proffered the file and Walker took it, flicking through the sheaf of pages. Even on casual inspection it looked useful stuff – more than useful. 'Thanks, sweetheart, I really appreciate it.'

He gave her a hug and in return she presented a business card. 'If there's anything else, just give me a call. Got to get back to work now.'

'OK, cheers, Liz.'

She left him and Walker found a vacant park bench, where he sat leafing carefully through the file. It was very good stuff. First there were several letters and forms signed by Ben Duffield, and other paperwork connected with the trust fund. Next he found a list of investments and assets at the bank, with a valuation at the time the trust was framed. He brooded on all this, then circled several numbers in one of the letters in Liz's file: two bank account numbers and a bank sort code. He grinned happily. This was priceless information if you knew what to do with it. He flipped open his mobile phone and punched a number. 'Satch, it's me. Can you talk?'

From the acoustic, it sounded as if Satchell was in the open air. 'Yeah, I'm just on my way to work. Are you back?'

'No, I've got to stay for a funeral. George Connelly's been murdered.'

'What?'

'I don't want to go into that now. But I need you to do me a big favour.'

'Ye-es?' Satchell was cautious, as you had to be with Walker. His tiny favours were often enormous: what would this 'big' one be?

'Look,' Walker went on. 'You know I wouldn't ask if I wasn't desperate, but I need to get information about transactions from a certain bank account.'

'And how the hell am I supposed to do that?'

'Well, I thought you might be able to get that woman who's after your body to help. Mad Mel, isn't it? I thought you said she could hack into MI5?'

'That was a joke, Mike.'

'So you're saying she wouldn't be able to hack into a simple bank account?'

'No, I'm saying I'm not sure I'm prepared to risk my manhood finding out!'

'Yes you are. You got a notebook with you? Then write down these numbers.'

CHAPTER 21

SUNDAY, 2 JULY, EVENING

SATCHELL STOOD on Melanie Crass's doorstep with a bottle of wine and a bunch of flowers. He braced himself, took a deep breath and rang the doorbell. Years ago a bright young history teacher had made Satchell's class learn the words: *Greater love hath no man than he who lays down his life for his friend*. He remembered those words now, with feeling. Melanie was simply not his type – too clever, too well educated, too all over him.

The door was opened almost immediately by the woman herself. Satchell opened his arms, flowers in one hand, wine in the other, and looked delighted to see her. 'Melanie!' He gulped. 'You look fantastic!'

He wasn't lying: fantastic was one way of describing it. He had only seen Melanie in dowdy, conventional business wear but tonight she was transformed, wearing vivid makeup and a tight, bright pink PVC trouser suit that was almost a catsuit. Her smile was half kitten, half predator.

'Not quite the formal me you're used to, hey? Come on in!'

He stepped through the front door like a condemned man approaching the gallows. 'Here, these are for you,' he said gallantly, thrusting the flowers and wine forward. She squealed with delight.

'Oh, David, you *shouldn't* have.'

North and Watkins, having met to indulge their mutual taste for corny romantic films, were leaving the cinema. North still had a half-empty popcorn carton as they passed through the foyer and into the street. 'It's so easy for the women in films like that. Even if they do have jobs, their careers get conveniently airbrushed out just before it's happy ever after. Hard-pressed woman police officer has triplets before going on to become police commissioner! It couldn't happen, no way!'

She and Watkins both laughed. 'I seem to remember Detective Lacey getting pregnant a lot.'

North shook her head. 'Somehow I have always seen myself as more of a Cagney.'

Watkins took a pinch of popcorn as they walked out into Leicester Square. 'If you want to go back to work you'll have to find a nanny. You can't do it all, Pat.'

'I know, I know. God, there's so much to think about. I don't feel like I'll ever be ready for this baby. I mean, the list is endless.'

'If you go back to work after what, three or six months, you'll be knackered and you'll probably feel guilty. You've got to be organised, maximise your time with the baby.'

'Well, Mike'll help.'

'Trust me, you think he will, but the responsibility will all come down on your shoulders. It'll be you that has to think ahead, Pat. Are you going to find out what it'll be? Boy or girl?'

'I don't know.' She giggled foolishly, girlishly. 'I don't know what I'm doing.' She looked at the popcorn. 'All this eating's not helping either. I must be out of my mind.' She stuffed the carton into a nearby bin, scattering bits of popcorn around their feet.

'No you're not,' said Watkins. 'But it'll be a change in your life all the same, and one that I envy.'

North put her hand on her stomach. 'I know. I still can't believe it.' She smiled, slipping her arm through Watkins' as they walked away to find the car.

Satchell perched nervously on a sofa in Melanie's sitting room. All around him was evidence of the woman's mysterious craft: circuit boards, computer terminals, modems, hard drives, printers. Their owner-operator was searching for a corkscrew.

'If you want to stay one step ahead of the game, so to speak, you've got to get your head round this new software.'

'Yeah, well, like I said on the phone, I've been having real trouble working through some of the coursework.'

Melanie unearthed a corkscrew and passed it, with the bottle, to Satchell. She came and sat closely beside him. 'So you want private tuition, do you? Or do you have an *ulterior* motive for coming here?'

Satchell was methodically sinking the screw into the cork, his heart sinking with it. 'Kind of . . .'

Melanie was up again, fetching a pair of none-too-shining wine glasses. She placed these on the low table in front of them expectantly, while Satchell went on uncorking the wine with tortuous deliberation.

'I've got a girlfriend and, er, we live together so it's not . . . It's something more . . .'

Melanie moved her butt a fraction closer to his on the sofa. From her face Satchell could see she was hugely enjoying herself. She gently pressed her crimson fingernail into his leg just above the knee, drawing a sinuous figure of eight there. 'Dave, I've got a cat. But *I* don't brag about my pussy. What is it you want?'

The direct approach tripped Satchell into immediate disclosure. 'Erm, I need you to hack into a bank account for me, as a matter of fact.'

Melanie shrank back in mock horror. 'A bank account? Well, David, you know that's illegal and, for an inferior Merlot and a bunch of flowers from the corner shop, I'm not sure I'd be prepared to risk it.'

Miserably, Satchell popped the cork of his inferior Merlot. 'There's no risk,' he said. 'We're not going to be breaking into the Bank of England. It's only to check up on something personal.' He poured her a glass and met her gaze, opening his eyes sincerely wide. 'I'd really appreciate it, Melanie.'

Melanie laughed wickedly. She crossed to her PC, woke it up and turned back to Satchell, who had got up and was brushing the copious moulted fur of Melanie's cat off his suit. She beckoned him imperiously and he picked up both wine glasses before joining her. She drew up two chairs, lovingly patting the seat of one meant for him. Then she put on a pair of thick-rimmed glasses. 'Sit your tight little arse down next to mine, Detective Sergeant Satchell. Breaking into someone's bank account is a risk, personal or not. Of course I've spent years networking my contacts, so let me explain the intricate art of hacking to you.'

Which she proceeded to do. And, soon, he was astonished at the ease with which an expert could access bank accounts. The speed of change in personal banking, away from high-cost high-street branches and towards cheap, personnel-efficient cyber-banking, had far outstripped the development of secure encryption systems. Nowadays all customers were encouraged to access their accounts through phone or computer links so that, from a security point of view, the banks' central computers had become, in effect, honeycombs, with as many access points as they had customers. Hackers who got in through one of these entry points could then use increasingly sophisticated encryption-cracking programs to roam around the bank's main computer, peering into any account that took their fancy. It was beginning to make keeping your cash under the mattress look like Fort Knox.

Satchell handed Melanie the numbers which Walker had dictated to him. She nodded her head, noting the sort code, and turned to her keyboard. For about twenty minutes she loaded programs and sent data to various cyberlocations. She picked up a couple of replies. Then she opened a new application, entered some more figures, and pressed return.

'It may take an hour or two to churn through a few billion encrypted combinations,' she said. 'Plenty of time for us to get to know each other a little better, wouldn't you say so, David?'

Satchell's mouth was dry with fear as he nodded dumbly.

CHAPTER 22

MONDAY, 3 JULY, MORNING

FUNERALS HAD never featured high in Walker's list of favourite entertainments and, as today was also the start of McCready's appeal hearing, he was having trouble concentrating on the cremation of George Connelly. His mind was principally on Satchell. Many hopes were pinned on his friend's success with the famous, fearsome Melanie Crass. He'd phoned Satchell first thing on Saturday, to be told Ms Crass was away teaching a weekend course in Ireland and Sunday was the earliest he could see her. Walker had spent an impatient weekend but he knew by now Satch would have results for him – if he was going to get any results at all.

As the curtains whirred together and Connelly's mortal remains were conveyed into the fire, Walker was first out of the building. He was already punching Satchell's number into his mobile as he cleared the porch of the crematorium chapel and stood in the hot sunlight. He dragged a pair of sunglasses from his breast pocket and put them on. 'Come on, come on,' he muttered in time with the ringing tone. As he waited, a thin thread of mourners began filing out of the building and gathering outside. It had not been much of a turnout.

Satchell's answering voice sounded thick and bleary. 'Man, you owe me big time! I was with Mad Mel until two this morning. She never drew breath then almost raped me! I couldn't get away.'

Walker cut his complaints short. 'Yeah, yeah. Did you get anything?'

Satchell yawned. 'You bet I did! Suit full of cat hairs and—'

'Satch!'

'OK, OK, you ready for this? Duffield has power of attorney over both McCready's money and Fiona's inheritance, right?'

'Right.'

'So, Mel hacked into Fiona's trust account and we discovered that there has recently been one very interesting and quite substantial pay-out . . .' His voice faded out momentarily into fuzz.

'What?' yelped Walker. 'What you got? Go on.'

'Hold onto your hat. Fifteen grand to a Vera Collingwood!'

'I knew it! The bastard's bribing her to change her statement.'

'Listen, Mike, you've got to tread very carefully on this one. If you want to use this information, you'll have to get a Section 8 under PACE otherwise it won't be admissible evidence in court.'

Walker was nodding. He knew all this. 'Right, right. Anything else?'

'Yep. We also hacked into McCready's account and traced it back to when computer records began. Right up until McCready was sent down, there was a big regular payment going out to an account in Florida.'

'Florida? You get a name?'

'Yes. Sheila Connelly. You know her?'

Walker looked around at the other mourners. One stood out and apart. She wore what even to Walker's untutored eye looked like a designer coat. She was still blonde and sexy at forty. He said hurriedly to Satchell, 'I think I'm looking at her. Thanks, Satch, I'll call you later.' He snapped shut his phone and hurried towards Jock Connelly.

'The blonde woman – is it who I think it is, Jock?'

'Ay, it's Sheila herself. Never thought she'd show up. Must have been her wreath weighing the poor bastard down. What a waste. If she'd come over earlier, maybe she could've helped him.'

Walker followed Sheila Connelly with his eyes. She was hurrying towards a waiting taxi, as if particularly anxious not to have to socialise. Suddenly Walker took off after her.

'Sheila, SHEILA!' he called. 'It's Mike. You remember me? Mike Walker.'

Sheila stopped and turned to look at him, still ten yards away.

'I spoke to George just before he died,' he said.

She appraised him for a moment with distaste, as if he were a particularly slimy form of pond life, then spun around and walked on. Walker caught her up, reaching to grab her arm. She shrugged him away.

'What do you think you're doing?' she said.

'It's what you've been doing that interests me, Sheila. Nice coat, but then you've been living a cushy life for years, haven't you?'

Sheila managed to look genuinely affronted. 'I don't see that's any business of yours.'

'Don't you? Poor George was always crazy about you. He spent twelve years behind bars for you.'

Moving away again, almost shouting back over her shoulder, Sheila was angry. 'Nobody forced him to do anything. He did it for drugs.'

The waiting taximan started his engine. Sheila went to open the door of the taxi but Walker got there first. 'You left him to rot when he got out of prison, why come back now?'

'I wanted to say goodbye to my husband.'

'You certainly got here fast. Who told you he was dead?'

'Jock called me.'

'I don't believe you.' There was a momentary stand-off. Then Walker played his ace. 'I've got details of the money paid to you by James McCready. You've been bleeding him dry for years.'

'I don't know what you're talking about.'

'Don't you? Come on, Sheila, why did McCready keep paying you, even after George was released?' Sheila reached around Walker and grasped the car's door handle. He had to move as she yanked it open. 'What did you have on McCready, Sheila?' Sheila gave him no reply. She simply dived into the taxi and pulled the door to. He did not hear her instructions to the driver.

In frustration, Walker watched the cab pull away. He looked around, spotted a battered black Mercedes waiting to take mourners to the wake and sprinted across, showing his warrant card. The driver looked like a man whom nothing could surprise. 'I need you to follow that taxi,' barked Walker, pointing at Sheila's cab, which had stopped on a red light.

The driver shrugged. 'Well, depends how far, pal. I've got a wedding at two.' It was only eleven. Disdaining to reply, Walker dived into the car ahead of a small group of mourners whose car it was. They were left wondering how they would ever get to the salmon-paste sandwiches.

Drumchapel, the neighbourhood they were driving through, was known to Walker only too well. They passed the crumbling bricks and slipped slates of the primary school he'd attended, one class ahead of George Connelly. He had a sudden memory of the pungency of the morning milk, and the hollow putter of the children's straws as they sucked up the last drops from their half-pint bottles. Next, he saw the small corner bakery, to which his ma had sent him for a loaf of bread every day before school. At some point since, as evidenced by a crudely hand-painted shop sign, the old bakery had sold bric-a-brac. But it was now padlocked and shut up with damp-stained chipboard. The residents had been drifting away for years. Those that stayed shopped for bread at the local superstore and didn't require bric-a-brac. As they left this landmark behind, Walker caught a glimpse of the place where he used to sneak a smoke at the age of eleven, a narrow alleyway behind a brick electrical substation. Curiously, this was one of the best-preserved buildings in view.

He looked ahead for Sheila's taxi. It was parked and she was heading on foot across a patch of rough ground, where an entire block of buildings had been demolished. Walker told the driver of his battered limo to pull up beside the waiting taxi. He leapt out to speak to the taxi driver and was directed to the concrete tower block on the far side of the waste ground. Walker started to run across it, after Sheila.

The tower block had been uninhabited for some years. On the front door notices had been pasted by the City Council, warnings against vandalism and unauthorised entry. But the door had been smashed in anyway. Walker shoved through and listened for sounds at the staircase. He could hear Sheila's high-heeled shoes clicking up the steps. He set off upwards behind her.

Walker found Sheila where he knew he would, in the wrecked front room of a ruined flat on the third floor: once this had been the Connellys' address. Floorboards were caved in, walls had shed huge slabs of plaster, every window was smashed. She was standing at one of the broken windows, staring out. She jumped when she heard Walker's tread.

'Come back for something, Sheila?'

Sheila spun around and stared resentfully at Walker. Then suddenly she laughed ruefully. She should have known. Even in the old days you didn't walk away from Mike Walker. She relaxed slightly and turned back to the sorry urban view. 'You forget how bad it was. My kids are at college now, even got American accents. Come a long way from here.'

'And you've come a long way to come back.'

She was playing with an unlit cigarette, as if unsure whether to light up or leave immediately. Instead of doing either she allowed a long silence to hang between them. 'Everyone always underestimated George,' she remarked at last. 'But he would have done anything for our kids, he loved them so much. I really believed George would come out to Florida to be with us when he got out.'

'What stopped him?'

Sheila shrugged, as she must have done over George many times before. 'He was on drugs in prison. I got myself clean, but he never did, even when he was released.'

'What did you have to make McCready pay you cash for years?'

Sheila stared stubbornly ahead.

'Sheila, were you blackmailing him?'

She turned and faced him now, fiercely defending herself. 'What business is it of yours? McCready was scum, still is. The bastard even threatened – actually threatened to *kill* – my little girls.'

Walker met her look with one of equal intensity. 'George was murdered, Sheila.'

She nodded. She was not surprised. 'I didn't come back just for the funeral. Jock told me about the appeal. If that bastard gets out, he'll come after me too.'

'Why?' Walker lifted his arms from his sides. 'What are you doing here, Sheila?'

She sighed and then crossed to the fireplace. 'I'll show you.'

She picked her way towards the fireplace. The gas fire which had once stood there had been removed, the copper pipes were twisted and the glazed tiles of the hearth were broken. The fireplace itself was filled with rubble. Sheila knelt in front of it and reached up into the flue. 'Might not still be here, you know. After all, it's been years.'

She pulled a face as she felt around in the cavity, soot and dust cascading down on her arm. She removed her arm and picked up a piece of broken floorboard, which she inserted into the hole and riddled around. More grime and dust descended in a shower around her. Suddenly there was a more serious avalanche of rubble, among which tumbled onto the floor a slim object in a filthy plastic supermarket bag tightly wrapped in masking tape.

Walker stooped and picked it up. 'What is it, Sheila?'

She said nothing, just watched complacently as Walker tore away the tape and revealed a switchblade knife. Sheila nodded at it. 'That's the knife McCready used on that young copper.'

Careful not to touch the handle with his fingers, Walker activated the sprung blade. He turned it in the light and saw the brown smears, definitely not of rust, still evident on it. This was Colin Hood's blood – and his too, perhaps. He pointed to his right eyebrow.

'And on me too!' he exclaimed angrily. Walker pocketed the knife. 'I'll have to get this to Strathclyde Police, Sheila. They'll have to re-open the case and it'll help focus their minds on finding George's killers too.'

She was brushing the dust from her hands. 'Good – that's what I want now. For George's memory, so he can rest in peace.'

Before they left, he took a last look around the flat. It had been the Connellys' place, but Violet had brought him up in one that was hardly different. It had been spanking new, still smelling of paint and plaster when he'd moved in as a six-year-old. Now the whole block was history and soon they'd detonate explosives and reduce it to a heap of dust and rubble. He touched the mouldy 1960s wallpaper, the plastic-veneered fitted cupboards, the tiled fireplace in which the knife had been concealed. Then he followed Sheila Connelly down the stairs.

CHAPTER 23

MONDAY, 3 JULY

A LITTLE EARLIER that same morning, at the Royal Courts of Justice on The Strand where all criminal appeals are heard, Rylands had gone down to see his client in the holding cells. The barrister was dressed for court with his usual elegance – blue shirt, white collar and bands, black silk waistcoat, the whole effect completed by a gold-chained fob watch.

The contrast with his surroundings, as he passed down the corridor, was striking. These basement cells were spartan in an old-fashioned, drably painted way, with fluorescent light and a minimum of furniture. McCready sat idly on a bench, listening to the sounds coming from the other cells – prisoners shouting, arguing or singing.

'Good morning, James,' said Rylands, breezing in. 'How are we feeling?'

'Nervous.' This didn't look quite true. McCready seemed utterly composed, more so even than Rylands.

'Quite, quite,' said Rylands. 'Well, I thought I'd come and tell you what's on the menu for today. At least we've got a goodish court.'

McCready looked momentarily concerned. 'I don't like the sound of the "ish" bit.'

'Well, we've avoided the obvious ogres, at least. We've got Lord Justice Bradpiece, sitting in the middle. Very courteous, very unstuffy, a top civil barrister in his time – he'll give us a fair hearing.

'Mr Justice Winfield on the right wing. He's a little trickier – if he doesn't like your case, he'll let you know fairly quickly. He was a good solid criminal man at the Bar and has seen it all before. At least he knows that criminal trials can and do occasionally go wrong.'

'So what's tricky about him?'

'Well, he tends to growl at counsel a bit, but that's my worry, not yours. On the left is Mrs Justice Piggott – Caroline to her friends. She's fairly new to the Court of Appeal but she's generally regarded as pretty clever.'

'How do I address them?'

'You don't. You say absolutely nothing. Just sit there and keep your head down. This is not like a trial, you know. We've only got leave to call our fresh evidence and witnesses Fiona and Vera Collingwood. Apart from that, they'll have read all the papers before they come in and have sorted out which bits they're interested in.'

'What? You mean, they'll have made their minds up before the off? That doesn't sound too encouraging.'

Rylands waved a hand in the air. 'No, not at all. Having read the skeleton arguments on both sides, they won't need to go through the details of every point in open court.'

'What's the prosecution barrister like?'

'Pembroke? Oh, you needn't worry about him. Quite a florid style and a deadly cross-examiner, but he'll have to be careful with a fifteen-year-old witness like Fiona. The court won't be overimpressed if he starts bullying her.'

'She can look after herself, Fiona can. You'll see,' insisted McCready.

'Good. Well, I must be getting up to court, make sure the witnesses have pitched up. They should have, it's twenty past.'

'I'm sure they'll be there.'

'Good, good. Well, fingers crossed, eh?'

McCready turned towards his barrister, his face radiating sincerity. 'I don't need to. I have every faith in you.'

They exchanged smiles and Rylands left. For a moment he paused outside the holding cell, as if some thought had occurred to him. Then, shaking himself out of it, he moved off at a fast pace towards the lifts.

Three judges entered the court and took their seats. At the centre was Lord Justice Henry Bradpiece flanked by two high-court judges: Mr Justice Geoffrey Winfield and Mrs Justice Caroline Piggott. Beside each judge rested a large filing box containing thick evidence files, each of them numbered. The same boxes, with the same files, were on both the defence and prosecution benches.

McCready entered the court, flanked by two security guards. From the dock he could see at one glance all the personnel who would be concerned in his appeal and, at first, it seemed a disappointing turnout. He remembered his trial, when the jury and the swollen public and press galleries had made the numbers a good deal more impressive. Here he had no jury. His fate was effectively decided by the three bewigged individuals on the bench.

In Rylands' team were his junior, James Bunn, and McCready's own solicitor, Ben Duffield, fidgeting with files and sheaves of paper and directing anxious smiles towards McCready from time to time. Willard Pembroke, leading for the prosecution, was a top-flight silk. He was known for his plummy, humorous manner. Beside him sat Ashley Freeman, his junior counsel, and the solicitor from the Crown Prosecution Service was behind. Roger Barker sat in the public benches, as did Mr and Mrs Plover. Satchell had taken the seat on the end of a row of detectives. Zita Sallinger was also there, reading a thick file while she waited for the talking to begin. The press bench was well stocked with journalists.

The Clerk rose to his feet to start the proceedings. He cleared his throat and announced, 'The Queen against James McCready.'

Pembroke leant back confidently on his bench. Freeman lounged beside him. Both looked as if they were enjoying themselves. Pembroke murmured behind his hand, 'Altogether too many queens in this case. Going to get very confusing.'

Freeman shook his head. 'Now, now!'

The Clerk turned to McCready. 'Are you James McCready?'

'I am.'

'Please be seated.'

McCready sat, staring straight ahead. On the bench, Bradpiece settled himself and then looked over his half-moon glasses to Rylands. 'Yes, Mr Rylands?'

Pembroke nudged Freeman. 'Here's another one!'

Rylands rose to his feet and paused to add that element of drama. There was a bang and a journalist arrived late. 'My Lords, My Lady, I appear for this appellant, together with my friend

Mr Bunn. The Crown are represented by my learned friends Mr Pembroke and Mr Freeman. This case comes before the Court, the single judge having granted leave to appeal in February of this year. The appellant was convicted of murder at the Central Criminal Court as long ago as September 26th 1992. The single judge granted an extension of time of some eight years.'

The latecoming reporter opened his notebook, whispering a question to his neighbour. Duffield scribbled a note for Rylands. In the public section, Plover patted his wife's hand.

Bradpiece squared his shoulders and spoke up in sonorous tones. 'Mr Rylands, you may take it that we have read the transcripts and your grounds and the skeleton submissions and are familiar with most, if not all, of the papers in this case. It comes to this, does it not? The appellant was convicted of the murder of his partner, Gary Meadows, who died from a single stab wound to his back, penetrating up into the heart. No one else other than the appellant was in any way involved in the incident which led up to that injury being sustained. You now, with the leave of the single judge, seek to call fresh evidence, principally from the deceased's daughter Fiona, who was present in the caravan at the time, and also from a neighbour, Vera Collingwood. The evidence is said to support the defence given at trial but rejected by the jury, that the injury was, or may have been, the result of an accident, pure and simple. That the deceased's injury was, in short, self-inflicted.'

Rylands bowed. 'My Lord, as ever, puts it in a much more succinct way than I could possibly have hoped to.'

'That,' Pembroke murmured again to Freeman, 'is why he sits up there and you, Rylands, are down here among us lesser mortals. I *do* hope we're not going to have to listen to his endless brown-nosing before we get down to the evidence.'

From the bench, it was now Winfield's turn to speak. 'You further complain that evidence relating to a brandy glass was not disclosed at trial, and that its disclosure would have been of material assistance to the defence. Is that the way you put your case, in a nutshell?'

'My Lord, precisely.' Rylands subsided into his seat, a little red-faced. On the bench, Bradpiece conferred briefly with Piggott and Winfield.

'Winfield's a great one for nutshells,' remarked Pembroke. 'I expect he was a squirrel in a previous incarnation.'

'He's certainly bright-eyed and bushy-tailed this morning,' said Freeman.

Mrs Justice Caroline Piggott now turned to Pembroke. 'Mr Pembroke!'

Pembroke got up, slightly startled. 'My Lady?'

'Could you help us? What is the Crown's position in relation to the brandy glass? You concede, do you, that it was clearly disclosable?'

Pembroke nodded his head gravely. 'We do, of course. But we go on to say that it could not have contributed in any significant way to the defence case, nor in any sense could it have weakened the Crown's case. Our position is therefore: "disclosable but immaterial". The glass should clearly have been disclosed at trial in whatever state it was in, broken or intact.'

'Yes, thank you. At this stage we simply want to know whether we may consider it as a piece of evidence. What weight it has will be a different matter.'

'My Lady, yes.'

He sat and Piggott turned to Rylands. 'Mr Rylands, are you content with that?'

Rylands rose. 'Well, the appellant would contend that its non-production was as a result of bad faith on the part of the officer in charge of the investigation.'

'For my part, I would say you will have an uphill task to establish that any officer in this case has deliberately withheld this piece of evidence knowing that it might affect the outcome of the case. That is really what you contend, is it?' The judges, in particular Winfield, appeared to have formed a more favourable opinion of Pembroke than of Rylands.

'Well, we say that is a possibility,' said Rylands. 'It clearly was withheld and clearly should not have been.'

'Shall we proceed for the moment on that basis?' determined Bradpiece, 'and leave to one side any issue of bad faith, which we can return to later if it becomes necessary?'

Rylands bowed. 'Of course.' He picked up a sheet of paper, took a sip of water from the glass in front of him, and continued. 'The glass could well have confirmed the defendant's account, given in interview; that Meadows' injury was received entirely by accident. Having made up, McCready told officers that he and his partner surveyed their respective wounds and went to bed, where they shared a glass of brandy. Had that glass been examined for saliva and for blood, and had it shown that both had drunk from it at a time after there was blood on both men, the jury may well have been reluctant to conclude that one had stabbed the other to death.'

McCready looked at the judges. They were listening carefully, pens poised over their notepads. Would they have the same reluctance after hearing Rylands' arguments?

'A drink shared after the accident would be quite inconsistent with the Crown's case, of one man stabbing another to death.'

'Mr Rylands,' broke in Winfield, 'are you really on solid ground here? Supposing the glass had been produced at trial, and it did indeed have fingerprints, lip marks, saliva, blood or whatever from both parties, I imagine the Crown would say that the appellant, after stabbing his friend, tried to revive him with a medicinal brandy. What is there to prevent such a scenario?'

Pembroke hid a smile behind his hand and whispered again to Freeman. 'The squirrel strikes back! Well spotted, old boy. This looks like it may save a few red faces among the officers.'

'Well, there's nothing to support any such analysis.'

'And you are asking us to reach an opposite view on speculation. I am not overly impressed by the potential of the brandy glass. As I see it, the mainstay of this appeal is limited to the fresh evidence.'

'Yes, My Lord.'

He dropped the paper he was consulting and picked up another, studying it for a few seconds before starting up again. 'As we see it there are three important points in this case. Firstly, the account presented at trial was precisely the account given by the defendant upon his arrest, at a time when he could not have known what investigators would find. Secondly, there is not a single piece of forensic evidence available to contradict his account. So much was conceded by the exhibits officer in a "highly complex scene", as he characterised it.'

The court was listening intently.

'It was replete with what one might describe as clues in the form of drops and smears of blood originating from both parties but principally from the appellant, distributed around the caravan in a sequence which matches the appellant's account.'

At this point Piggott broke in. 'I'm sorry, Mr Rylands, can you tell me which are the relevant photographs of the scene?'

'Certainly.' He turned to Bunn, who handed him a bundle of photographs.

'Seventeen to thirty,' Bunn told him audibly.

The judges opened the ring binders which contained the photographs in the case and flicked through them.

'Seventeen to thirty,' repeated Rylands, waiting for a few moments to allow the judges to find the right numbers. 'Of course, the one thing the photographs can't tell you is the sequence in which the blood came to be deposited round the mobile home. What they do confirm is that the defendant's account of his own movements and, to a lesser extent Meadows' movements, were consistent with the pattern of bloodstaining found by the exhibits officer.'

'And of course your point is,' commented Piggott, 'that when he gave that account he had not seen any photographs and could not possibly know what the evidence at the crime scene would indicate.'

'And, reasonably, the DNA testing was not done until some time later.'

'Precisely. Then there was the highly significant fingerprint on the blade of the knife, depicted as photograph number twenty-nine.'

Winfield snorted as he looked at twenty-nine. 'The appellant's fingerprint on the murder weapon!'

'Well, on the kitchen knife,' said Rylands lightly. 'It was, in fact, his right thumbprint. The print was pointing up the blade, consistent with him taking hold of the knife, being proffered to him by Meadows, in his uninjured hand and then placing it in the sink.' Rylands picked up a ruler from the table and demonstrated the action he described.

'And you can tell all of this from *one* fingerprint, can you?' demanded Winfield.

Rylands remained impassive. 'Dr Foster, the prosecution pathologist, confessed at trial that the act of inserting a knife into a body would effectively clean off any prints which were on the blade. The blade, as we can see from the photograph, does not appear to the naked eye even to have blood on it. It was, in effect, "wiped off" as the blade was withdrawn from the wound.' Again he demonstrated with his ruler, pulling it through his closed fist to show the wiping.

'Have a care not to injure yourself with your ruler, Mr Rylands,' warned Bradpiece, with a judicial smile.

Rylands smiled slightly in answer and nodded at Bradpiece, then turned back to Winfield. 'In answer to My Lord's question, the print on the knife blade undoubtedly got there after the stabbing. As a matter of comment, in the ordinary course, a man would pick up such a knife by its handle if the handle were available. There is an inference that McCready's print got onto the knife when Meadows proffered it to him after injuring himself with it.'

'Was there any scientific evidence from the knife handle?' asked Piggott. 'Prints, for example?'

'No, My Lady, only that the handle was not a receptive surface for fingerprint purposes.'

'So the only identifiable print on the knife was your client's right thumbprint, on the blade.'

'That is correct, My Lady.'

'Do go on, Mr Rylands.'

'We submit that the chances of the appellant giving his account at the very outset, and the Crown being unable to contradict that account in such a complicated crime scene, is highly significant.'

'Yes,' she returned. 'All that appears in the cross-examination of the exhibits officer, which I have noted.'

'Surely that's not right, Mr Rylands?' put in Winfield. 'The Crown's pathologist contradicted that account, did he not, in the transcript of his evidence? File two, page fifty-three, letter B.'

Everyone reached for the appropriate file, except Rylands, who went instead to his notes. 'Yes, but he was himself flatly contradicted by two very eminent experts at transcript page one hundred and six, letters A to D and pages one hundred and eighteen to nineteen respectively.'

'Yes,' Piggott came back. 'I noted those passages as well.' Bradpiece and Winfield evidently had not. They flicked through the files, trying to locate the relevant pages.

'So, in summary, we have firstly the appellant's account given at the very outset. Secondly, the fact that every single piece of forensic evidence found was consistent with that account. And thirdly, the curious circumstance that the Crown was able to produce no timetable of what they say happened within that caravan, no sequence of events.'

'Well,' said Winfield drily. 'I believe that the Crown says the appellant simply stabbed his friend in the back. Do they really need to go further than that?'

'But, My Lord, for all the exhaustive work of forensic scientists, there was no compelling evidence to support what the Crown said happened leading up to what they called the murder.'

Winfield nodded. 'All right. I see your point, Mr Rylands. Continue, please.'

CHAPTER 24

MONDAY, 3 JULY

WALKER DELIVERED the knife to the Strathclyde Police and gave them a rapid résumé of Colin Hood's murder: McCready and the Connellys, the fatal fight, the conviction of Connelly and his discovery of the weapon. When asked for more information about Sheila, Walker explained – quite truthfully – that he had no idea where she was. Knowing she could be charged for withholding evidence, not to mention perverting the course of justice, Sheila had refused to go anywhere near a police station. Walker deliberately did not force the issue. As far as he was concerned, it was unimportant. Only McCready mattered.

Travelling back from Glasgow, he phoned North from the train, knowing she had taken a week's leave and would be at home. She picked up the bedside phone. 'Hi, sweetheart,' he said.

She could hear the syncopation of the train's wheels under his voice. 'Mike, I've been waiting for you to call. You didn't switch your mobile on.'

'I'm on my way home. I need you to get a message to Pembroke.'

'Yes?'

'Could you go to the court, find him and tell him I've got even more evidence against McCready? I've got the knife he murdered Colin Hood with and, you won't believe it, it's been well preserved. My guess is McCready's prints are all over it.'

North thought the note of triumph in his voice was premature. 'Mike, listen to me! You know they won't be able to bring that up in the appeal. It'll have no bearing.'

'Maybe not, but I'll tell you what will . . . Duffield using Fiona Meadows' inheritance to pay off Vera Collingwood!'

This did impress her. '*What*? Do you have proof?'

'Not yet. I'm getting it, though.'

'But that still doesn't explain why Fiona's so keen to come forward now.'

'You interviewed her. What do you think?'

'Well, she did say she'd blocked it all out and it only came back when Duffield approached her.'

'Well, there you go. Duffield's obviously the key.'

'Why would Duffield risk so much to help McCready?'

'They're old pals, and he's probably making some money for his troubles.'

'I don't know, Mike. Fiona seemed pretty convinced it was an accident.'

'Yeah, well, I don't think we should underestimate the power of suggestion.'

'Maybe.'

'Listen, I need you to get over to the court. I'll meet you there. I've . . . missed you.'

'Me, too. OK, I'm on my way!' North smiled. Walker was unstoppable in certain moods. She replaced the phone just as she heard the kettle boiling in the kitchen. She hurried to the stairs but got only halfway down when, out of nowhere, a cramp slashed at her stomach. She doubled over and put a hand on the wall to steady herself, breathing deep. The pain did not stop. If anything it was intensifying. Slowly she tried to continue down the stairs. The agony was great and the stairs steep. Halfway down came another blazing assault of pain, which seemed ten times greater than the other. She swayed, her foot slipped and she fell, pitching forward. Instinctively her hands went to her swollen belly as if to protect it as she tumbled. Her head was unprotected. It struck the stair post with a crack and she lay still.

With every appearance of supreme confidence, Rylands continued his submission to the court. It was difficult to gauge the feelings of those he had to convince. The three judges each thought independently and did not necessarily respond to the same arguments in the same way. 'My Lords, My Lady, there was evidence at trial of the behaviour of McCready and Meadows towards each other that evening. The appellant has never, at any time, denied that he and his partner had been drinking that night. They'd had, in his own words, more than a "skinful". That night they had been out with friends at Butterflies.'

Winfield looked at the Queen's Counsel with bemused interest. From his reading of the documents in the case, it had not appeared quite clear to him what exactly this 'Butterflies' establishment was. Rylands enlightened him while the journalists scribbled furiously. 'It's a club in central Soho, famous for its transvestite cabaret acts. Gary Meadows and James McCready were regular customers and were both well liked. That evening was particularly memorable as McCready had joined in the cabaret.'

McCready remembered the evening well. He had been good that night. His last night of freedom, as he now thought of it. Nothing hanging over him, no one pursuing him. Just lots of booze and the pulsing karaoke. It had been amateur night and most of the acts had been crap, really laughable. But he took his Blondie dead seriously and no one laughed at him except for pleasure. The drag queens, the leather boys and their subs, even the scattering of bemused Japanese tourists standing uncertainly at the back of the crowd greeted him with cheers when he strode out to mime 'Atomic' as Debbie Harry – the silky-straight, almost white wig, the miniskirt, the Lycra stockings covering what he knew to be convincingly shapely legs. The manager had told him afterwards he was virtually professional standard.

'By all accounts,' Rylands told the court, 'Meadows was in high spirits after they left Butterflies. Witnesses from the club that night recalled him saying he was proud of his partner's, the appellant's, impromptu act. They were both eager to enjoy the rest of the evening, but knew they should return home to care for Fiona, Meadows' seven-year-old daughter. They did, however, call into their local pub, the Frog and Ferret, only a few minutes' walk from their home, at around closing time.'

In his mind's eye McCready could see the pub lights shining invitingly. It was a private party – how could they resist? Neither of them really wanted to stop drinking. He was still high after his performance and Gary was stumbling around giggling uncontrollably.

'The bar licence law closes public bars and pubs at eleven. The landlord of the Frog and Ferret did indeed obey the law, but continued to serve drinks to a few regular customers, as his private guests. This is apparently known as a lock-out.'

Winfield smiled and adjusted his half-moon spectacles. 'I think you'll find it's a lock-*in*, Mr Rylands.'

Rylands paused and then nodded as McCready remembered the party. He had played the piano and there had been more singing – not Blondie, but old cockney songs. He and Gary had not stayed long, but long enough for him to sink a few more whiskies and whirl a very drunk Eva Widelski around in an inebriated dance.

'My Lord, I am grateful,' said Rylands. 'A lock-*in*. He, the landlord, recalls that both the appellant and the deceased were still in high spirits. At eleven forty-five the appellant and Mr Meadows left the pub ...' Rylands shuffled his papers and selected a new page. 'Can I move to the next area which causes the Crown difficulties, namely the injuries suffered by the appellant? These were the deep cut to the right upper arm and the cut to the left palm. The Crown at trial were not able to give any sensible explanation of these and indeed were reduced to suggesting that they may have been deliberately self-inflicted by the defendant. The appellant's account of the injuries was that Meadows was in a highly excitable state and, having armed himself with the kitchen knife, started waving it around. The appellant sought to disarm him by going for the knife and in doing so suffered the cut to his left palm, an injury described as a "classic defence" injury.' Again using his ruler, Rylands demonstrated the action for the judges.

'In the ensuing fracas Meadows again caught the appellant on the arm. This all occurred before the stabbing. Had it occurred as the Crown contended – after the stabbing – the knife would presumably have borne traces of the appellant's blood on its blade. The Crown could show no evidence of this—'

Piggott frowned and interrupted. 'Surely your best point, Mr Rylands, is that if your client had indeed inflicted these wounds on himself in order to make it look as if he had come under attack and defended himself, the very first thing he would do would be to say as much. To put it bluntly, he would be shouting self-defence from the rooftops, and that is precisely what he did not do.'

'That is quite right, My Lady. Far from proclaiming that he was acting in self-defence, he told police that he did not believe Meadows had intended to hurt him, and then went on to say that he was stupid to have tried to take hold of the knife. "Not very smart of me," was how he put it in interview.'

Rylands waited while Mrs Justice Piggott wrote some further notes. 'Had he gone to the extreme lengths,' she said, looking up at last, 'of inflicting these injuries on himself to found a false defence, he would hardly have stopped short of telling the police about it at the first opportunity and making it the mainstay of his defence.'

Delighted he had got this central, but slightly elusive, point across, Rylands nodded emphatically. 'Absolutely. And what he did here was to deny throughout that he had the knife in his hand, depriving himself of any issue of self-defence, or indeed provocation, and simply stating that it was an accident and indeed an accident that he himself had not properly seen. Hence his failure to appreciate the depth of the knife wound and the severity of the internal injuries, and the consequent failure to call an ambulance.'

Now it was Bradpiece's turn to be interested. 'So you would say it was not just an accident, but a whole series of accidents.'

Rylands did not respond to this immediately. He was searching for another piece of paper from his voluminous bundle. After a pause Bradpiece looked at the court clock: five past one. 'Seeing the time,' he said, pronouncing the lunch interval in the time-honoured way, 'I think that would be a convenient time.'

The three judges started to rise and Bradpiece said shortly, 'Two fifteen.'

'All rise!' called the court usher and the judges made their exit, Bradpiece and Winfield through a door on the right and Piggott through one on the left. Rylands lingered at his place, still sorting documents. He and McCready exchanged a nod, a cool smile, as the prisoner was led out.

The judges, minus their wigs and gowns, sat at a small table set with glasses of water and paper napkins. An usher brought in a platter of assorted sandwiches. 'Thank you,' said Bradpiece to the usher and then, to his colleagues, 'it's just sandwiches, I'm afraid. If I eat too much it makes me want to sleep. Mind you, with Mr Rylands that's easy on an empty stomach!'

'Yes,' agreed Winfield. 'I think he's practising his oratory skills for the house! He's gaining quite a reputation for being a champion of gay liberation rights. He was excellent on the television documentary, very precise, lots of charm.'

Piggott poured herself a glass of water. 'I saw the documentary when it aired. These programmes should take more responsibility. It's so easy to distort the facts to make sensational viewing.'

Bradpiece was sorting through the tray, trying to determine what sandwich fillings had been provided. 'The appellant wasn't on it, was he?' he murmured.

'Only in old footage,' Winfield told him. 'From before his original trial. Perhaps I'm wrong. I switched channels after a while . . . The Kentucky Derby was on the racing channel if I remember rightly.'

Now Bradpiece was passing around the sandwiches. 'There's beef and tomato, prawn cocktail or ham and lettuce.'

'I'm the cocktail,' claimed Piggott.

'I'm a tuna man myself,' remarked Winfield, as he, too, helped himself and bit deeply into the sandwich.

Bradpiece was still thinking about the television documentary. 'Do you have a copy here?'

'Yes,' said Piggott, chewing vigorously. 'But I'm not sure if it'll make exciting viewing when you've had to sit through the case all day.'

* * *

Watkins walked up the pathway to Walker and North's flat. She studied the intercom and rang the bell of number six. There was no reply. She rang again and, still getting no response, was about to turn away when the door opened. A woman with a shopping trolley came out quickly, letting the door slam behind her.

'Hi,' said Watkins, 'do you know if there's anyone at home, flat six? Pat North? I'm a friend of hers. Only I've been trying to call and . . .'

The woman was brisk. 'Don't know. Call the caretaker, he's flat two. I can't let you in . . . security.'

Watkins produced her warrant card. 'I'm a police officer.'

But the woman was already on her way to the shops. 'Ring for the caretaker!'

After keeping her waiting for what seemed a long time, the caretaker appeared at last. 'Hi, I'm a friend of Pat North in flat six,' said Watkins. 'It's just that she was supposed to be at home this morning and she's six months pregnant. I've been ringing and ringing with no reply.'

'You better come in,' he said gruffly.

Watkins rang hard and long on the flat doorbell, noting that the milk and a newspaper still stood by the door. 'There's something wrong. Could you get some keys?' She showed him her ID and he grunted, moving off to his lair.

As he ambled back, Watkins flipped open the letter box and looked through. She could see North's head, the hair unmistakably that of her friend, resting on the floor near the bottom of the steps.

'Hurry!' she called out. 'I can see her, she's lying on the floor. Quickly, open the door.'

She called through the letter box. 'Pat? PAT!'

But there was no answer from the figure lying at the foot of the stairs.

CHAPTER 25

MONDAY, 3 JULY, AFTERNOON

McCready sat with his tray of food untouched, chewing gum. With the adrenalin filling his stomach he was not hungry, although on the outside he showed his usual insouciance. He heard the peephole flap go up and the cell's door being unlocked. Quickly he spat his gum into a piece of paper. It was Rylands. McCready stood to greet his lawyer, almost shyly. Nothing was said as the guard picked up the tray and stood with it near the door. McCready smiled at Rylands, who, apart from his wig, was still dressed in full court rig.

'How are you?' he asked.

'Fine, thanks.'

Rylands glanced at the uneaten tray of food. 'Good,' he said. 'I'll grab a sandwich and see you in court, then.'

The guard slipped back into the corridor, waiting for the barrister beside the open door. Rylands favoured his client with a confident smile but before he could turn back to the door, McCready had stepped towards him. His voice again had that shy, almost demure quality which stopped Rylands in his tracks for a moment.

'You look really handsome, you know?' said McCready. 'The wigs look daft on everyone else! But you also make me nervous. You have become . . . unapproachable.' He tipped his head to one side, appraisingly. 'Anyway, you're a lot more confident, in court. It's very sexy. The black silk waistcoat, the crisp white shirt, and I like the monogrammed gold cufflinks.'

Rylands flushed, embarrassed, and said with a slight, broken laugh, 'You're very observant.'

McCready was suddenly fervent. 'You hold my life in your hands! It must be a real power trip, to have someone totally dependent on you.'

Rylands just shook his head. McCready was making an absurdly blatant play for him. Was it simply shallow flattery – or something more? 'I believe you are innocent,' the barrister stammered. 'I'm just doing my job to, er, the best of my ability.'

McCready advanced further and stood right in front of Rylands. He suddenly put his hands on the barrister's shoulders and seemed, for a brief moment, to be caressing them. 'I want more than your best. You get me out, prove me innocent, because you know I am.' He rubbed his palms on the finely tailored cloth of Rylands' suit. 'Get angry for me, for eight wasted years. You'll make the front page of every paper. You'll become a hero.'

'Many have campaigned for you, Mr McCready.'

'But none with your high profile.' He smiled coyly and traced the lines of Rylands' shoulders with his palms. 'When you were blackmailed, forced into coming out, you proudly and publicly acknowledged your sexuality. I read about you, I know all about you, that's why I kept on writing to you. I admire you. You are not ashamed to be who you are.'

Rylands pulled away, yet almost reluctantly could not yet detach himself from McCready's words.

'I couldn't defend myself at my own trial. I wasn't able to defend myself on the documentary. I can't even defend myself here in the Appeal Court.'

'I really have to go—' Rylands nodded at the guard through the glass window on the door.

McCready's voice rose, still anxious to detain his barrister. 'I never defended myself over Gary. They gave me drugs because I was so crazy with grief. They made me sick. They could have injected anything into me at the hospital.'

'I *have* to go,' said Rylands. 'Please, we have discussed this, and believe me, I will use everything you did not have to defend you in your trial. It's imperative you just try to stay calm.'

McCready was very emotional now, close to tears. 'All my life I've been ashamed. Don't you understand why I admire you? I have been afraid to defend who and what I am.'

Rylands nodded and finally turned to the security guard outside the door. Before leaving, he looked back to McCready, who sat, head in his hands, at the table. 'Thank you for your honesty,' Rylands said.

McCready looked up, smiled. 'You go.'

Rylands consulted his watch. 'Yes, I really need something to eat before we go back into court. So, see you in there.'

The key turned in the lock behind Rylands. McCready remained still for a moment, then slowly relaxed. Staring ahead reflectively, he unwrapped the gum from its paper, put it in his mouth and, leaning his head back against the wall, again started to chew.

North came round before the ambulance arrived, Watkins cradling her head. The two ambulance staff lifted her efficiently onto a stretcher.

'Pat, I'll get your night things,' Watkins told her breathlessly. 'I'll sort everything out.'

'Call Mike, tell him.' Her voice was tiny and distant.

'Don't worry, he's on his way. You just rest now, don't worry, everything's going to be fine. Shall I stay with you?'

North managed a woozy smile. 'Just get Mike, thanks. Thanks, Viv. I'll be OK.'

She was raised and taken out to the ambulance. Watkins rapidly surveyed the scene. There was a pool of blood on the floor where North had been lying. It didn't look good.

In court, it was time for Rylands to present his witnesses and now Vera Collingwood was on the stand. She spoke clearly enough but occasionally was forced to take deep, rasping asthmatic breaths. Rylands took her through the fatal evening from her point of view. How she had been booked to look in on Fiona, had done so, nothing was amiss. She had then seen the two men returning at just before midnight and had subsequently seen them through the window of the mobile home, apparently drinking and dancing.

'So after you saw them sharing a drink, the light went out and you returned to bed?' asked Rylands, finishing up.

'Yes.'

'Thank you. Could you wait there, please?'

Pembroke rose just as Vera was seized by a new gasping fit. She wheezed and heaved her shoulders up and down.

'Would you like a glass of water?' asked Pembroke courteously.

But Vera was recovering herself. 'No, thank you.'

'Are you comfortable standing or would you prefer to sit down?'

'No, I'm all right, thank you.'

Pembroke glanced down at his notes and then looked his witness in the eye. 'Can you give a reason, Mrs Collingwood, why you did not tell the police what you have just told us when you were first questioned in January 1992?'

Vera's eyes flicked around the court. 'Well, I was asked questions and I gave a statement. I did tell them, they just can't have taken it down. I was so upset at the time and, as they never asked me about it again, I didn't think it was important.'

'You didn't think it was important?' he queried incredulously. 'Your friend is accused of stabbing another friend, his lover, both men you knew well, and yet you didn't think it was important to tell anyone what you saw and heard that tragic night? But now, eight years after the death of Mr Meadows, you suddenly have total recall of the night?'

Vera bristled. 'Yes. I mean, I believed he had done it, and it wasn't until that television producer came round asking me questions that I wondered if what I had seen was important.'

'So nobody has coerced you to say what we have heard you describe this afternoon?'

'No. I'm saying it because that's what I remember.'

'You don't have any other reason for adding to your statement?'

Vera was gasping again. 'No, I do not. I've said that I don't over and over. I told you what I saw, I told *him*.' She nodded at Rylands.

Pembroke turned blandly back to the judges. 'No further questions.'

They sedated North and put her on a glucose drip. Very pale, she kept hovering between sleep and wakefulness. Watkins sat by the bed for hours, holding her friend's hand. Then Walker arrived, breathing heavily. Watkins thought there was a terrible, bewildered look about him. 'How is she?'

Watkins spoke softly. 'Oh, she's doing fine now.'

'What about the baby? Is the baby OK?'

As gently as she could, Watkins shook her head. 'I'm sorry, Mike. She lost the baby.'

Walker stood for a moment in incomprehension. Watkins stood up and moved aside. He headed for the chair and sank into it and, trying to comfort him, she put a hand on his shoulder.

'Can I get you anything? Cup of tea?'

Walker didn't exactly shake his head, he seemed to let it wander from side to side. 'No, no, I'm fine, thanks.'

A moment later his awareness of Watkins returned. He said, 'Thanks for everything, Viv, thank you. I'll just sit here with her, no need for you to wait.'

'Are you sure?'

'Yes. You go on home.'

She picked up her bag and coat and moved gracefully to the door and murmured, 'I'm so sorry, Mike.'

Watkins quietly closed the door and left Walker looking steadily at North's pale face. She woke a few seconds later and was at first unsure of where she was. Then she slowly turned her head towards Walker and reached out to touch him. 'Mike.'

Walker leant forward, taking her hand. 'I'm here, sweetheart.'

'Did they tell you?'

Walker nodded, close to tears. What could he say, what could he give her to make it better? Clumsily, he could think of only one offer to make. 'Listen,' he said, 'we'll get married, we're going to get married.'

She smiled wanly. 'Bit late to be making an honest woman of me, isn't it?'

Walker became emphatic. 'No, it's never too late, and it might not be too late for us to start, er, you know, have another try. I mean, you're not too old.'

'Is that a back-handed compliment?'

'But I don't mind! If we can, we can. If we can't then that'll be fine too, because you are the most important thing in the world to me.'

He bent to kiss her forehead. 'I love you.'

At this, North's attempt at jocularity broke down and she was weeping openly. 'I'm sorry. I'm sorry, Mike!'

He stroked her face and whispered, 'I know, sweetheart, I know. Let it all out. Let it go.' He held her tightly while she wept, and he wept with her.

CHAPTER 26

TUESDAY, 4 JULY, MORNING

'How's SHE doing?' asked Satchell as he walked with Walker towards Pembroke's chambers.

'Not good. She lost the baby.'

Satchell stopped and touched Walker on the arm. 'Oh, man. I'm really sorry.'

Walker did not want to linger on this subject. He tugged Satchell along towards the entrance. 'Have you got the bank statements?'

Satchell delved into his pocket and pulled out a clump of papers. 'I got them. But are *you* OK?'

Walker shrugged. 'Not really, but we've got to get these to Pembroke. The sooner this is over, the sooner I can get back to Pat.'

A few minutes later the two policemen sat opposite Pembroke, who was in his shirt sleeves and tabs, exposing a pair of shockingly red braces. He was eating sandwiches for breakfast and sipping a large paper cup of coffee, as he told them how difficult it might be to persuade the judges to take this new evidence on board at such a late stage. But Satchell wasn't convinced Pembroke had grasped the import of the bank accounts and the possible implications for McCready's appeal. 'McCready's solicitor set up a company, Cornwall Communications,' he said, 'which he used to transfer money backwards and forwards.'

'Yes, yes, quite a paper trail,' said Pembroke sagely.

'And what about the McCready incident in Glasgow?' put in Walker. 'The knife should have his fingerprints on it. With that and Sheila Connelly's statement—'

'Yes,' Pembroke interrupted impatiently. 'But what you must realise is that it is a completely separate case.'

'I know that. But doesn't it give an insight into McCready's character – that he's killed before?'

Pembroke shook his head. 'We simply won't be able to get that in. We're dealing with this conviction, not a previous murder.'

Walker thought for a moment. 'Let's say you call me, ask me about the personal grievance McCready has accused me of having. Couldn't I slip it in then? That I now have proof that he has committed another murder in the past.'

Pembroke sighed. 'No, no, no. I am sorry. The only thing that we can use, and this will have to be divulged to Rylands, is that you have evidence to show that Duffield paid a sum of money to Vera.' Pembroke finished his sandwich and drained his coffee.

'Yes, out of Fiona Meadows' inheritance,' insisted Walker. 'You can't say that's not relevant to the bloody case.'

* * *

In spite of his earlier scepticism, by the time Pembroke went down to the courts and met with Rylands' junior, Bunn, he was in high spirits. The more he thought about it, the better these bank statements appeared. The two colleagues moved down the corridor, where groups of solicitors and gowned barristers had gathered, all carrying large bundles of papers and many with take-away coffees. Pembroke spotted Rylands and Bunn and veered towards them, wafting copies of the bank statements. 'And behold!' he crowed. 'A notice of additional evidence came winging down from on high, yea even after the eleventh hour. And it was laden with fire and brimstone and there was wailing and gnashing of teeth among the defence team.'

Rylands frowned. 'What *are* you talking about?'

'A copy for you, and one for your admirable junior. Bank statements, old boy. In a nutshell, as the phrase goes, McCready's been transferring the odd pound or two to a witness, on a date remarkably adjacent to her new witness statement. I suspect she may be in for a "wee spot of bother", as they say in Glasgow.'

Rylands took the statements and looked over them as Pembroke chortled to himself. Rylands' face had taken on an aspect of puzzlement and then outright disbelief which soon developed into stunned horror. Pembroke twisted the knife. 'I shall invite you to recall Mrs Collingwood for further cross-examination.'

They came into the court together, Pembroke surveying the public section and noting that both Roger Barker and Zita Sallinger had arrived. 'Failing that,' Pembroke went on gloatingly, 'I'll just apply to call the banking evidence. I rather feel they'll give me leave, don't you, by the time I've explained what it's all about? Oh, and we've highlighted the relevant entries, as the money goes in and out of the different accounts, in fluorescent pink. No social comment intended, it's the only colour I have that hasn't run out.'

Rylands was thinking hard. 'I may have to ask for an adjournment to look at all this. How come I only get it this morning?'

Pembroke shrugged. 'You got it about three minutes after I did, old boy.'

Rylands was allowed an hour's adjournment and, when this expired, Vera Collingwood was recalled to the witness stand. Rylands immediately yielded his witness to Pembroke, just as Walker eased into the back row of the police benches, joining Satchell and the other officers in attendance. Duffield was uneasy. He stared at McCready as if trying to convey his worries by telepathy but the prisoner did not glance towards him. He was looking fixedly at the witness box. In the momentary silence, the journalists' pencils could be heard chasing across their notebooks.

'Can I ask you about your present circumstances, Mrs Collingwood? You currently reside in the same mobile home park as you did at the time of the murder, but now have a new home.'

'That's right.'

'You moved into a new luxurious mobile home nine months ago, but I believe you were behind in the rent on your previous accommodation?'

'Yes, that is correct. I hated the place, it had bad memories for me of poor Gary. And it was damp.'

'Could you please tell the court how you were able to financially secure your new home?'

Vera's asthmatic wheeze was sporadic but her breathing would suddenly descend into alarming gasps, especially under pressure. This happened now. 'That's none of your business.'

She fought for breath, the court listening to every painful inhalation with riveted attention. 'If you must know,' she went on, 'I had private savings.'

Pembroke used his eyebrows expressively. 'Really? Private savings?' Pembroke's question was just short of outright sarcasm. 'Were you not on Social Security benefits and dependent on your pension until recently?'

Vera's breathing, amplified by the microphone, was squeaking. She sipped water and seemed almost physically deflated.

'Mrs Collingwood? Did you understand my question?'

'Yes.'

'Didn't someone else provide the money for you to upgrade to your rather smart new home?'

Vera bit her lip and turned to the bench. 'Do I have to answer that, My Lord?'

'Yes you do, Mrs Collingwood,' said Bradpiece, gently but firmly.

But still she said nothing. Pembroke gave her five seconds and pressed on. 'All right. Let me make it clear. Did Mr James McCready, via his solicitor Mr Duffield, assist you financially so that you could move from what you have described as a damp caravan to a nice new modern one with every facility?'

'He has always been very kind, very supportive to me.'

She was beginning to sound like a marathon runner at the twenty-two-mile mark.

'Just *how* supportive, Mrs Collingwood?'

'He helped me out.'

'He helped you out? Just how *much* did he "help you out", Mrs Collingwood?'

Vera Collingwood shrugged with attempted bravado. 'Few hundred. Nothing illegal about that!'

'A few hundred,' repeated Pembroke with magisterial emphasis. 'A new caravan. Nothing illegal about that. Would you please look at these bank statements, Mrs Collingwood?' He picked up copies of the bank statements acquired by Satchell as a result of a court order the previous day. He handed these to an usher, who took them to Vera, presenting them ceremoniously. Vera squinted at them.

'Would you please describe to the court what you are looking at?' asked Pembroke.

He was interrupted by an impatient Winfield, sick of listening to Mrs Collingwood's agonised respiration and Pembroke's flowery rhetoric. 'I don't think we need the theatrics, Mr Pembroke.'

'Yes, My Lord. Mrs Collingwood, are those copies of your bank statements?'

'Yes, but—'

'Which clearly show a large sum of money going into your account six months prior to Mr McCready's appeal?'

'Well, I . . . I don't know.'

'Well then, can you tell the court for what reason that sum was paid to you?'

'I don't remember.'

'You don't remember . . . Well, maybe I can help you out. Was it in any way connected to you *adding* to your statement regarding events on the night Gary Meadows died?'

Vera looked aghast. Her eyes searched vainly for help. Ben Duffield's head was bowed as he studied his shoes. Barker was riveted by the drama unfolding. He glanced at McCready, who seemed to shiver, as if touched by an icy hand. 'No,' Vera said defiantly. 'It was not.'

'You seem very sure about that, Mrs Collingwood, yet you are still unsure why that money was paid to you. I wish to remind you, Mrs Collingwood, that you are under oath.'

Winfield leant forward now and peered over his half-moons. 'Let me clarify exactly what Mr Pembroke is asking you, Mrs Collingwood. All he is asking you is whether you were paid money to add to your original statement.'

'No, I was not.'

Winfield stared at her impassively as Pembroke returned to the chase. 'Yet you decline to tell the court what this substantial payment was for?'

The witness wheezed. When she was able she said, resentfully, 'I've said it was a gift to help me out and that's the truth of it. You're trying to put words into my mouth.'

'Just like the words in your statement were put into your mouth by that payment? A payment made to you by a company called Cornwall Communications. Do you know Mr Benjamin Duffield, the owner of this company and solicitor to Mr McCready?'

'Mr Pembroke,' cautioned Winfield. 'I think Mrs Collingwood has made her position with regard to this payment clear. I think we must draw our own conclusions.'

'If My Lord pleases,' Pembroke conceded and, having nothing more to ask, sat down.

Barbara MacKenzie had known it was going to be a tough, not very interesting day, with two detailed interview reports to type up and, if there was time, the beginning of an article she had promised to do for one of the police trade papers on the careful handling of child witnesses. She had thrown her keys onto the desk, hung her coat, flicked the kettle on and turned on her computer. Routine.

There was a tap on the door and Charlie, her colleague from the Child Protection Unit training section, peered around the door. 'Morning.'

Barbara sighed. 'Morning, Charlie.'

'Just wondering if we still had a copy of that Rackham House documentary.'

Barbara yawned. 'Should do. It'll be on one of the shelves in Janie's office.'

'Great,' said Charlie. 'Thanks, Barbara.'

Half an hour later, Charlie was back. 'No luck?' asked Barbara.

'Yeah, I found it eventually, thanks. Just thought I'd drop these off – they'd been put in the wrong sleeves.'

Charlie deposited two videotapes on the desk and passed a third to Barbara. 'Isn't this the one you were looking for?'

Barbara stiffened as soon as she saw the name on the label: *FIONA MEADOWS*. A date and time was appended. It was the tape Mike Walker had asked her to find for him. After a few moments' thought, during which she considered dropping the video into the bin just to spite him, she opened her bag and rooted for the card Walker had given her. This was a question of justice: nothing whatever to do with what she sometimes thought of as her broken heart. She dialled Walker's mobile phone.

The Court of Appeal was ready to hear the fresh evidence of Fiona Meadows. Wearing her school uniform, glancing nervously around at Duffield and then up at McCready in the dock, she took the stand. When she sipped water her hand around the glass was shaking. She told the court of waking up and hearing a row outside her room. She had gone to the door and peeped out. Her father was holding a knife, McCready was trying to get it off him. Rylands gave her plenty of time, adopting a calming, coaxing manner.

'Can you go on for us, Fiona? I know this is very upsetting for you. What happened next?'

'Er, yes. Well, then my dad backed away and Jimmy seemed to trip on the carpet and Dad fell backwards. It all happened so quickly . . .' Walker had been out. He slipped into his place again beside Satchell, watching Fiona intently. 'Daddy said he was all right and went back to bed. Then Jimmy came over and kissed me, said not to worry, that we were all friends again and for me to go back to bed. Then he started looking for some bandages.'

'I'm sorry, Fiona,' interjected Bradpiece. 'I don't quite understand, who exactly was looking for the bandages?'

'Jimmy. Then I went back to bed.'

Suddenly Walker's face lit up as the door opened and Barbara came in. She was breathing hard, having run all the way into the building, and he could see she was clutching a video cassette. She scanned the room looking for Walker, then crossed to take a place immediately behind him. She leant forward and held out the tape. Walker turned and took it, gave her a peck on the cheek, then nudged Satchell with delight. He passed the tape forward to Pembroke's junior, who handed it on to his leader.

'And did you fall asleep directly?' Rylands was asking Fiona.

'No, sir, I was awake for a while listening to my dad and Jimmy talking to each other, then I went to sleep.'

'You were no longer afraid? No longer worried about your father?'

'No, sir, I wasn't. I thought he was all right.'

Pembroke and Freeman were having a whispered conference as Rylands asked, 'You were very fond of your father, weren't you?'

'Yes.'

'So there would be no reason for you to protect someone who hurt him?'

'No, sir.'

Coming to an end, Rylands closed his file. 'Fiona, could you wait there. I expect there will be some more questions for you.'

Pembroke rose with the air of a man with momentous news. 'My Lords, My Lady, before embarking on my cross-examination of Fiona, might I raise a matter, perhaps in the absence of the witness?'

'Yes, of course, Mr Pembroke,' said Bradpiece reassuringly. 'Usher, would you accompany the witness out of court and stay with her? Thank you.'

He said to the witness, 'I don't expect we'll keep you waiting for long. Would you go with the usher?'

Fiona hesitated. She gave an uncertain glance towards the dock before following the usher out. Now Pembroke drew himself up to his full height, brandishing the tape. 'My Lords, My Lady, I have just been handed a videotape which could prove to be vital evidence in this case. Fiona was seen by a Child Protection officer within a week of her father's death, and gave her account, recorded on video in the usual way. I am told, although I have not yet seen the video myself, that Fiona, aged seven, gave a very different account to the one we have just heard in court from Fiona aged fifteen. May I ask for a short adjournment so that I can see the video. I expect my learned friend Mr Rylands will want to see it as well.'

For a few moments, the judges conferred. 'I think we'll rise and give you, Mr Pembroke, an opportunity to get your house in order. Will you let us know, via the usher, how long you are likely to need?'

McCready was frowning. What the hell was happening? Everything had been going so well, and now this . . . Once the judges had gone he stared hard at Rylands, an accusatory stare, then allowed himself to be ushered from the court. Rylands approached Pembroke, who could hardly suppress his pleasure in the moment. 'Er, just exactly what use do you plan to make of this video?'

'Well, that rather depends on what's on it, doesn't it?'

Knowing Walker was in court, Watkins dropped in on North in hospital. As she came in, North had her eyes closed. Her complexion was pallid and waxy. 'The nurse said you refused breakfast and lunch.'

'I can't eat at that ungodly hour in the morning, and I don't fancy lunch at eleven thirty.'

'So apart from starving yourself, how are you feeling?'

'Oh, terrific. How're things with you?'

'Come on, Pat. I know what you're going through. I've been there, remember? Twice. You can't blame yourself, believe me.'

'But Mike warned me to take it easy!'

'Come on, Pat. It was an accident.'

'Yeah, I know. And I'll get over it.'

'Yes you will, but it'll take time. It wasn't your appendix you lost.'

'I know that! I just can't help feeling guilty. If only I'd . . .' She opened her eyes wide and turned them towards her friend. They were moist. 'I just can't believe it's really gone.'

Watkins sat on the bed and drew her friend close. A few moments later they were both crying.

CHAPTER 27

TUESDAY, 4 JULY

LOOKING DECIDEDLY pale, Rylands returned to the court with Pembroke. The video made by the Child Protection Agency eight years earlier had shaken him to the core. There had been no ambiguity about it as far as he could see and now, having championed McCready so forcefully, he had to face the fact that he'd been comprehensively hoodwinked. It seemed impossible that the court would take a different view of the tape, and if it didn't, the case was over.

The ushers were setting up a monitor and video recorder. Pembroke shimmied over to them and apologised for all this last-minute trouble. 'That's all right, Mr Pembroke. We're used to you by now,' was the cheery response.

Rylands looked around for Walker and saw him sitting with another plainclothes officer, deep in conversation. The bloody man looked smug. It was not entirely true. As the judges filed back in, Walker felt tense but was trying to conceal it. 'Shame McCready's not here to watch this,' he told Satchell, who was sitting beside him. 'I'd love to see the look on his face.'

But Satchell nodded to the door which led down to the cells. 'You're just about to. Here he is.'

McCready was being led back into court looking, for the first time, less confident. He took his place in the dock and stared with curiosity at the video equipment, which had been set up in such a way as to give the whole court a view of the screen. Pembroke rose. 'My Lords, My Lady, thank you for the time. My learned friend and I are both agreed that the video should now be played. The ushers have managed to conjure up the necessary equipment at short notice.'

He gestured towards the screen. Winfield looked aside at his fellow judges and turned back to Pembroke. 'And why wasn't this video disclosed at trial?' he asked.

Pembroke had his answer ready and delivered it hastily. 'My Lord, the Senior Investigating Officer was advised that Fiona was too young and too vulnerable to be cross-examined and in consequence she was not called.'

Winfield smiled thinly, his scepticism apparent. 'That doesn't quite answer my question, Mr Pembroke. Whether used or not, the video was clearly disclosable.'

'My Lord, certainly,' admitted Pembroke. 'Inquiries will be made.'

'Shall we get on, then?' He turned to the usher. 'We'll need the witness back in court.'

McCready looked nervously towards the main door, through which Fiona would enter.

Fiona returned to the witness box, serious-faced. But it did not look as if it would be hard to ruffle her composure. Winfield addressed her kindly. 'Fiona, please be seated. We're going to watch a video taken of you some years back. Can you see the screen properly?'

She nodded and looked up towards McCready. He caught her glance and smiled bleakly.

'Thank you, usher,' said Pembroke. 'Could you do the honours? The tape is rewound, I think.'

The usher pressed the play button on the remote-control unit. The video footage was in black and white. At the edge of the screen a caption stated that the date was 20 January 1992, beside which the display gave clock time and elapsed time. Young Fiona sat on the floor of a plain, carpeted room beside a low play table. Children's drawings could be seen on the wall, toys were scattered on the floor. Barbara MacKenzie was squatting next to the child. To the layman she might have been a primary-school teacher or play leader, instead of a police officer trying to coax out vital evidence.

'Fiona,' she asked, 'do you know the difference between truth and lies?'

Fiona nodded her head gravely.

'Let's see, then. I'm wearing a skirt. Is that true, Fiona?' Barbara was wearing trousers and a shirt. Fiona shook her head. 'OK. I'm wearing a long dress. Is that true, Fiona?' Again, Fiona shook her head, more emphatically this time. 'I'm wearing trousers. Is that true?' Finally, Fiona nodded. 'Yes, that's the truth! Well done.'

Fiona smiled. She was not finding this too difficult so far but she was obviously concentrating hard.

'Now we know what is the truth and what is a lie, I want you to tell me the truth about what happened to your daddy last night. Please tell me everything you remember. All that matters is that you don't make anything up or leave anything out. This is very important.' Fiona picked up a woolly haired Cabbage Patch doll from the toybox. 'You can hold onto dolly,' reassured

Barbara. 'She's a lovely dolly. You keep hold of the doll and tell me what you saw last night. Can you do that?'

Last night. The words obviously terrified Fiona. She clutched the doll, as shock stole over her, her eyes wide and her mouth trembling. She suddenly jumped to her feet and was running up and down the room in silence. Barbara remained where she was. She said coolly, 'Where are you running to? Come and sit here with me, Fiona. Tell me what you saw last night.'

Fiona stopped for a moment, swung her head from side to side and immediately began to run up and down the room again. She still said nothing at first. Barbara gave her time – ten, twenty, thirty seconds – then suddenly Fiona screamed. The sound cut through the attentive courtroom like a lightning strike. 'Don't hurt Daddy, *please*! Don't hurt Daddy . . . Daddy, come to bed. DON'T HURT DADDY. DADDY. NO! NO!' The scream reached a higher and higher pitch of hysteria which echoed around the hushed courtroom.

Rylands winced fractionally, as pale as paper, while Pembroke watched with satisfaction. Walker and Satchell leant forward simultaneously and Fiona herself had let her mouth fall slightly open. She put her hands to her head as she tried to remember in real time – the occasion of the interview with Barbara and, before that, the night of her father's death. She was shaking her head, not in denial but out of confusion and inner turmoil.

The whole court seemed to turn towards McCready. He tried to remain impassive but inside he was churning. He looked at Fiona and she glanced back at him. Their eyes locked for a moment. *Christ!* he thought. *She's getting it all back*. He, of course, knew exactly what had happened that night. But he'd thought he was the only one who knew, absolutely and for certain. Now, watching her younger self acting out the stabbing had made Fiona remember everything. All McCready's hope, all his expectation of triumph and imminent freedom, crumbled to dust inside him.

Far from being two jovial, drunken guys stumbling home together in a haze of alcoholic bonhomie, Gary Meadows and Jimmy McCready had arrived back at the mobile in an ugly, explosive mood. Meadows especially was resentful at the attention McCready had been attracting all evening.

'Spoilt the whole bloody evening,' McCready shouted. 'Moody bitch.'

Meadows pushed him away. 'I just want to be left alone, right?'

'Right! So you should be. You've been a miserable bastard all evening.'

'Oh yeah? If anyone spoilt the evening, it was you with your . . . your pathetic grandstanding.'

McCready had noticed Vera hovering around between their two homes, a space illuminated by two porch lamps. 'Get out of here, you nosey bitch!' he snarled. He pulled out a five-pound note and crumpled it before throwing it to her. 'Here, take your money and piss off!'

Vera was not fazed by this verbal assault. 'You drunken buggers!' she hit back. 'You shouldn't be allowed with that kid, I'll report you.'

McCready sneered. 'You wouldn't dare! Now go home.'

McCready lurched after Meadows through the door of their home and slammed it behind him. Meadows was in the bedroom, heading for the sound system. He switched on a pulsing rock and roll track at ear-splitting level, swiped a bottle of brandy from a shelf and started dancing around, swigging from the bottle.

McCready followed him into the bedroom, holding out his hand. 'You've had enough, Gary. Just give me the bottle. Give it me.'

Meadows smiled and pulled a demonic face. 'Yes, I've had enough – of *you* ordering me around, I've had enough. You get out and leave us alone, I mean it. I hate you poncing around those clubs, making me look like a dumb piece of shit.'

McCready almost spat. 'You're only jealous. You hate it when I get all the attention.'

'No, I hate it when you smother yourself in makeup and prance around like an arsehole! I want you out of here. Pack up and get out.' He jerked his thumb towards the door. The movement made him spin round towards a side table, from which he picked up an ashtray and hurled it in the direction of his lover's head. It missed, smashing a mirror on the wall immediately behind.

'Make me!' McCready challenged. He felt powerful still, the darling of the crowd, impregnable. But Meadows had disappeared into the kitchen and McCready could hear the sound of drawers being opened and slammed shut. He followed into the hall, meeting Meadows, who was now wielding the large stainless-steel kitchen knife.

'Come on, then, come on,' he said, almost sing-song. 'Why don't you try to kill me? You got away with murder once, but you won't again.' Meadows danced around in front of McCready, waving the knife. McCready tried to grab it and received a slash to his left palm. He recoiled with shock and held his hand. Gouts of blood were welling around his gripping fingers.

'You stupid idiot! Look what you've done!'

Meadows froze, looking at his handiwork with awe. Suddenly came a door's click and Fiona was there, looking at them. Meadows tried to still his spinning head. 'Go back to bed, honey,' he said. 'We're just playing. Go on.'

But it was McCready who went to Fiona and scooped her up in his arms. Meadows didn't like that. He looked at his lover with unconcealed suspicion. 'Put her down, James,' he yelled. 'Put her down or I'll cut your throat. PUT HER DOWN!'

'Make me!' goaded McCready for the second time that night. His tone incensed Meadows, who started cursing incoherently. Fiona, too, began screaming and wriggling violently to free herself. McCready couldn't hold her and she broke free, running up and down the hallway, screaming. McCready saw that her father was momentarily distracted and went to grab the knife. The two men grappled inelegantly as Fiona stopped her running and froze, rabbit-like.

'Let *go*, Gary! For God's sake, put it down!' McCready had felt there was reason still in his voice. He wasn't goading but placatory now. But then the knife, still under the partial control of Meadows, slashed down on McCready's right forearm. This enraged him. With a desperate twist of Meadows' wrist, McCready pulled away, now holding the knife in his own bleeding hand.

Meadows' facial expression went from belligerence to fear. He turned to where his daughter was standing, his back to McCready, as if to protect her. Exactly at this moment, McCready jerked forward, making a savage, darting movement with his arm, the blade flashing as it plunged into Gary Meadows' back. Meadows spun round in terror and Fiona saw, inches from her face, the handle of the knife protruding from her father's back.

The victim's face was one of amazement. McCready could see no pain there. He saw him feel behind his back, his fingers fluttering to get the knife, finding it and wincing as he pulled it out of his own flesh. He did not look at the weapon, sticky with blood, but only at McCready. He was struggling to believe what had just happened. 'What have you done? What have you done?'

McCready, too, was shocked but he managed to shake his head. 'Nobody fucks with me, Gary.'

Meadows' eyes closed and opened again. He had begun to feel the wound throbbing now. He stumbled back against the wall. He saw McCready looking at Fiona and suddenly tried to push himself forward again to separate them. 'Dear God, let her go! Please, please don't hurt my baby, please.'

But McCready could not be stopped. He dragged the child by her hair into her bedroom. He slammed the door shut, turned back and grimly took the knife from Meadows' unresisting fingers. Carrying it by the blade, in his right hand, he took it to the kitchen sink. Then he helped Meadows into the bedroom and heaved him onto the bed, turning him over slightly to inspect the knife wound. It looked OK to him, a clean slit, with a rim of blood around it, nothing gory.

'You're fine, Gary,' he said coldly. 'It's not even bleeding.' He had left Meadows then, to see to himself, finding a bandage in the kitchen and cutting and wrapping it around his arm and hand. He came back to the bedroom and picked up the brandy bottle, roughly trying to pour the liquor into Meadows' mouth. 'Drink! Come on, Gary! You'll be fine. Come on.'

But Meadows was by then already too weak to drink. McCready himself took several gulps from the bottle and, giving way to rage again, he slammed it down on the glass-topped dressing table. The glass shattered into a web of cracks. McCready found a glass and poured the last of the brandy into it. He drank again, then looked drunkenly down on Meadows lying prone on the bed. He tried again to force him to drink from the glass but the brandy only dripped down Meadows' chin. 'Come on! Come on!' McCready shouted.

But Meadows still showed signs of life. Feebly he managed to lift his hand up and push the glass away. McCready steadied himself. He took a couple of deep breaths. Then he put the glass and bottle down beside the bed and got in beside Meadows, who was now making slight grunting sounds. McCready took no notice. He lifted Meadows' head and jammed a pillow under it, which he thought made him look more comfortable. McCready smiled and drew the bedclothes around himself, then turned out the light. 'G'night, Gary,' he murmured. 'I love you.'

In the dark, Meadows for a few moments faintly gasped for breath. There was a gurgling sound, then silence. Lying beside him, McCready closed his eyes and slept.

'Jimmy angry! Jimmy angry!' The little girl in the video had stopped running and was staring straight ahead.

Barbara said, 'What is Jimmy doing, Fiona?'

Fiona turned the doll over in her hand and stabbed it repeatedly in the back with a crayon she had grabbed from the table. 'Jimmy did this to Daddy. Jimmy did this to Daddy. Jimmy did this to Daddy.' She went on stabbing at the doll, then stopped and turned the crayon on herself, jabbing it into her shoulder and her arm. At last she stood, her jaw frozen, locked in a silent scream.

Back in his holding cell, McCready sat with his hands clenched and head bowed. Rylands posed stiffly by the cell door.

'So, what now?' McCready's voice was a whisper, hardly audible.

'What do you mean, what now? Your witnesses have just been blown out of the water, James. Both Fiona and Vera now face perjury charges. As for Duffield, he'll be struck off and probably charged with perverting the course of justice.'

McCready slowly raised his head and stared at Rylands with those wide-open eyes. Suddenly he smiled and said softly, 'Can't blame me for trying.'

But Rylands did. Rylands was seething. 'You've dragged everyone down to your level. You even had me fooled.'

McCready got up. His smirk was pure impudence now. 'Well, you know the saying. Money talks.'

'Really?' Rylands' voice was soft and lethal. 'Then you should have paid Sheila Connelly more.'

McCready faltered. 'What?'

'She's handed over the knife you used to kill that young police officer.' Rylands watched McCready squirm anew. He'd made witnesses do this many times in court and he even enjoyed those fleeting moments of power. But he felt only bitterness now. He turned and walked back to the cell door.

McCready's normally quick mind was dulled by the knock-back he had received from the court. He reacted slowly to Rylands' move. 'Robert, Robert!' he called out. 'Wait!'

Rylands, however, kept on going. He didn't look back as the cell door was slammed shut.

'Hi, sweetheart, how are you doing?'

North was doing OK. She was sitting up in bed reading a magazine when Walker arrived with a bag of grapes and a gigantic bouquet of flowers. 'Better.' And he could see it was true. Some of the sparkle had come back. 'They've said I can go home next weekend,' she told him.

Walker put down the flowers and fruit and clapped his hands. 'They have? That's wonderful!' He was beaming. North settled back in the bed. 'So, how did it go?'

'Beautiful. Soon as the judges saw the video it was all over.' He sat on the bedside. 'Plus with the new DNA advances, if McCready's prints are on that knife, Forensics'll find them. So he's looking at another life sentence for murdering Colin Hood. Bastard won't get out for a long time.'

North accepted his gentle kiss on the cheek with a smile. He transferred to the chair beside the bed. 'So,' she said, 'it's obvious now why Vera changed her story. But Fiona seemed so genuine when we interviewed her.'

'Yeah, I was watching her in court. She was truly shocked by the video. I think Duffield had managed to convince her that the accident story was the truth. Wouldn't have been too hard if she really had blocked out what had happened.'

'Poor girl.'

'Eh, and I tell you what. I get a tap on my shoulder coming out of the court, and there's the Chief himself, he'd slid into court. He shakes my hand, then he says, "Sorry about the problems you've been having; PCA have completed their investigation and fully exonerated you. Obviously, the suspension is lifted and . . ." Well, then he says there's a whopper of a case he'd like me to take over. I'm back, Pat! I'm back on top and ready to roll!'

'That's marvellous, Mike.' And in truth North felt a tiny stab of happiness. Walker grabbed hold of her hand and squeezed.

The moment was shattered as Satchell strode in, also with a huge bouquet of flowers and, in his other hand, a bottle of brandy. 'These are for Pat, and this is for you, Mike.' He presented the bottle of brandy to Walker as if it were the FA Cup.

Walker's face split in a laugh as he took the bottle and twisted off the top. A moment later he was splashing brandy into a hospital tooth-glass. 'Thanks, I need it. Hey, Satch, she's coming home at the weekend.'

'They don't like you to take up a bed for too long,' murmured North sleepily. 'But I'm going to take it easy.'

'Hey, you got another glass, Mike? You want a drop, Pat?' asked Satchell.

'No, I'm OK, help yourself.'

But there was only the one tooth-glass.

'Don't worry,' boomed Walker, 'we'll share this one. To Pat and her complete and fantastic recovery.' He gulped and watched North contentedly close her eyes, letting the tension go. Walker held up the glass, and passed it to his friend. He stood back and pushed the air with both hands in a warning gesture. 'Careful with that glass, Satch!'

Dear Reader,

Thank you very much for picking up *Appeal*, the fourth book in the *Trial and Retribution* series. I hope you enjoyed reading the book as much as I enjoyed writing it.

It has been a pleasure to revisit *Trial and Retribution* after its television series and I am so fortunate to continue writing these novels – of which there are six in total. Do keep an eye out for news about the next book in the series, *Justice*, which will be coming soon. And if you haven't had a chance yet to read the first three books, *Trial and Retribution*, *Alibi*, and *Accused*, they are available now in paperback, eBook and audio.

In *Appeal*, a man was convicted of killing his partner but when new evidence comes to light, he wins his appeal for a retrial. When the assigned detective discovers that it was her partner that led the original police inquiry, she finds herself having to ask questions of him she'd never thought she would. What did you think of the way this relationship played out? What would you have done if you found yourself in the same position?

If you love crime and legal thrillers you may enjoy my podcast, *Listening to the Dead*, which I co-host with former CSI Cass Sutherland. We explore the fascinating world of forensics, from the science behind the headlines to the evidence that cinches a conviction – with world-class experts discussing their most well-known and shocking cases. All episodes are available now on all podcast platforms.

You may also enjoy my *Jack Warr* series, the first five books – *Buried*, *Judas Horse*, *Vanished*, *Pure Evil* and *Crucified* – are available now. If you want to catch up with the *Tennison* series, all ten novels – *Tennison, Hidden Killers, Good Friday, Murder Mile, The Dirty Dozen, The Blunt Force, Unholy Murder, Dark Rooms, Taste of Blood* and *Whole Life Sentence* – are available to buy. I've been so pleased by the response I've had from the many readers who have been curious about the beginnings of Jane's police career. It's been great fun for me to explore how she became the woman we know in middle and later life from the *Prime Suspect* series.

I am also very excited to share the news of my memoir, *Getting Away with Murder*. It has been a very time-consuming and astonishing process recalling my past for this book. It seemed I was capable of remembering every title and character from all my novels and television series but had no memory of rather important personal events. However, after a lot of encouragement and family albums, I have slowly started to enjoy recalling some sad times, some awful times and some hysterically funny times. I am hoping that sharing my life with you will make for an enjoyable read.

Looking ahead, I'm very glad to announce the news of my next series, starring Jessica Russell, an experienced CSI. Introducing a new female detective is no easy accomplishment but I have found writing Jessica to be a joy and I'm excited to explore her world more in future books.

If you like more information on what I'm working on, the *Trial and Retribution* series, the *Jack Warr* series or my memoir, you can visit www.bit.ly/LyndaLaPlanteClub, where you can join my Readers' Club. It only takes a few moments to sign up, there are no catches or costs and new members will automatically receive an exclusive message from me. Bonnier Books UK will keep your data private and confidential, and it will never be passed on to a third party. We won't spam you with loads of emails, just get in touch now and again with news about my books, and you can unsubscribe any time you want. And if you would like to get involved in a wider conversation about my books, please do review *Appeal* on Amazon, on Goodreads, on your social media account or talk about it with friends, family or reader groups! Sharing your thoughts helps other readers, and I always enjoy hearing about what people experience from my writing.

With many thanks again for reading *Appeal*, and I hope you'll return for the next in the series.

With my very best wishes,

Lynda

Keep reading for an extract from the first book in Lynda's brand new crime series, introducing CSI Jessica Russell . . .

The husband of a prominent and infamously ruthless barrister is found in horrific condition after a robbery and brutal assault. Now in a coma, a major investigation is launched using the newly formed, experimental Metropolitan Police Serious Crime Analysis Unit.

Jessica Russell is an experienced CSI with degrees in psychology and criminology with an exceptional Master's in Investigative psychology and behaviour analysis. But Jessica's first job as team leader of MSCAN is entirely new to her: to bring together a team of three trusted officers.

Between them, the team has dealt with every kind of murder and major crime scene – their expertise ranges from forensic DNA to blood spatter analysis, digital forensics and beyond.

Now they must piece together the complex puzzle at the heart of this brutal crime. If it was a robbery gone horrifically wrong, what was so important to have been stolen?

AVAILABLE NOW

CHAPTER ONE

Jessica Russell woke at 7 a.m. and spent the next hour in the living room doing her daily yoga and meditation, hoping it would help calm her nerves before her interview at Scotland Yard. When she'd finished, she rinsed the dirty crockery her twin brother David had left in the sink the night before and put it in the dishwasher. Then, she wiped down the work surfaces and table before making her daily breakfast of granola, yoghurt and blueberries. She was making herself a ginseng tea when David walked into the kitchen wearing a T-shirt and pyjama shorts.

'Not at work today then?' she asked, surprised to see him.

'I wouldn't be here if I were, would I?' He yawned and scratched his backside.

'I was just asking, that's all . . .'

'I had hoped to have a lie-in, but all your chanting woke me,' he grumbled.

'Sorry about that. Is the day off to escape that little Chihuahua that keeps attacking you on your rounds?' she laughed.

'It's not funny. The bloody thing's mad. It's bitten me twice now. I daren't give it a kick in case it drops down dead.'

'Tell the owner to keep it indoors.'

'I have, but she's eighty-six and doesn't know what time of day it is . . . she's as mad as her dog.'

'So why the day off?'

'I'm going to look at a racing bike in West Wickham. It's a Fairlight Strael, a year old and hardly used, or so the seller says.'

'How much is it?'

'Two grand.'

'For a bicycle!'

He frowned. 'They're nearer three thousand new. I'll use it for the Ride London event if I buy it. I'm doing it for Cancer Research in memory of Mum, so it'd be nice if you'd sponsor me.'

'Of course I will. Have you raised much so far?'

'Nearly three grand. A lot of my postie colleagues have donated online. I've also been a bit cheeky and asked people on my mail round.'

'Are you allowed to do that?'

'No, but I stuck to people I know well who are unlikely to report me. They've all been very supportive actually.'

'Well done, you. Send me the link and I'll donate. How far is the ride?'

'Hundred K. We start in central London, cycle into Essex and finish at Tower Bridge.'

'Do you want anything?' she asked, getting the granola from the cupboard.

'Finding your own place to live would be good,' he said, po-faced.

Jessica wasn't sure if he was being serious. 'I meant some breakfast.'

'No thanks. All I want is some water and more sleep,' he replied. As David reached for a glass, Jessica noticed him wince and then rub his lower back.

'You all right?'

'I pulled something pushing my mail trolley around.'

'I thought they were meant to make your job easier.'

'They're still bloody heavy when they're full.'

'Maybe you should ask your manager about working in the sorting office if your back's playing up.'

'No way. I like being outside in the fresh air.' David turned the cold tap on too far, splashing water everywhere.

'Mind what you're doing, David, I just tidied up.' She grabbed some kitchen towel and placed it on the floor.

'What is it with you and tidiness?'

'Old Chinese proverb says a tidy house is a happy house.'

He grunted. 'Less of your silly yoga chanting will keep me happy.'

'I've got my big interview today. I was trying to calm my nerves.'

'It's not like you to be nervous about anything. It's just another job, isn't it?'

'It's more than just a job. If I'm selected, it will be a big step forward in my career, running a team of forensic experts.'

'You'll smash it. You're bloody good at what you do.'

She smiled. 'I'm meeting some colleagues after the interview. I should be home between three and four.'

He started to walk off, then turned around. 'I was joking about you moving out. You know I appreciate everything you've done for me since Mum died, but I'm better now, so if you did want to find a place of your own, I wouldn't be upset, that's all.'

'That's OK. I'm happy here with my adorable little brother,' she replied.

'You may have popped out twenty minutes before me, but people say you look a lot older,' he said with a grin.

'And wiser,' she responded.

He yawned and rubbed his lower back as he left the kitchen.

* * *

Jessica could feel her nervousness mounting as the train arrived at Charing Cross just after 10.15 a.m. It was a cloudless but slightly chilly May morning, and the streets were bustling with people. As she joined the crowd, she couldn't help glancing at her watch again, knowing she had plenty of time.

Arriving at Scotland Yard, Jessica showed her Kent Police civilian identity card to one of the armed officers. He nodded, stepped aside and let her in. She then gave the receptionist a copy of the email from Commander Mary Williams confirming the appointment. The receptionist checked Jessica's name against the list, ticked it off and handed her a visitor's lanyard. 'Take the lift to the fourth floor, then turn left. Commander Williams' assistant's office is at the end of the corridor.'

Jessica nodded her thanks, checked her watch one more time, then went into the Ladies opposite the lifts. In the toilet, Jessica checked herself in the mirror to make sure she looked professional. She was wearing a navy-blue trouser suit, white silk blouse and block-heeled court shoes. Her thick, curly red hair was tied up in a bun. She touched up her makeup and then washed her hands. After carefully drying them with paper towels, she used the towels to clean the sink and taps.

Exiting the lift, Jessica made her way to Commander Williams' PA's office where a tall, dark-haired, good-looking man in his mid-forties was sitting behind the desk. 'I'm Jessica Russell. I've come for the Murder and Serious Crime Analysis Team Leader interview.' She handed over the confirmation email and showed him her identification card.

'I'm Jordan, the Commander's PA. You're nice and early.'

'Gives me more time to compose myself before I enter the lion's den,' she joked.

He smiled. 'I think you'll find it less formal than you're expecting. So that you know, the panel likes to call it MSCAN for short . . . it's less of a mouthful. The waiting room is just across the corridor. Help yourself to a hot or cold drink. I'll come and get you when Commander Williams has finished interviewing the other candidate.'

'Thank you. Can you tell me who else is on the panel with Commander Williams and what their rank and department is?'

Jordan smiled. 'Well done, you're the first person to ask. They all work in the homicide and major crime command. DCI John Anderson is the small bald chap. He's a Senior Investigating Officer on the Barking homicide team. The other officer is DCS Morgan. He's based here at the Yard and is Commander Williams's deputy.'

'How many people are they interviewing?'

'Eight in total, and you're the last.'

'Thanks.' Jessica entered the waiting room and got herself a bottle of water. Thankfully she already knew Commander Williams from when she was a DCS in the Kent Police before she got a promotion and transferred to the Met. Jessica had been the crime scene manager on Kent homicide cases when Williams was in overall command. She was a highly respected, no-nonsense detective with a successful track record and the Met had recruited her to improve the efficiency of investigative and forensic work in homicide and major crime investigations.

Jessica removed her phone from her handbag, switched it off, and looked at the time again; it was 10.45 a.m. She had thirty minutes before her interview and decided to review the notes she'd made in preparation. Jessica read a couple of pages, then realised it was making her anxious again, so decided to do some deep breathing instead. She was just exhaling when the door opened and Jordan entered.

'The panel is ready to interview you, Miss Russell. Sorry it's a bit earlier than expected. The last candidate's chances were pretty much over before the interview began. Commander Williams does her homework on all the applicants. She discovered the chap had made derogatory remarks on Facebook and X about the Met's senior management. He tried to deny it but had to fess up in the end.'

Jessica shook her head. She wasn't on social media herself, and couldn't believe how foolish some people could be. Jordan took her to the Commander's office, and she took a deep breath as she entered.

Despite Commander Williams's desk being positioned in front of the windows, Jessica was surprised to find her sitting in a comfortable armchair and the two male officers seated on a matching three-seater sofa.

'Nice to see you again, Jess,' Williams smiled. 'I don't expect you're used to being interviewed this way, but I prefer a less formal surrounding as it helps candidates feel more at ease.' Williams smiled, gesturing for Jessica to sit in the other armchair. Morgan nodded in agreement, but Jessica noticed Anderson's dour expression as he picked up his clipboard and pen from the coffee table.

Williams's opening question was to ask her if she knew who the other officers present were, and Jessica was immediately thankful for Jordan's tip as she reeled them off.

'And what do you know about MSCAN?'

'It was your vision to create a team of the best crime scene examiners working alongside a behavioural psychologist for the homicide and major crime command. They will deal with all forensic matters throughout an investigation, from crime scene to court. This will include crime scene analysis, reconstruction, victimology and suspect profiling. They will also consider the value and limitations of the available evidence, as well as suggesting any additional investigative and forensic opportunities.'

Williams nodded with a look of approval and wrote something on her clipboard.

DCS Morgan raised his pen. 'The Commissioner was initially reluctant about Commander Williams's idea as the Met already has its own forensic lab and crime scene managers. He was also concerned about the running costs. How do you think MSCAN will bring value to major crime investigations?'

'Having a specialised unit of experts on hand to identify and optimise the best forensic opportunities in the early stages of an investigation should ultimately be more cost-effective.'

Williams smiled. 'That's pretty much what I told the Commissioner. That said, he decided MSCAN would be evaluated after a year. If it isn't cost-effective and producing results, it could be disbanded. How would you feel about that?'

'I'd like to think that won't happen, ma'am. If selected for the team leader role, I know I can run a unit that will get results and prove its worth.'

Williams and Morgan nodded. The expressionless Anderson twirled his pen between his fingers, then pointed it at Jessica. 'What makes you think you'd be a good team leader?' he asked bluntly.

Jessica took a deep breath. 'I have good communication skills, a strong work ethic and the ability to empathise with others. Good leadership is about supporting the people around you, trusting them, and allowing them to contribute their expertise so the team can be successful.'

'Yes, I'm sure I read that definition in a manual somewhere,' Anderson glibly replied. He then flicked through a couple of pages on his clipboard before continuing. 'You are only thirty-four, and according to your CV, have been a crime scene manager for two years, which isn't a lot of experience in managing people.'

Jessica wondered if he was just trying to unsettle her or was totally against her leading the MSCAN team. Either way, she was determined he wouldn't get to her. 'The director of forensic services in Kent was the referee for my MSCAN application. He recommended me for the position and commended my crime scene management and forensic investigation skills,' Jessica replied calmly.

Anderson was about to continue, but Williams raised her hand to stop him. 'Tell us about your academic qualifications, Jessica.'

'I have a joint first-class honours degree in Psychology and Criminology and a master's degree in Investigative Psychology.'

'Was criminal profiling part of your degrees?' Williams asked.

'Yes, ma'am, for my Master's, but it was called Behavioural Investigative Analysis.'

'We haven't selected a behavioural psychologist for the team yet. How do you think they will assist murder and major crime investigations?' Morgan asked.

'Essentially, behavioural analysis studies an offender's motivation and method by examining their verbal and nonverbal actions during and after the commission of the crime. Identifying these behavioural clues at a crime scene is fundamental to developing an accurate profile of an unknown offender. It's a valuable investigative tool that detectives can use to narrow down a list of suspects.'

'Some say it's nothing more than guesswork,' Anderson said.

'A behavioural adviser should only base their conclusions on the information and documented evidence they receive from investigators,' Jessica replied calmly, not taking the bait.

Morgan nodded and made a tick mark on his clipboard.

'Do you find your behavioural knowledge helps as a crime scene manager?' Williams asked.

'Undoubtedly. I try to get inside the offender's head, to think and act like them in order to identify the correct forensic approach.'

'You have impressive qualifications, but my question is this. Have you ever actually given behavioural advice on live or cold case investigations?' Anderson asked.

'No, sir, but I have been involved in a case where a behavioural adviser was called in and . . .'

Anderson shook his head, 'The National Crime Agency has an approved list of highly qualified behavioural investigative advisers that senior investigators can contact for advice on major investigations. Is your name on that list?'

'No, sir.'

Anderson frowned. 'Then you have no recognised expertise in using or giving detectives behavioural advice.'

Jessica noticed Williams's expression tensing. Anderson was about to continue, but again Williams stopped him. 'That's not necessarily correct, DCI Anderson. Tell me, Jess, the case where the profiler was involved, was it the murder of a young woman in Maidstone?'

'Yes, ma'am, she was strangled to death in her own house with a pair of tights. I was the crime scene manager.'

'As I recall, the senior investigating officer went with the profiler's theory, which was . . .' Williams deliberately paused. 'The husband had snuck home during a night shift, murdered his wife for the life insurance, then staged the scene to look like someone had broken into the premises and killed her. You told the senior investigating officer you disagreed with the profiler and thought someone else might be responsible, but he ignored you.'

'In fairness, he listened to what I had to say but disagreed and charged the husband.'

'But you were right, and he was wrong. Tell us why,' Williams asked.

Jessica nodded. 'For me, the crime had none of the hallmarks of a staged scene. I considered that it might have been a burglary gone wrong. A rear window was broken using a lump of wood, which we recovered nearby. I had the window pieced together, found an ear print on it, and the scientist recovered black woollen fibres on the wood, which made me wonder if someone wearing black gloves had been listening for any movement inside the premises, as a burglar might do. The husband went to work at 7 p.m. He said his wife told him she was tired and would have an early night. It was possible the wife had gone to bed and turned all the lights off, leaving the premises in darkness and I . . .'

'How could you know she was in bed at the time?' Anderson scoffed.

'I didn't, and I could still be wrong. However, I noticed the duvet on the left side of the bed was thrown back, and one of the bedroom curtains had been pulled open. Her bedside cabinet had been knocked sideways, and a glass of water was spilt on the floor. I considered the possibility the victim had heard the window break, woke up startled, jumped out of bed and looked out the front bedroom window, thinking the sound had come from the outside. The suspect heard her moving about and entered the bedroom. A brief struggle ensued beside the bed, knocking the cabinet out of position. He then took her into the living room and strangled her with a pair of tights.'

'The person who killed her could have pulled the curtain open,' Anderson suggested.

'I agree that was possible. However, I considered it unlikely that someone who had just committed a murder would pull a curtain open so wide to look outside. If this were the case, I would have expected the curtain to have been pulled back just a few inches.'

'That makes perfect sense to me. Was any property stolen?' Morgan asked, while Anderson huffed.

'The jewellery she was wearing and her mobile phone, which was on a charger in the living room.'

Morgan nodded slowly. 'And what was the evidence that led you to her killer?'

'Although we didn't find any DNA evidence to link another suspect to the crime scene, his mistake was leaving the tights around the victim's neck. I considered they might not be hers and had the crotch area tested for DNA. The vaginal fluid didn't match the victim, but it did match a local woman who had a criminal caution for a minor assault. Her boyfriend, who had a record for burglary and assault, was arrested, and his right ear matched the print on the broken glass. We also found black woollen gloves at his flat, matching the fibres on the wood used to break the window.'

'Did the girlfriend assist the investigation?' Morgan asked.

'Thankfully, yes. She said he had come home drunk on the night of the murder and had a scratch on his face. He said he'd walked into a low-hanging tree branch and became physically aggressive when she questioned him further. She also said he had sexual fetishes and liked to put a pair of tights around her neck and tighten them during sex. On one occasion, she found a pair of her tights in his jacket pocket . . . his excuse was that it made him feel she was always close to him.'

'Did he admit the murder?' Anderson enquired.

'No, he tried to blame the victim's husband but was found guilty and sentenced to life imprisonment.'

'Why do you think he killed her?' Morgan asked.

'He was a heavy drinker with a short temper and sadomasochistic tendencies. It's possible she may have seen his face and recognised him. He then panicked and strangled her, which may also have given him some sexual gratification.'

'Was the victim sexually assaulted?' Morgan asked.

'I think she may have been, but there was no forensic evidence to support that conclusion.'

'Then I guess we'll never know if your profile was correct,' Anderson said smugly, leaning back in his chair.

Jessica had finally had enough of his demeaning remarks. 'The jury convicted him on the evidence presented to them . . . not my theory alone.'

'How did you feel when he was convicted?' Morgan asked.

'I felt proud that our scene of crime and forensic teamwork had saved the husband from possibly going to prison for a crime he didn't commit.'

Williams nodded in agreement. 'Did you receive any recognition for your work on the case?'

'Yes, the trial judge commended my crime scene investigation, and I was also awarded a Chief Constable's Commendation.'

Morgan flicked through the papers on his clipboard, then looked at Jessica. 'Are you a modest person?'

She was confused by his question. 'Well, I'm not a bragger.'

Morgan continued. 'You never mentioned the commendations or the case involving the profiler on your CV. Why was that?'

'To be honest, I thought it might reflect badly on me as I disagreed with a senior officer and I . . .'

'It was exceptional work, and disagreeing with a senior officer is never easy, regardless of rank,' Morgan remarked.

Commander Williams continued. 'We will also be recruiing two forensic experts for MSCAN. If you were selected for the team leader role, is there anyone in particular you would like to work with?'

'Yes, ma'am. Diane Thomas. She's a forensic scientist specialising in DNA, blood pattern analysis and fibres. I have worked alongside her many times at major crime scenes and her knowledge and skills have been invaluable.'

To Jessica's surprise, Anderson nodded. 'She lectured on my senior investigators' course. She impressed me; her blood pattern work has solved some big cases. Who would be your second pick for the team?'

'Stephen Jones. He's a fingerprint expert who also specialises in footwear, tool and weapon mark comparisons. He's worked on numerous murder and terrorist cases.'

Williams nodded. 'They've both applied to be on the team. I've spoken to colleagues, and they are both highly respected. Have you spoken to them about working on MSCAN?'

'Yes, ma'am. I felt I should get their approval first if asked to put any names forward.'

'Would they still be interested in joining the team if you didn't get the job?' Anderson asked.

'Of course. They see it as an opportunity to get more hands-on experience rather than being called in as and when for their expertise. I'd love to work with them more permanently, but that's not for me to decide.' Jessica smiled at Anderson, who frowned and looked at his clipboard.

'Your CV states that after completing your master's degree, you worked as a trainee probation officer in Southwark, supervising young offenders to help them avoid re-offending. Is that correct?' he asked.

'Yes, sir. It was challenging as the kids I dealt with were often impulsive and tested boundaries at every level. But it was also very rewarding.'

'So why did you leave after only a year in the job?' Anderson asked, looking at her pointedly.

Jessica knew she could have just said she didn't feel it was the right job for her but decided to be open and frank with the panel. 'I was sexually assaulted by a fifteen-year-old boy I was supervising. Unfortunately, he wasn't charged, but I'd rather not go into all the details. At the time, I couldn't handle the emotional distress it caused me and found it difficult to concentrate on my work. I decided on a different career path and joined Kent police as a scene of crime officer.'

Anderson and the others looked shocked. 'I'm sorry. I didn't know that, um, you know . . .' Anderson mumbled.

'It's not something I'd want to put on my CV. Bad things happen, but you learn to deal with them.'

Anderson didn't ask another question during the remainder of the interview, which focused on Jessica 's personal life and interests. She told them that she currently lived with her brother, but was looking for a place of her own. She also explained that due to her long hours as a crime scene manager, she didn't have much of a social life but enjoyed staying fit and practising yoga to relax and stay focused.

Williams looked at her watch and said she had a couple more questions. 'If you are not selected as the team leader, would you still be interested in being a crime scene investigator on the team?'

‘Yes, ma’am, I’d welcome the opportunity to be on such an elite unit.’

‘And if selected for either role, how long would it be before you could start?’

‘The Kent director of forensics is aware of my application, and I’d have to hand over my current cases, but I think two weeks would be a fair estimate.’

Williams nodded. ‘You’ll be contacted with the panel’s decision on Friday.’

‘Thank you, ma’am.’ Jessica shook hands with each officer before leaving, and Williams and Morgan wished her well. As he gave her a limp handshake, Anderson said nothing.

* * *

Once Jessica had left the room, Williams turned to her colleagues. ‘I have to say Miss Russell impressed me. She has all the requisite skills, and her knowledge of behavioural analysis is definitely an asset. What did you think of her choice of Diane Thomas and Stephen Jones as part of the team?’

‘I wouldn’t argue with that. Five of the eight candidates said they would like them on the team,’ Morgan said, and Anderson nodded his agreement.

‘If Miss Russell was on or leading the team, there could also be a cost-saving opportunity,’ Williams remarked.

Anderson looked confused, but Morgan could tell what she was considering. ‘Are you thinking about giving Miss Russell a dual role?’

Williams nodded. ‘Yes, as the team leader, she can also be the behavioural adviser and a CSI.’

Morgan nodded. 'A team of three will certainly be more cost-effective than four.'

Anderson frowned. 'Just because it would save money doesn't mean Russell is the right choice.'

'What is your problem with her, John?' Morgan asked, clearly exasperated.

'I don't have a problem with her. She's clearly an excellent CSI, but she's not on the NCA-approved list as an analyst. I believe employing her as a behavioural analyst is a massive risk and could do more harm than good.'

Williams stood her ground. 'Behavioural advisers do not have Russell's crime scene skills and forensic knowledge. They are generally called in by an SIO a few weeks after a murder or rape by an unknown offender and never visit a live scene. They base their analysis and conclusions on scene photographs, police and witness statements. Russell would be there right from the beginning.'

'Sounds like you've already made up your mind,' Anderson grumbled.

'I haven't. I'm merely pointing out her all-round abilities. We need to discuss our notes on all the candidates before making a final decision.'

Don't miss out on Lynda La Plante's inspiring memoir . . .

Actor, Writer, Producer, Author. Lynda La Plante is a creative force to be reckoned with.

Best known as the writer behind TV's *Prime Suspect, Widows* and *The Governor*, being a bestselling crime writer is actually Lynda's third career. Having worked as a jobbing actor, Lynda decided she wanted to write the fierce, flawed and deep roles for women that weren't available in the '70s and '80s, and in doing so, broke through the glass ceiling and changed TV drama for ever.

From studying drama at RADA with the likes of John Hurt and Ian McShane to treading the boards in musical comedy; from typing her first ideas on spec to running her own award-winning production company; from mixing with the Mafia in Italy to shadowing a private detective in Los Angeles, this is a book filled with hilarious and surprising stories told with Lynda's trademark wit and style.

Always a maverick, always pushing boundaries, always standing strong where others would have wilted, Lynda remains at the very top of her game and *Getting Away with Murder* shows exactly how shedunnit.

AVAILABLE NOW

BEFORE PRIME SUSPECT THERE WAS

TENNISON

DIVE INTO THE ICONIC *SUNDAY TIMES* BESTSELLING SERIES.

And coming soon
the final Tennison thriller . . .

WHOLE LIFE SENTENCE

THE THRILLING NEW SERIES FROM THE QUEEN OF CRIME DRAMA

Lynda La Plante

IT'S TIME TO MEET DETECTIVE JACK WARR

OUT NOW

THE

INSPIRATION

FOR THE MAJOR MOTION PICTURE

OUT NOW

Eight years ago, James McCready was convicted of killing his partner, Gary Meadows. But McCready has always claimed that the stabbing was a tragic accident and, when fresh evidence comes to light, he wins his appeal for a retrial.

Detective Inspector Pat North is assigned to the reinvestigation. But when North discovers that her partner, Detective Superintendent Mike Walker, led the original police inquiry, their fledgling relationship is put to the test – particularly when she starts to suspect that he is covering something up.

Could Walker have tampered with evidence to frame an innocent man? And if so, who is the real killer?

PRAISE FOR LYNDA LA PLANTE

'The UK's most celebrated female crime author'
DAILY MAIL

'Lynda La Plante practically invented the thriller'
KARIN SLAUGHTER

DISCOVER THE GRIPPING TRIAL & RETRIBUTION SERIES

£9.99 www.bonnierbooks.co.uk

ISBN 978-1-80418-949-8

9 781804 189498

FSC

At Bonnier Books UK, we are committed to publishing sustainably. Find out more here: bonnierbooks.co.uk/sustainability